PANDORA'S EYES
The Alex Cave Series book 5.

Written by James M. Corkill.

I0589906

Chapter 1

GROOM LAKE, NEVADA:

Ex-CIA operative and geophysicist Alex Cave stepped into his friend's office. "What's going on, Doc?"

Doctor Henry Heinz, the base director, waved Alex over to a chair beside him to look at a monitor. "I received this recording from the International Space Station. It was taken after the launch of a new satellite called the SV1, for Space Vacuum One. It is supposed to be an efficient way to collect the orbiting space debris."

"Sounds like a good idea."

"Yes, but what they are using to do it got my attention."

Alex watched the recording, showing an eight foot long, octagonal cylinder with solar panels, floating among the stars, then a knot formed in his stomach when he saw the twenty foot long, torpedo-shaped device protruding from the center, and pointed to the monitor. "That looks like one of the alien weather control devices that nearly caused a new Ice Age, and I barely managed to get all four of them under control. Let's go, Doc. I need to make sure we're missing one."

They hurried down the hallway to the large commercial elevator, where Henry entered a code and stared into the retina scanner. The outside door opened, and then Alex grabbed the interior mesh door and slid it up. Once he and Henry stepped inside, Alex repeated the process to go down.

The elevator stopped at the lowest level, where Alex opened the doors and led the way along a wide corridor. When they reached the large door at the end, Henry entered a code and stared into a retina scanner again. The lock clicked and Alex shoved the door open, then rushed into the room and slid to a stop when he saw only one cylinder in the metal rack. "Damn it, Doc! This is supposed to be a secure facility. How can two of them be missing?"

"I will find out how someone managed to steal them. Your job is to get them back before he causes a global catastrophe."

Neither Alex nor Henry spoke until they entered the office, where Henry sat down and typed a command into his computer before looking at Alex while they waited. "You did not finish telling me about these devices."

"Oh, right. They were designed to attract pollutants from the atmosphere, but whoever is in control thinks it's going to attract the debris in space."

"I believe it is a good idea. All that rubble has to be tracked, and it has already caused millions of dollars in damage to several satellites, spacecraft, and even the International Space Station."

"You're right, Doc, if they know what they're doing. All the information about how they operate is on board our spaceship, so how could they possibly know what they're doing with that device without some kind of instruction manual? They don't realize they're meant to work in unison, all connected somehow."

Henry heard a beep and turned to the monitor. "One of our people here at the base signed for all the devices. Wait a minute. He quit eight months ago, right after the arrival date."

"That still doesn't explain how they know about its operating system."

Henry entered a command. "I had David make a copy, and I uploaded the information." When he saw the new data, he leaned back in his chair. "Someone hacked into my computer and made a copy of the data."

Alex stood and pulled his phone from his front pocket. "I'll call Martin right away."

On the first ring, the secretary for the Director of National Security answered. "This is Alex Cave. Is Director Donner available? Okay. Please have him call me right away." He looked at Henry. "He's in a meeting."

"I wish we had left them in the ocean, Alex. I have a very bad feeling about all this."

"We didn't have a choice, Doc. In order to get rid of the devices, they all must be together in one place."

Henry stared up at his friend. "Will you ever tell me your secret?"

"If what I suspect happens, I might need to tell all of you."

"Perhaps the Director could find out how they were stolen."

His phone rang, and Alex recognized the picture of the Director of National Security. "Hey, Martin. You're on speaker with the Doc."

"Hi, Alex. Are you getting settled in okay?"

"I'm getting there."

"What can I do for you?"

"Three of my devices never made it to the base, and their operation manual was copied. Now one of them is in orbit, called the SV1. Do you know anything about the company who owns it?"

"Yes, they're a reputable company with several military contracts. Have you ever heard of the DAR Corporation?"

Alex's posture stiffened when he thought about his unscrupulous dealings with the owner not too long ago. "I have. I thought they were demolition and reconstruction contractors."

"That's only a subsidiary of the main company. Their goal is to collect the billions of dollars' worth of precious metals from space. In fact, they're doing the first orbital test this afternoon, about 4:00 PM your time. The crew on the space station will send a live broadcast of the event."

"That's only six hours from now. You have to stop them, Martin. They have no idea how dangerous they could be."

"I believe you, Alex, and I'll do what I can, but one of these days, you had better tell me more about them."

"I know. In the meantime, could you send me all the data you have on DAR and the SV1?"

"I'll have my secretary send it to your private email account."

"Thanks, Martin."

Henry waited until Alex put his phone away. "Is there anything I can do to help?"

"Yes. Set up a remote video camera on that remaining device and monitor it during the test."

Henry thought about it for a moment. "If they are as dangerous as you claim, perhaps we should move it to the surface, away from the base."

"We're better off keeping it where it is. They were built to react with the environment, and there is less air in the vault."

"Very well."

"I'd better call Okawna. I hope he can have Bett pick me up in Seward." Alex selected the contact, then a moment later, he recognized the image of his best friend. "Hey, Okawna. Where are you right now?"

"I'm on the Mystic and we've just refueled in Seward. We're getting ready to head back out to resume the search for the last device. Why?"

"Don't leave."

"All right. How about a little more information?"

"Have you heard about the SV1?"

"No. Is there a problem?"

Alex told him about the missing devices and explained his concern. "The problem is the one in the water. When they activate the one in space, the one in the water will start freezing the ocean at an incredible rate, and you don't want the Mystic to be in the vicinity."

"How do you know about all this stuff, Alex? Oh, right. It's super top secret."

"I'm really sorry, my friend. If things develop like I think they will, I'll explain everything."

"Is there anything I can do to help?"

Alex thought about the *Mystic*'s helicopter pilot, Betty Mason, a feisty little woman married to Joshua, the ship's technical expert. "Is Bett on board?"

"Yeah, do you need a ride?"

"I do, but not from here. I'll meet you in Seward."

"Okay, I'll be waiting."

Alex put away his phone. "I need to borrow the jet. I'm meeting up with the *Mystic* in Seward, so I can keep an eye on what happens with the device in the Bering Sea when they activate the one in space."

"Yes, of course. Would you like to take David with you?"

"No, he should keep working on the cloaking system in spacecraft. Okawna and I can handle it."

"Of course. Keep in touch."

"I will."

***

EASTERN WASHINGTON. SV1 CONTROL CENTER:

Paul Carter was standing behind a young man, Scott Brackenbury, and a woman, Teresa Taylor, who were sitting in front of computer monitors. He looked at the large television mounted to the wall, showing a live image from SV1's on-board camera, and placed his hand on Scott's shoulder. "All right. Let's see what she can do."

Teresa turned to look at Paul. "You've decided the SV1 has a sex?"

"Fine. See what *it* can do. Are you happy now?"

She grinned. "Yes, thank you."

She turned to Scott, one of the engineers on the SV-1 project. "Ready when you are. Let's fire it up."

Scott placed his finger on the enter button of the keyboard and felt his heart rate increase. "Thrusters on standby. Sending command now."

Carter stared intently at the image from the camera showing the small end of a spinning, funnel-shaped distortion off the pointed end of the device. "Good work. Let's start with the harmonic resonance frequency to attract carbon atoms."

Scott entered the command into his computer. "All set."

Teresa studied the data on her monitor. "Verified. It's on."

The television showed a flash of reflected light, and then a slowly rotating silver object entered the distortion. "That looks like some kind of wrench."

Scott looked up from his monitor. "The field is holding. We've caught it!"

Teresa captured a still image of the wrench and did a recognition comparison. "It's one of the tools used by the Hubble telescope repair team."

Scott adjusted the camera for a wide angle view. "We're attracting more material, and at this rate, we should have this section cleared in a few hours."

A soft beeping came from the computer speaker and Scott saw a second resonate frequency, oscillating 180-degrees out from the one in use by SV1, then a moment later, it was gone. "That was strange."

***

NORTH OF DARRINGTON, WASHINGTON:

Rita Harrow stared up at the pewter-colored torpedo-looking device pointed up into space, then at the small monitor for the control computer. When the seconds vanishing on the digital clock reached zero, she pressed a key, and the device shut down and she looked over at Steve Preston, the owner of the DAR Corporation, and her lover. "The effect should be over."

Preston looked over at the tall woman with red hair. "Are you sure you have this thing under control? I mean, your first test altered the jet stream over the Northern Pacific Ocean, and now California is suffering a massive drought. Will it return to its original course?"

She crossed her arms over her chest and stared down at the ground. "I hope so. I didn't mean for that to happen."

"Are you ever going to tell me how you know so much about these devices?" He noticed the rage in her eyes when she looked up at him. He could tell whatever caused it was still bothering her.

Rita put her hands on her hips. "Why not? I was on a research ship called the *Mystic* off the coast of Washington, when a man named Alex Cave suddenly showed up and I was fired. I couldn't complete my mission, and it pissed me off. A friend did a background check on him, and it turns out, he's a close friend of Martin Donner, the Director of National Security."

Preston stared at her, waiting for her to finish. "And?"

"The *Mystic* belonged to millionaire Mike Tanner, who evidently became Cave's good friend. I figured my being fired meant they were up to something big, and I've been keeping track of Tanner's different ships to find out what it is. It turns out one of them recovered another device like this one and we took it. That's the one you have in orbit. One of our spies working at Groom Lake told us another one had suddenly arrived there, and a third one was being shipped from Adak Island in Alaska." She tilted her head toward the trailer. "You're looking at it."

"I see. How did you know what it does?"

"We managed to get our hands on the instruction manual."

"Don't tell me. Your spy at Area 51."

Rita didn't reply and pressed a button on the control panel, and then the twenty foot long torpedo-shaped device slowly dropped back down into the custom trailer. Another button closed the top, and then she shut the side door to the control panel and turned back to Preston. "I can hit anywhere at any time."

Preston stared back. "I'm not so sure."

"Now that we have one in orbit, I can hit with pinpoint accuracy." When his eyes remained uncertain, she turned back to the trailer. "Fine. Believe what you want."

Preston looked at his wristwatch. "I'd better get going. I need to be the first person to sign the contract to do the search and rescue, with a clause that says my company gets the contract for the cleanup. I'm going to make a fortune by controlling the weather and getting paid to clean up the mess I created. Isn't that a kick in the ass?"

"I know, and I get twenty-five percent."

Preston's smile faltered for a moment. "Even so, we're talking millions of dollars."

When Preston turned and climbed into his silver SUV and drove away, Rita stared after him for a few moments, wondering why he didn't kiss her before leaving. She hurried to the customized motorhome that towed the trailer, climbed inside, and then headed north toward US Interstate 5.

***

EAST OF DARRINGTON, WASHINGTON:

State Patrol Officer Harry Clemens was driving along the freeway when he noticed four dump trucks and construction equipment parked in front of his grandfather's abandoned drive-in movie theatre, but as far as he knew, his family did not intend to tear it down. He took the next off ramp, drove across the overpass, and headed back to the theatre down a side road. He stopped near a large motorhome, where a dozen men were sitting under the awning and studied the men for a few moments before climbing out.

Paul Simms glanced at his men and then stood as he waited for the highway patrol officer to walk over. "Can I help you, Officer?"

"I was just wondering why you're here. Are you staging for a job?"

"Yes, but not for this property. I'm just waiting to hear from my boss. We shouldn't be here for more than a few hours."

Clemens was about to ask him more questions when a voice from his portable radio interrupted, then stepped away from the group to answer. "This is Clemens. Go ahead."

"We have a report of a tornado touching down just north of Monroe and it's headed south. We need you to help the local police shut down the exits off the Interstate highway in that area until the storm passes."

"Are you kidding? We don't get tornadoes in this part of the Pacific Northwest."

"Listen, Harry. This is not a joke, now get moving."

"I'm on my way."

Clemens glanced back at the truck drivers, then climbed into his patrol car and drove back to the Interstate highway. He still couldn't fathom the idea of a tornado in Monroe.

When the patrol car drove away, Simms sat down and looked at his crew. "It shouldn't be much longer now."

***

MONROE, WASHINGTON:

Mayor Carl Barstow scratched his head through his gray hair as he watched the patrol cars and ambulances begin to arrive from nearby towns after the three-story apartment complex just south of the small town was nearly destroyed. He looked over at his friend, Officer Clemens. "I can't believe this just happened, Harry. Look how it ripped up the building. Yet just a quarter mile away, there was no damage. Like it touched down for a minute and then just disappeared."

Clemens looked down at the dry flakes of blood on his fingers and heaved a deep sigh as he shook his head. "I've found seven dead, and a lot of serious injuries. Many of the masonry walls held together, so there could be some survivors underneath the pile, but it's going to take some time before we could get some equipment here to start digging through the wreckage. We're just so ill prepared for such a disaster. Tornadoes just don't pop up in our neck of the woods. And they definitely don't just appear out of nowhere. There weren't even any storms around. It's a perfectly sunny day with maybe a few clouds in the sky." He thought about all the construction equipment stationed at the theatre. This was an emergency, and he was going to put them to work. "I have an idea. I'll be back in a moment."

Clemens hadn't taken a step before he noticed the silver Cadillac SUV leading the way for the construction equipment from the theatre. When the vehicle stopped beside his patrol car, a tall man wearing gray slacks and a black shirt climbed out and walked over to greet him and the Mayor.

Preston held his hand out to the officer. "Do you need some help?"

The Mayor hurried past Clemens and grabbed the man's hand. "I'm the Mayor, Carl Barstow. We sure could. We have people trapped in the debris, so you need to hurry."

Preston suppressed a smile. "Sorry to hear about that. I'm Mister Preston, owner of the DAR Corporation. My people would be glad to lend a hand. Let's go to my car and you can sign a waiver of liability for my company so we can get started."

"You bet."

Clemens found it extremely odd that this Mister Preston just happened to have his equipment waiting nearby, but there was no way he could have known this would happen. At least as far as he knew, anyway. For the moment, he needed their help, so he let go of the idea that this was not just a coincidence.

Chapter 2

BERING SEA:

Alex sat alone in the passenger compartment of the Gulfstream jet, oblivious to the soft whine of the engines. He just couldn't figure out how DAR could know what the devices could do in only nine months. He thought back to the Red Energy operation, but the recovery of the devices from the oceans was top secret, and not even the military knew what they were doing. Only the crew of the *Mystic* and his friends at Groom Lake knew about the four devices.

Skip Johnson, the pilot, walked back from the cockpit to his only passenger. "We'll be on final approach to Seward in five minutes. Do you want us to stick around?"

Alex stood to stretch. "That would be great, Skip. At least until after the test."

Skip chuckled. "You mean the SV1? They call it a space vacuum, but I doubt it will work with no air to suck the debris inside."

"Perhaps you're right. We'll know in about an hour."

When Skip returned to the cockpit, Alex sat down and buckled up, then stared out the window as the jet swung around directly over the harbor to line up with the runway, and he saw the *Mystic* anchored offshore. She was a tri-hull, and the blue-and-white contrasts of her paint job enhanced her sleek design. When she was underway, the main ship was supported by the two outside pontoons, which ended in a vertical V to slice through the water instead of going over the waves. They also housed the turbine engines and water jet pumps.

The jet made a gentle landing and taxied to the small private air terminal. When it stopped, Alex got up and moved to the front of the plane, where the pilot open the door and lower the steps. "Thanks for the ride, Skip. The test is in thirty minutes, so I'll call you once I know the situation."

He grabbed his small suitcase from the storage rack in case he ended up staying, and when he turned back to the door, a tall man with shaggy blond hair and brownish-green eyes was standing at the bottom of the stairs.

Okawna looked up at the tall, dark-haired man standing in the doorway. "Hey, buddy. Good to see you again."

Alex went down the steps and walked beside his friend towards the blue-and-white, six-person helicopter. "I know you have a lot of questions, but I'd rather wait until we get back from the test before I explain everything."

"Fine by me. Mike is in Seattle and won't be back for a couple of weeks."

Alex set his bag down on the asphalt when a small woman with short blond hair reached up to give him a hug. "Hey, Bett. How have you been?"

"Doing just fine. Josh is looking forward to seeing ya again."

Alex enjoyed her Texas accent while he glanced at his watch. "How long until we reach the open water of the Bering Sea by helicopter?"

"About twenty minutes."

"Are you fueled and ready to go?"

"Yeah, why?"

"We need to head out right away if we want to get there before the test."

She shrugged her shoulders. "All right, let's get started."

Alex tossed his bag into the rear passenger compartment and climbed in, while Bett climbed into the pilot's seat. Since he was a good helicopter pilot himself, Okawna sat in the copilot's seat. When the copter leapt into the air, Alex put on his headset and leaned forward between the two seats. "Sorry to drag you away from watching the test of the SV1, but it's important we're near the device in the water when it happens."

Okawna turned in his seat to look back at Alex. "So, you're expecting to see the ocean turn into a giant ice cube?"

"I hope not."

"I was just thinking about all the commercial ships in the Bering Sea. Have they been warned to leave the area?"

"No, I couldn't do that without raising a lot of unwanted questions. If I'm wrong, no one will be the wiser. If I'm correct, they'll be the least of our problems."

Alex leaned back in the seat, and no one spoke as the helicopter flew over the Aleutian Islands into open water. Without knowing the exact location of the weather control device, he had no Idea where the freezing might occur. He kept looking at his watch, and when it showed three minutes until test time, he leaned forward. "Take us up to a higher altitude so we can see more of the surrounding water."

When the alarm on his watch beeped, Alex slid back and forth across the bench seat to stare out the side windows. "Okay, Bett. Swing us around in a circle."

***

SV1 CONTROL CENTER:

Paul Carter stood behind Teresa and Scott, staring at the information on the monitor, hoping this second test would go as well as the first one had. "All right. Turn it on." He looked across at the image on the wall monitor, waiting for the funnel to appear, but when nothing happened, he looked down at the data in front of Scott. "Is that what I think it is?"

Scott didn't look up. "Yes, it's the second signal, and it's interfering with our controls. I suggest we shut it down until we can determine the source."

"All right."

Carter leaned over Scott's shoulder as the young man entered the command, then the second signal disappeared. "That's just too much of a coincidence. The problem has to be here on our end. Run a diagnostic on our software to find out where that second signal is coming from."

Scott looked up at Carter. "I don't think we're causing it."

"Just run the test."

Scott entered the command into the computer, and a few moments later, the data on the monitor showed no malfunction or the source of the second signal. "I told you so."

"It has to be us. Keep searching while I call Preston and let him know what's going on."

When Carter left the room, Scott leaned back with his hands behind his head and looked over at Teresa. "I'm telling you, that signal isn't coming from us."

"I agree, but Paul is under a lot of pressure to make this work. We just have to figure out where it's coming from."

Scott released a deep sigh of frustration, dropped his arms onto the desk, and typed commands into the computer. "I think our software has a mind of its own, like artificial intelligence."

"That's a scary thought."

"Well, get used to it, because someday it will happen and we'll lose control of everything we take for granted."

***

BERING SEA:

Alex could not stop glancing at his watch as they waited for something to happen, but after fifteen minutes, when the SV1 was supposedly activated, the ocean lay undisturbed. "This is one time I'm happy to be wrong. We might as well head back to Seward."

Alex stared out the side window of the helicopter, positive the SV1 was one of the missing devices, but he needed information on how DAR managed to get their hands on it, and who copied its operating system. The only way that could happen was with help from his friends.

Okawna turned to look back at Alex. "We still need to recover this device, and we don't have that much area left to search. Could you stick around for a day or two?"

"I don't have anything else going on at the moment, so sure. I'll give you a hand. I'll call the plane and tell Skip he can head back to the base."

***

SEWARD, ALASKA:

The helicopter approached the open stern deck of the *Mystic*, and Bett gently brought them down between the fifteen foot submarine called the *Wizard*, and the nineteen foot motorboat. The whine of the turbine engine died to a whisper, and then everyone climbed out. Alex was greeted by a big man with a thick red beard and hair named Joshua Mason, Bett's husband, who was the electronics specialist of the crew. When Joshua held his arms out, Alex stepped forward and accepted a hug. "Good to see you again, Josh."

"Hey, Alex. I've set up a secure connection, and notified everyone on your list about your conference. They're waiting for you to make contact."

"All right. Let's get started."

Alex reached back inside to grab his bag, and then followed everyone through the rear doors into the main hallway, past the stairs up to the bridge, and into a large open lounge with a big-screen TV on the wall. Once everyone was seated at the table, he indicated for Josh to connect them to Director Donner and his team at Groom Lake. A moment later, the screen was divided with Donner's image on one side, and Henry, Jadin, and David on the other side. "First, I'm glad to say nothing happened up here. At least for now. What happened to the device in the vault, Henry?"

"Nothing. It remained just as we saw it."

"That's good news."

Donner had gotten a background check on Preston, which seemed legitimate. "Are you positive about the one in space, Alex?"

"Ninety percent, so I'd really like to see it up close to make sure."

"Well, I can't let you take your spaceship up to check it out. I'm having a hard enough time keeping it a secret from the public, but I'll get you some photos of the SV1."

Henry held his palm up. "We have re-vetted the remaining employees here at the base, and everyone is cleared, Alex."

"Good. I guess it's time for you to know the truth. For the past several months, all of you have been patient with my being so secretive on how I know so much about these devices and the spaceship, and I would like to explain why. I was sworn to secrecy by a time traveler named Paladin."

Alex studied their reactions, and Donner stared back quizzically, but the others just grinned, including his friends on the *Mystic*. "I'm telling you the truth."

Okawna placed his hand on Alex's shoulder. "After everything that's happened in the past few months, I believe you, buddy. I'm grinning because I'm looking forward to the rest of the story."

Alex smiled. "All right. It all started right after the Dead Energy Operation. These devices were built by the first race of humans who occupied this planet, one hundred and eighty million years ago. They were forced to abandon this world in a hurry and didn't have time to take all their advanced technology with them, and over the past few millennia of tectonic shift and volcanic activity, these devices, and the spaceship, were brought to the surface." He explained everything that had happened up to the end of the Red Energy Operation, leaving out the personal details of his relationship with Rita. "That's when I was sent back in time to stop the *Mystic* from testing their new ultrasound locator. Therefore, you see, this is a new timeline for me. Hell, for all of us." He waited for a response, but they seemed in shock. "Well?"

David broke the silence. "Wow. I hope you plan on making that story into a book."

Alex felt a sense of relief when everyone seemed to believe him. "I'll think about it. For now, we need to locate this device in the ocean."

He noticed Donner was still grinning. "What?"

"It never ceases to amaze me how many times you get involved in unusual situations. Did Paladin tell you why they had to abandon everything?"

"Apparently, they were testing a new piece of equipment in the Mariana Trench when something went wrong. The explosive force was enough to cause a shift in the tectonic plates, setting off hundreds of eruptions around the world. Only the people on the surface made it off the planet, and I'm guessing the people in the trench were destroyed by the magma."

Donner's grin slipped away. "Wow, Alex. I can see why you're worried about Preston having one of these devices. All right. Let me know if there is anything you need."

"Thanks, Martin. We'll continue the search for this device until something changes."

When everyone signed off, Alex looked around at his friends and noticed the broad grin on Okawna. "What's so funny?"

"I was a hero in all the timelines."

"Yes, but you're a hero in any timeline."

"Thanks, Alex. Listen, we don't have too big an area left to search with the sonar and we should be done by tomorrow morning. We just need to secure the helicopter so we can get underway."

"I'll give you a hand."

Chapter 3

NORDVULC, (NORDIC VOLCANOLOGICAL CENTER), REYKJAVIK, ICELAND:

Estelle Burkhart was at her computer station when she saw a flashing warning light on the monitor. A large geologic disturbance had just occurred under the frozen Arctic Ocean, one hundred miles north of the Beauford Glacier. She hurried from her lab down the hallway to the Director's office and tapped on the open door. "Do you have a minute?"

Jeffery Sliven was sitting at his desk and looked up from the computer monitor. "Of course."

"We had a significant seismic event one hundred miles north of us. Oddly, it was only a surface disturbance, about one hundred meters below the ice."

"That is strange. Is there any sign of volcanic activity?"

"Not that I can tell. It lasted thirty-seven seconds and stopped."

"All right. Let's send a ship to check the area for anything unusual. Who do we have available?"

"I think the American, Terry Hardin, and his people are doing research not too far from that area."

"Ah, yes. Mister Harden. I'll have him stop and check it out before he heads back. Hopefully, it is not a prelude to a new volcano forming above that section of the rift."

***

THE NORDVULC RESEARCH SHIP VULCAN, 100 MILES NORTH OF ICELAND:

Terry Hardin steadied himself against the railing in rhythm with the slight movement of the deck as he stared through his digital binoculars. With the bridge of the ship four meters higher than the ice sheet, he saw three massive white spires rising above the flat surface, as if something had punched a hole up through the thick ice. He looked down at the three teachers and seven students on the main deck of the one hundred and fifty foot ship and hollered down to them. "Let's fly one of our drones over the ice sheet to see what happened."

Hardin waited as the group left the deck to go inside so they could watch from the classroom. One person came out with the small quad copter and let it fly away, before hurrying back inside. Hardin stepped back into the bridge and joined his first mate, Tim Black, and then they watched the image from the drone's camera on the overhead monitor as it approached the ten foot vertical edge of the ice sheet, which appeared to have been sheared off by a giant chisel. As the drone gained altitude, he saw three massive triangle-shaped blocks of ice at a slight upward angle, with the points meeting in the center.

According to the readout from the drone, the extrusion was one-hundred-meters due north from the ship. As the drone moved around the thick blocks, small flashes of sunlight appeared to reflect up through the narrow gaps between the wedges of ice. Hardin stepped outside and told them to bring the drone back to the ship, and then Tim joined him. "I'll call NordVulC and tell them what we've discovered. These recordings are going to blow their minds."

Hardin went back into the bridge and grabbed the satellite phone to call the director. He was hoping to get onto the ice sheet and go down inside the opening for a closer look, but Director Sliven ordered him to bring the students and recordings back to NordVulC immediately. When he finished, he strolled outside for a last look at the ten-foot wall of sea ice. "Take us home, Tim."

Hardin remained outside at the lookout station, tucked behind a slender wall with a window. He had no intention of letting NordVulC be the only group to see these recordings. In three hours, he would be back in the harbor, and the second thing he was going to do was contact MUFON. He grinned at the irony. His friends in the Mutual UFO Network were looking to the skies, and he found one right here on the planet we live on.

Chapter 4

BERING SEA. THE *MYSTIC*. 5:00 AM:

It was Alex's turn on watch, and he studying the pictures of the SV1 Donner had sent to him, and there was no doubt it was one of his missing devices. According to the report, DAR's corporate headquarters was on Fidalgo Island, near Anacortes, Washington. He was familiar with the area from his time growing up in the Pacific Northwest.

When he heard a soft beep, he studied the return from the transducer on the monitor. The computer was set to notify him if it located the item programmed into its software, but the *Mystic* was nearing the end of the last run, and there was no sign of the device. When the grid image slid down the screen, he released a deep sigh of frustration they could not locate it. He pulled back the throttle and stepped out of the cabin into the cool morning air. "Damn!"

He knew it had to be in this area, because in the other timeline, this was the end of the massive ice sheet it had created. He stared out across the water toward the sun rising over the Taylor Mountain to the east, and when a sudden chill blew across his cheek, he turned to the north. "Well, I'll be damned." He hurried back into the bridge, grabbed the microphone for the intercom, and then called Okawna's cabin. "Are you awake?"

"I am now. Am I late to relieve you?"

"No, but we're searching in the wrong place."

"I'll be up in a second. Make sure there's some coffee for me."

Alex grabbed a small plastic cup of ground gourmet coffee from the shelf, put it in the machine, and set a mug in place beneath the spout. He turned back to the navigation system and brought up the charts for the Arctic Ocean on the monitor, then entered the coordinates and checked the quickest route to the Arctic from the Bering Sea. He looked up when Okawna came up the stairs, his hair tousled, and his eyes still swollen from sleep. "Your coffee will be ready in a moment. Take a look at these charts."

When Okawna was beside him, he indicated an area on the south end of the Polar Ice Sheet. "In the other timeline, that's where it started. That's where we'll find the device."

"Could you be a little more accurate? It would take an entire fleet of boats blasting away with ultrasound to cover that much area."

Alex realized he was right and sat down on the stool. "There has to be another way."

Okawna stepped over to the coffeemaker and grabbed the mug of steaming, dark liquid. "Could you find it with your spaceship?"

Alex chuckled. "It's not mine anymore, and Donner would never allow it out of the hangar."

Okawna turned to the front window and stared east at the sun's reflection rising on the smooth surface of the water. "If they're as dangerous as you say, maybe we're better off leaving it where it is."

Alex stood and his eyes bunched together in thought as he typed information into the computer. "We need a satellite image of that section of the arctic. When the SV1 was activated, the freezing could have occurred up there instead of down here."

Joshua Mason came up the stairs and saw his friends leaning over the keyboard. "What's going on?"

Alex looked up at the big man, who looked more like a lumberjack than a techno-wiz. "I'm trying to find the latest satellite image of the Arctic Ocean near the ice sheet, but I'm not accessing NASA's system."

Josh moved over to join them. "Let me try." He sat down to be more even with the console and entered several commands. A moment later, he indicated the screen to Alex. "That's it. What are you expecting to see?"

"A massive ice cube."

Alex studied the image, but the surface of the ocean was empty, so he looked over at his friends. "I guess it didn't activate. I'm sorry I wasted your time searching the wrong area."

Okawna shrugged. "And we'll never be able to find it without your spaceship, so we should just leave it there."

Alex knew that wasn't an option. "I'll try to convince Donner to let us use the spaceship."

"Should we head back to Seward before we head back to Anacortes?"

"No. If Bett flies Okawna and me back to Seward, we'll catch a flight there and meet up with you later. That way, you won't have to detour."

"Not a problem."

***

ANACORTES, WASHINGTON. DAR CORPORATE HEADQUARTERS. 9:00 AM:

Okawna drove the rental sedan up the winding road through the fir trees and stopped when it ended at the office. From the outside, it resembled a large modern home perched on the solid rock mountaintop, with a magnificent view of the Strait of Juan de Fuca, the San Juan Islands, and Vancouver Island, British Columbia.

Alex admired the modern architecture of the building. "The report indicates when it comes to profits, Preston plays hardball."

"This should be fun."

They climbed out and strolled up the stone walkway to a large glass door, with the letters D.A.R. etched into the frosted surface. He rang the doorbell and looked up at the camera and speaker. A moment later, Preston answered.

"Hello, Alex. I'll be right there."

Alex saw movement on the other side of the glass before a handsome man dressed in pastel colors opened the door. He appeared to be in his early forties, and clean shaven, with trimmed hair.

Preston smiled at his guests. "I've been looking forward to meeting you both. Come in and we'll talk."

Alex led Okawna through the doorway and held his hand out to his host. "Thanks, Mr. Preston."

Preston accepted. "Steve is fine. Have a seat and tell me what I can do for you."

Alex sat in one of two recliners, facing a beautiful view of the San Juan Islands. Tinted skylights made the room bright, but at a comfortable temperature. Okawna remained standing, looking around the interior. "Nice place you have here, Stevie. Can I call you Stevie?"

Preston's gaze at Okawna hardened. "No, you may not! You can call me Mr. Preston."

Alex grimaced just to keep from grinning at Preston's reaction. "I must apologize for my friend. Some people don't care for his sense of humor."

Okawna grinned. "Just messing with you, Steve. No harm intended."

When Okawna sat in the other recliner, Preston remained standing and turned to Alex. "What can I do for you?"

"I'm interested in your SV1. It's quite a piece of technology, and I noticed from the pictures that the main body appears to be a single object, like a torpedo. Would you mind telling me how you acquired it?"

Preston gave him a sly grin, turned to press the intercom button, and spoke into the microphone. "Why don't you come down and join us?"

Preston stepped back and looked at Alex. "Have you ever heard the term a woman scorned?"

Alex wasn't sure what he meant until Rita walked into the room, and then his hands clinched into fists on the armrests. He had learned what type of person she really was during the Red Energy Operation, where she had kidnaped his friend, shot down a Coast Guard helicopter, and caused the eruption of the Yellowstone Super volcano, killing his girlfriend and her daughter, and thousands of other people. Even though he had stopped her and changed the future, he could not forget what happened in the other timeline, so he remained seated when Okawna stood.

Okawna smiled at the attractive woman with red hair he almost had an affair with when they were on the *Mystic* together. "How have you been, Rita?"

Rita placed her hands on her hips and smiled at Okawna. "I see you're still getting lots of sun."

Her smile slipped away when she noticed the anger in Cave's eyes, but she locked stares with him as she moved around to face him. "What's your problem, Cave? Why did you get me kicked off the Mystic without an explanation? I've never even met you until you came on board."

Alex's fists unclenched, and his expression softened. He knew if Rita were involved with the SV1, he would need her cooperation. "You're right, Ms. Harrow, but I'm sworn to secrecy, so I'm not able to give you an explanation. And for that, I apologize."

Rita kept her hands on her hips. "What do you want?"

Alex took a moment before responding, and knew the time for playing softball was over, so he stood. "I know you did not design and build that piece of equipment you have floating in space." He noticed the surprise in Preston's eyes. When his host turned to look at Rita for an explanation, he realized Rita was the thief, not Preston.

Rita crossed her arms over her chest and scoffed. "You know nothing, Cave. Steve's company holds the patent rights. You can check for yourself."

"That may be, but it's not yours."

When Rita smirked, Alex got in her face. "Did I say something funny? Because even if you didn't steal it, you have no idea what kind of fire you're playing with."

Preston eased Rita away and indicated the door to his guests. "We're through here, gentleman. You know the way out."

Alex glared at Rita and Preston. "I'll be seeing you two again." He spun around and shoved the glass door open, hearing Okawna's footsteps right behind him. Once outside, he climbed into the passenger seat of the sedan and stared through the front window while he waited for Okawna to get in. He knew he was right about the device in space, but for the moment, there was not a damn thing he could do about it.

Okawna climbed in and started the engine. "What's next?"

"I don't know. Since I'm in the area, I wouldn't mind seeing my family in Sparrow Valley before I head back to Groom Lake." He noticed Okawna's pleading eyes and smiled. "Want to come along?"

"You bet I do. I like your father, and the kids are great."

Okawna backed out of the parking spot and headed down the mountain toward the marina. He knew this time of day the traffic would be light, so they should reach Sparrow Valley in an hour.

***

Rita plopped down in the chair. "Cave is going to be a problem."

"What about his friend?"

"Okawna's okay. At least, he was when we were on the Mystic."

"I don't like him."

She stood. "I want to run another test on the device this afternoon."

"I don't have any crews available at the moment. We'll have to wait until I can set up a contract with another company."

"You won't need them. It would be too suspicious if you and your equipment suddenly showed up in Cave's hometown."

"Where is it?"

"An old lakebed on the western side of Mount Baker. A quaint little place called Sparrow Valley."

Preston smirked. "A woman scorned, all right." He stared after her and grinned as she headed for the door. His grinned slipped away, hoping she was correct about her ability to control the device precisely.

Chapter 5

WASHINGTON STATE:

Inside the rental car, Alex and Okawna sat in comfortable silence for nearly an hour, and then the corners of Okawna's lips curled up into a grin. "Rita sure looks good. When we were on the Mystic, I was about to make my move on her when you showed up and kicked her off the ship."

"I did you a favor. You wouldn't have liked her once you got to know her." He reached over the back seat and grabbed a manila envelope, opened the flap, and slid the pictures and a small stack of papers onto his lap. "According to this report, Preston's research facility is in Eastern Washington. That must be where they're controlling the space vacuum. Could you be away from the Mystic for a few days?"

"Sure. I told Mike we've called off the search, so nothing for me to do until he gets back from the Environmental Conference in Vancouver. I'm ready for a little excitement."

***

FIDALGO ISLAND, WASHINGTON STATE:

Rita climbed out of the motor home, taking a deep breath of fir-scented air as she slowly scanned for witnesses around the dry lakebed. The information on the realtor's website was very helpful in finding this location for her local tests, since the only thing in the area was a dilapidated bait and tackle shop, which was about to fall over, and the pilings for what used to be a dock.

She moved to the side of the trailer and opened the door on the control panel. When she flipped a switch, the quiet purr of the generator was the only sound for miles in every direction. When she entered a command, the cover opened and device rose up out of the trailer, but when she activated it, she felt a strange tingling sensation in her teeth, something she didn't feel the last time the machine was on. She studied the readout and noticed a second frequency oscillating 180-degrees out from hers. "That shouldn't be here."

***

SPARROW VALLEY:

Their vehicle reached the rim of the ancient volcanic crater, where Alex and Okawna were about to drive down into the valley, when Alex noticed what appeared to be a large dark cloud with a hole in the center, and then realized it was forming on the southern side of his family's ranch. Alex glanced over at Okawna and pointed through the window. "That's an interesting cloud formation."

Okawna barely managed to catch a glimpse before the angle changed as they headed down into the valley. "Could it be a wind shear effect around the mountain?"

"Possibly, though I've never seen one like that."

"Maybe it's a contrail from a passing jet?"

Alex didn't answer when he noticed a small disturbance below the opening in the cloud, and the pointed outline of a transparent funnel slowly descended toward the ground. "What the hell?"

"Is that what I think it is?"

"A tornado! Hurry, it's headed for the ranch!"

***

Robert Cave kept his phone against his ear as he opened the screen door and stepped out onto the back porch. "I see it, Alex. It looks like a tornado."

"It is, and it's heading right for you. Are the kids there?"

"No, they're in school. I'd better bring the horses up from the pasture."

"Forget about the damn horses, Dad, just get in the truck, and get out of there! We're headed your way and will meet you on the road in a few minutes."

Robert hurried down the steps. "All right."

***

When Alex and Okawna turned off the highway onto the road leading to the ranch. They could see the tornado moving through the forest on the other side of the large pasture, and it was headed toward the barn, but there was no sign of his father or his old blue pickup on the road. When Okawna parked in front of the house, Alex leapt out and looked around, but didn't see his father. "Robert?" He ran up the steps and entered the kitchen. "Dad? Are you in here?"

The sound of the wind howled louder and louder as he hurried from room to room. When there was no sign of Robert, he ran back outside and down the steps, while branches, grass, and leaves began pelting him hard. He held his arm up to block the small pieces of flying debris as he joined Okawna to search the area for Robert. "He might be in the old garage. That's where he keeps his truck. Let's go!"

When they ran past the barn, Alex saw a strange mass of spinning trees and dirt in a cloudless tornado. The bottom of the transparent funnel was carving a meandering fifty foot wide swath of destruction through the forest, ripping trees apart and clearing the ground beneath them as it surged in his direction. He ran into the garage and saw the truck, but not his father, so he hurried to the back of the building, where a storeroom had been dug out of the hill. It had originally been used for storing vegetables. When he threw open the door, he was blinded by the beam of a flashlight. "Dad! Are you all right?"

Robert stood up from the wooden bench seat. "Yeah, the truck wouldn't start."

"Come on! We need to get out of here and we don't have much time!"

Okawna was staring through a small gap between the large wooden sliding doors when Alex and Robert came out of the room. "We're too late! It's tearing the siding off the barn and we'll never make it to the car."

Alex put his hand on his father's shoulder. "Let's get back into the storeroom! It's our only chance!"

Alex grabbed a length of slender rope and a shovel while Okawna followed Robert into the small room. He tied one end around the handle, closed the door on the rope, and pulled the shovel against the outside of the door to hold it closed.

An instant later, the roar from the tornado was nearly deafening, and they heard objects slamming against the truck. The wind threatened to tear the door off the small room, and it took all of Alex's and Okawna's strength to hold it closed. When the side mirror of the truck punched a hole through the door, the strain on the rope was gone, and then the roaring wind suddenly vanished, replaced by the sound of huge objects slamming onto the roof of the garage.

***

Derek Cave sat on the edge of his motorcycle, talking to Jessica Parker in the parking lot of the high school, when he noticed the strange-looking tornado moving toward his family's ranch. He tried calling his grandfather, but there was no answer, and he swung his leg over the seat and sat down. "That's not good, Jessica. I have to go!"

He started the engine, gunned it a few times, then released the clutch and raced out to the main highway near the small town. When he turned onto the dirt road leading to the ranch, the tornado was ripping the siding off the barn, but it didn't occur to him racing toward the destruction would put his life in danger. His only thought was to find and save his grandfather.

***

FIDALGO ISLAND:

Rita flipped another switch, and once the device was safely tucked into its trailer, she shut down the generator, closed the side door, and climbed into her motorhome.

She sat in the driver's seat for a moment, with the engine still off, and thought about what had just happened. After several moments, when she had no idea why there was a second frequency, she started the engine and headed back to Dar headquarters.

***

INTERNATIONAL SPACE STATION:

Commander Ethan Short heard a soft beeping and studied the digital readout on the station's main computer, then turned to Anatole Bonich, his Russian friend. "Take a look at this. We're getting some kind of E.L.F. signal, but I can't tell where it's coming from."

Anatole pushed himself away from the viewing port, floating the short distance across the small room to join Ethan. "I have seen that signal before. It happened when they activated the space vacuum."

"I read a report about a government project called HAARP, for High Frequency Active Auroral Research Program. They used extremely low frequencies to study the behavior of the ionosphere, but some respected researchers allege that powerful E.L.F. signals could be used for weather control."

When the signal abruptly stopped, the men looked at each other, and Anatole grinned. "You see. Nothing to worry about, comrade."

***

SPARROW VALLEY:

Everything seemed deathly quiet after the tornado had passed, and Alex tried to open the door, but it wouldn't budge. When Okawna was beside him, they both kicked against the wood, but it was like hitting a brick wall.

Robert was standing a short distance away and saw the concern in his son's eyes, so he tried to put a positive spin on the situation. "At least the tornado has moved on."

"Yes, but if we can't get out of here, we'll run out of breathable air in about thirty minutes."

Chapter 6

WASHINGTON:

By the time Derek was near the ranch, everything had stopped swirling and fell from the sky, as if someone had flipped a switch and turned off the tornado. He just hoped Robert had left before it tore the place apart. When he turned the corner onto the circular driveway, he noticed the house was barely damaged, with only two broken windows in the kitchen, and everything else was miraculously intact. He stopped the motorcycle next to a strange car and saw pieces of barn wood on the trunk and roof. He shut down the engine and set the kickstand before climbing off and running up the steps into the kitchen. "Grandpa? Are you in here?"

He hurried through the rest of the house and then ran back outside to look around. Most of the barn was still intact, and he ran down the road and looked through the opening where the doors used to be, but the loft had collapsed, covering part of the stalls. "Grandpa? Are you in here?" He stepped back and cupped his hands around his mouth. "Robert? Can you hear me?" When no one answered, he thought his grandfather could be dead, and his heart felt as though it was being crushed as he turned and moved away from the barn.

***

Alex was using his pocketknife to carve a small hole in the door panel when he heard a voice, and stopped scraping and listened. "That sounds like Derek." He knelt down and looked through the tiny opening, then heard his nephew's voice again. "Derek! Over here! We're in the garage!"

***

When he didn't get a response, Derek felt a sense of panic, the suddenly remembered Robert had kept his old truck parked in the garage, and looked across the dirt road at what was left of it. The entire roof was gone, and the sliding doors had crashed into the blue pickup. He ran to the old building, hoping his grandfather was not inside the truck, crushed to death. As he got closer, he heard a familiar voice call his name. "Alex? Is that you?"

Alex sighed with relief. "Derek! Over here! We're trapped in the storeroom. Can you get us out?"

Derek assessed the situation and saw the driver's side window of the blue pickup had been pushed up against the entrance to the storeroom. "It looks like the truck is against the door. Let me see what I can do."

Derek cleared a path through the debris leading up to the truck, moving most of it out of the way by hurling boards, shingles, and tree branches to the side. One of the large wooden doors lay across the back of the cab and pickup bed, and the other was leaning against the passenger door.

He grabbed the edge of the wooden door and tried shoving it past the vehicle, but there was too much debris piled up against it. He tried standing it upright, but it felt like a million pounds of dead weight. He took a deep breath, gritted his teeth, and pushed with all his strength, then squeals of protest erupted from the old nails holding the wooden planks together as the door slowly became vertical. With one final shove, it dropped away from the passenger door and crashed onto the shattered timbers on the floor. "I'm almost there!"

He grabbed the door handle and pulled, but the door refused to open. He squirmed through the window opening and carefully crawled over the shattered glass on the bench seat to the driver's side window, which was already down. "I'll have you out in a minute. Is Robert with you?"

"Yes, and Okawna."

"Is everyone okay?"

"Yes, we just can't get out on our own."

"Okay, sit tight. I'll find something to bust out the door."

Derek knew his way around the garage and hurried across the debris to a small locker on the floor in the corner. He tossed the busted boards out of the way and opened the door, then grabbed a ten-pound sledgehammer and carried it back inside the truck. "Stand back!"

Derek rammed the steel head against the wood several times until it punched through, and then kept beating away sections of the door until it was larger than the window opening before reaching inside. "Give me your hand, Grandpa, and I'll pull you through."

Alex knelt down so his father could stand on his knee, and once Robert had crawled out the other side of the truck, he squirmed through the window. When he was out, he saw Okawna coming through the cab of the truck. He looked around at what remained of the garage and thought it was a total disaster, but when he looked across at the barn, he was surprised to see its siding had been ripped away, but the heavy timber frame was still intact. "What about the house?"

"It's still pretty much okay. A couple of windows were busted out, but that was about it."

Okawna studied the garage door lying on a pile of thick wooden rafters and then heard a creaking noise from one of the standing walls. "Let's get out of here."

The foursome hurried outside and strolled up the road to the house, and everywhere they looked was like a war zone. Trees ripped up, roots and all, and strewn across the pasture. Boards, branches, and random debris were scattered across the property, and then Okawna stared off into the distance behind them. "Would you look at that?"

Everyone turned around and saw what had caught his attention. It was a definitive path through the forest and pasture left behind by the tornado.

Derek closed his slightly opened mouth. "I've heard stories of destructive tornadoes leaving behind a literal path of destruction. I've even seen video footage during the aftermath of a tornado, but the enormity of it all doesn't sink in until you see it firsthand."

Alex noticed the two broken windows on the house as he climbed the steps onto the back porch and stepped into the kitchen. He flipped a switch on the wall and the ceiling light came on, and walked through the rest of the house, then went back outside to his father. "It's safe to enter. I don't know how, but you still have electricity."

"The power company buried the wires after the flood last year." Robert surveyed what remained of the barn and the torn up forest and pasture. "What in the world is going on, Alex? It was a beautiful day, and there wasn't even any rain or thunder. It just came out of nowhere. We don't even get that kind of stuff out here."

"We're not sure what's going on exactly, Dad. I'm glad we showed up when we did, though."

"Yeah, why is that? I didn't know you were in town."

"Right, sorry about that. It was a last-minute thing. We were in the area and thought we'd stop by for a quick visit. Okawna and I are actually headed over to eastern Washington to check on something, but we can stick around and help you clean up this mess."

"We'll be okay, son. I'll call the insurance company before we do anything. You go ahead and take care of your business. I'm sure it's important."

Okawna dragged the boards and pieces of barn siding off the rental car. The damage wasn't too bad, lots of scratches, but no major dents, then looked over at Alex. "I'll let you explain this to the rental company."

Alex hugged his family, and then he and Okawna climbed into the sedan and drove back to the main highway leading to eastern Washington. They continued through Mount Baker State Park and over the continental divide, where fir trees were replaced by pine trees, and Alex stared thoughtfully through the front window. "What are the odds this would happen just after we see Rita?"

"She seemed pretty pissed at you, but I don't see how she can be responsible for this mess. No one can control the weather like that. Right?"

"I suppose so. I'd better call Martin. Maybe he has some intel that could shed some light on things for us."

Once Alex got through to Donner, he explained what had happened with the tornado. "I think it has something to do with the SV1, but I'm not positive."

Donner thought about a recent call he received from Harry Clemens, a deputy sheriff. "Listen, a friend of mine just told me about a tornado in Darrington last Monday. A tornado appeared out of nowhere and demolished an apartment complex, then suddenly stopped. It turned out Preston had a crew standing by when it happened and got the contract for the rescue and cleanup, and I don't think it was a coincidence."

Alex didn't like where this was leading. "Neither do I, but that would mean they did it from space, and I can't see how that is even possible. We're headed to Preston's facility in eastern Washington to see if we can get inside."

"Don't do anything illegal, Alex. You're listed in our records as a geologic consultant. It's already getting harder and harder to explain why a rock hound is breaking into classified facilities and leaving a trail of bodies, so be careful."

"I will, Martin. I always am." Alex smiled as he hung up the phone and looked over at Okawna. "It seems I getting a reputation as a bad ass geologic consultant."

Chapter 7

FORTY MILES SOUTHWEST OF SPOKANE, WASHINGTON:
Dry grasslands stretched away into the distance on both sides of the gravel road as they drew near the facility. Tall security fencing with lighting and cameras formed a large square around the compound, and in the center was a one-hundred-foot square concrete building. More cameras and sensors were mounted around the roofline, and a large satellite dish and a tall antenna were mounted on the roof. The only colors were the dark awnings shading the windows of the guard shack and the vehicles parked near the entrance to the SV1 control center on the other side of the fence.

Okawna stopped at the security gate, where a man behind bulletproof glass stared back at them. When the man spoke, the voice came through a speaker below a video camera.

"State your business."

"We'd like a tour of your facility."

"We don't allow tours. If there is nothing else, please leave. Have a nice day."

Alex leaned across in front of Okawna to look at the guard. "Call Mr. Preston and tell him Alex Cave and Okawna are here."

Okawna chuckled. "I wish I could see the look on Preston's face when he gets the call."

"I bet he lets us in. If he's hiding something, he won't want to make us any more suspicious than we already are."

After several minutes, Okawna heard the guard tell him to enter, then the gate moved to one side, and he drove through. "I guess you were right."

They drove into an open parking space near the front door, and when they climbed out, a casually dressed man stepped out from the building and Alex held out his hand. "Nice of you to let us take a look around. I guess you already know our names."

The man stared back evenly as he shook hands. "I'm Paul Carter. I manage the control center."

Carter stared at the two men, sizing both Alex and Okawna up. Preston had forewarned him these two could pose a problem if provoked, so he knew he had to tread lightly.

"Follow me and I'll show you around."

They followed him into the building, past a room with security personnel monitoring the cameras and dozens of racks of computing hardware. When they entered the main control room, they saw a young woman in a security uniform standing just inside the door. They moved further into the large, air-conditioned room, and Alex noticed a young man, about David's age, concentrating on the desk monitor above a control console.

Carter waved his hand at two large wall mounted televisions. "As you can see, this is where we monitor and control the satellite."

Alex noticed the female guard smiling at Okawna and suppressed a smile himself when he turned back to Paul. "Where do you do all your research and development?"

"DAR has a partner with a large compound in Nevada."

"Who would that be?"

"I don't know all the details. Someone named Essex."

Alex glanced at Okawna, who had stopped smiling at the girl when he heard the name. "Interesting. Listen, we saw a strange weather event just on the other side of the mountains recently. A nearly transparent tornado formed below a strange cloud and tore up my father's ranch. Could the SV1 have something to do with it?"

"No, that's impossible. Nobody can control the weather."

The young man stood and stepped closer, shaking hands with the newcomers. "I'm Scott Brackenbury. Pardon me, but it is possible. If you apply the right resonant frequency, you could stimulate the molecules in the ionosphere and affect the direction of the jet stream. The SV1 uses specific frequencies to attract certain molecular combinations, and another frequency to fuse them into a solid mass, so it could be programmed to emit an ELF to affect the weather."

Okawna thought about Christmas. "I'm sorry. An elf?"

"It stands for extremely low frequency."

Carter had heard of the theory. "Even so, you would have no way of creating an isolated weather event, much less a tornado here on the planet." He noticed Scott was deep in thought. "What's on your mind?"

Scott looked at Alex. "What time did you see the tornado?"

"Exactly 9:47 this morning. Why?"

"When we first fired up the SV1, I noticed a strange frequency 180-degrees offset from the SV1's operating frequency. It was like an echo, but it wasn't coming from the SV1. I think it was coming from somewhere on the planet. It happened again this morning, about the same time as your tornado."

"I see. There was a similar tornado in Darrington right after you turned it on the first time. You have no idea where these signals came from?"

"No, they didn't last long enough for me to run an analysis. The recording was too short."

Alex had a thought and looked at Paul. "How did you plan on getting all that junk down from space?"

"Preston has a recovery vehicle standing by at the Nevada facility."

Alex looked down at Scott. "Is there any chance you could call me if you detect the second signal again?"

Scott looked at Paul, who indicated approval. "Sure. What's your number?"

Alex told him and watched him write it down. "Thanks. I guess we'll let you get back to work. I appreciate you giving us a tour, Paul."

Carter bent down to the pen and paper. "Just a minute, Alex."

Carter wrote his name and number and then ripped the sheet from the tablet. "This is too much of a coincidence. Here's our private number. Call us if you hear about another tornado or another strange weather anomaly."

Alex took the paper. "I appreciate your interest."

Carter waved the female guard over. "This is Debra. She'll escort you back to your car."

Okawna strolled beside Debra as they left the room, and once outside the building, he kissed the back of her hand before she went back inside. He climbed into the sedan but didn't start the engine. "I thought Essex was arrested for kidnapping."

Alex knew John Essex's major flaw was his fanatical obsession with going into outer space. He wasn't interested in money, but Janice Sloan, the woman who had kidnapped Fala and her daughter, had enticed him with the promise of a piece of advanced alien technology to help him get into space. She also threatened to cut off his manhood. "I guess you didn't hear. His attorney pleaded he was coerced into helping Sloan under a threat of death. He didn't go to jail, and is out on bond until his trial."

"That reminds me. How come you didn't mention the other missing device at Preston's place?"

"Just playing a hunch. If they have it, they would never admit it, and I would imagine it's at Essex's compound."

Okawna's lips formed into a sly grin. "We already know our way around. Let's check it out."

"I'll call and book us a flight to Reno, Nevada."

Okawna backed out of the parking space and headed for the airport in Spokane, while Alex called and made reservations, but they only had an hour to check in. He told Okawna, who pressed the accelerator to the floor, and they were racing along the road across the open grasslands at full speed.

***

FIDALGO ISLAND. DAR HEADQUARTERS:

Preston was upstairs in his office when the security system let him know one of the garage doors was opening. He looked over at the monitor, seeing Rita's troubled expression gazing up at him. He pressed a button for the lock, then stood and hurried down the stairs, and met Rita coming in from the garage. "What's going on?"

Rita hurried past him to the bar, grabbed a beer from the refrigerator, and then took a deep swallow. "There's something wrong with my device."

Preston stared at her as she took another deep swallow. "Would you care to elaborate?"

"There was a strange signal piggybacking on mine while it was on, and the oscillations made my teeth vibrate." She noticed the concern in Preston's eyes. "What's going on, Steve?"

"SV1 control noticed the same thing, but it only lasted a few minutes. Not enough time to figure out what caused it."

"What was the exact time it happened?"

"9:47 this morning."

"That's when I was trying to destroy Sparrow Valley."

Preston thought he heard wrong. "Tried? Didn't it work?"

"In a way. I couldn't hit the town, but I tore up some of Cave's property."

"I thought you said you had pinpoint accuracy."

"It has to be that second signal causing some type of interference."

"Maybe it's your signal bouncing off the SV1."

"No, this one is the complete opposite of ours. Like an echo. I put the trailer in a secured storage building until we can figure out what's going on."

"Good idea. Let's see if it happens again without your device."

***

GROOM LAKE:

Brian Carver thought the video image of the strange-looking torpedo appeared to be crooked, so he entered the number for Doctor Heinz and waited. The more he studied the picture, the more it appeared the concrete walls were straight, and the torpedo was at an angle. He picked up the phone and pressed a button. "Director, it's Brian, over at security. You should check on that torpedo you have us watching. I think it might have fallen over."

***

Henry hurried from his office and along the hallway to the elevator. He performed the usual security check, then the door opened, and he stepped inside. He selected a floor, and then the doors closed. Once the elevator stopped, he stepped out and hurried down the hall to the vault, but his jaw dropped open as he suddenly stopped. "Good grief!"

Chapter 8

NEVADA:

Okawna turned off the asphalt onto a well-maintained gravel road, while Alex enjoyed the panoramic view of the open desert, and the aroma of sage filling the air coming through the open windows. It was a long drive to Essex's compound, located south of the Naval Air Station in Fallon, and it brought back sad memories for both of them. Driven by his desire to design an economical means of space travel, Essex had purchased the land and leased test sites from the government after the Cold War. More importantly. He wanted to mine the moon.

Twenty minutes later, they arrived at the expansive facility and Alex looked around to see if anything had changed. The last time they were here, they arrived by parachute at night.

The ten foot tall, barbed wire fences still stretched out across the desert on either side, but the guard shack was gone, and the single pole across the entrance was replaced with a massive steel gate. ESSEX SPACE RESEARCH AND DEVELOPMENT CORPORATION was stated in large stainless steel letters above the tan-colored security building.

Okawna parked in an empty space in front of the structure, and then they climbed out and stood in front of a camera, then Alex pressed a small button below the speaker. While he waited for someone to answer, he noticed Okawna staring at him. When he turned to look at him, saw a mischievous glimmer in his eyes snd smirked at him. "What are you thinking?"

"Do you think he'll be glad to see us again?"

Alex chuckled. "Not likely. We caused him a lot of grief the last time we were here."

"Yeah, well, his greed got him in trouble, not us. We just ruined his plans."

They were interrupted by a voice from the speaker. "State your business."

Alex looked at the camera. "We're here to see our good friend, John Essex."

"Is he expecting you?"

"No, we were in the area and decided to stop by to say hello."

"What are your names?"

"I'm Alex Cave, and this is Okawna."

"Do you have a last name, Okawna?"

Okawna's hands clenched into fists at his side. "Yes, Okawna. Got it?"

"Stand by."

Alex thought about the man who had gotten them out of the facility the last time they were here. "I wonder if Jim Coburn got fired for helping us."

"No, I can't see how. Nobody saw us together, so I bet he's still here."

The door opened, and then a serious-looking man dressed in SWAT gear stepped out and put his hand on the butt of his sidearm. "You'll have to leave any weapons in your vehicle. No one will bother them."

Alex knew this would happen, and they had already locked their pistols in the console between the seats. "We're good."

"You'll set off the metal detector if you're lying."

Alex stared back evenly. "I said we're good."

The man could tell Cave didn't like being called a liar. "No offense, Sir."

When the man stepped aside, Alex entered the building and walked through the metal detector without issue, as did Okawna. The guard stayed back while they stepped up to the check-in desk, where a big man was waiting on their side of the counter. Not wanting to arouse suspicion, Alex and Okawna tried not to show any sign of recognition of the familiar face.

"I'm Alex Cave and this is Okawna." Alex stared at the man's name tag. "Mr. Coburn. We're here to see John."

Jim suppressed a smile. "Yes, he's expecting you." He held out two visitor badges. "Keep these with you and follow me. I'll drive you to his office."

None of them spoke when they stepped outside, where Alex climbed into the front passenger seat of the SUV, with Okawna directly behind him. Once they were driving away from the building, Alex smiled and reached across to shake Jim's hand.

"It's good to see you again, my friend."

"You too, Alex. I never thought I'd see you guys again."

Okawna reached over the seat to do the same. "I hope we didn't get you into any trouble the last time we met."

"Not at all. Essex was grateful I understood his predicament. However, he has a new partner, since you killed Sloan. I guess you noticed all the beefed up security measures."

"Yes, I heard he's working with Steve Preston on the SV1 project."

"That's right. Preston did an extensive background check on each one of us, but I knew my crew was vetted. He added three new men to my security team without even asking me if I wanted them."

Alex noticed Jim's knuckles turning white on the steering wheel. "Okawna and I are following a lead on two strange tornadoes in the Pacific Northwest. His project manager at the control center told me they happened while their SV1 was working. That's how we ended up here."

"I see. I'm sure Essex isn't looking forward to seeing you again."

"You're probably right. I'm hoping he might let you show us around."

"I'll tell you what. If he won't, I will."

"I appreciate the offer, but we don't want to get you in trouble. Let's just play it by ear."

Jim parked in front of the glass-spired structure that was Essex's office and living quarters. When they climbed out, they were surprised to see the small man hurrying out through the front doorway.

John Essex stopped in front of his visitors and crossed his arms behind his back. With his most serious expression, he stared up at Alex and Okawna. "You have a lot of nerve, Cave. When I found out you were here, I called Preston, and he warned me about what you two were up to."

Okawna bent over to be even with Essex's face. "Then why did you let us in?"

Essex smiled and tried to grab Okawna's hand to shake it. "Because I'm excited to show you what I've accomplished since Preston became my partner. I am actually going to get into space! Isn't that wonderful?"

Okawna stood, but did not take the little man's hand. "You're just full of surprises, aren't you, John?"

Essex turned to Alex, but when he saw him shake his head no, he didn't reach out to him. "I'm really sorry about what happened. I wasn't lying when I said she was going to kill me if I didn't go along with her plan to kidnap your family. Anyway, let's all get in so Jim can drive us around and I'll show you what I've built."

Essex started to climb into the front passenger seat next to Coburn, but hesitated when Okawna stepped in front of him. "Fine. I'll ride in back. It's a short drive to the rail facility."

On the drive through the vast compound, they listened to Essex's excited descriptions of the various projects he was working on. "I'll tell you this much, Alex. After what happened with Sloan, I lost all my other contributors and Steve helped keep me out of jail. Without his financial support, I would have lost my dream."

Alex noticed the glimmer in Essex's eyes and knew the man was on a mission of passion. "I understand you have a vehicle for collecting the space junk."

"Yes, that's where we're headed. It's in the last hangar." He leaned forward near Jim's ear. "Skip the rest of the tour. I can't wait to show them my spaceship."

Alex recognized the elevated electro-magnetic launch system extending from the end of the hangar, but this time, the other end was somewhere over the horizon. Jim pulled over next to a small door on the side of the large structure, and then they all climbed out.

Essex couldn't stop smiling as he ran ahead to open the door, and Alex thought he was like a little kid, excited to show his parents what he had made all by himself. They followed him through the doorway into a massive open bay., where Alex nearly ran over the little man when he saw the exotic-looking machine perched on the magnetic launch platform. "Wow, John. She's a beautiful craft, all right. Would you mind if we take a closer look?"

"Of course not. Please, go right ahead. Let me show you what I've built."

Alex grinned at Okawna, whose mouth was still open, then climbed up the steps to a platform next to the cockpit. It was a two-seater and looked more like a short-winged drone than a spacecraft. He looked down at his friends and then climbed inside.

A moment later, Okawna's smile couldn't get any wider as he climbed in beside Alex in the two-person cockpit and studied the labels on the dark video screens built into the stylish console. "Too bad we can't take it for a ride."

"I hear you." He looked up at Essex on the platform. "How do you overcome the extreme G-force on launch?"

"Pressure suits, of course, but we limit the acceleration to the max a fit person could handle. That's why the track is ten-miles long."

Okawna studied Essex's small frame, and he didn't appear to be fit for a maximum G-ride. "Do you need an astronaut?"

"No. Most of the work will be done with thrusters and robotic arms, so no space walking."

"Hell, I'm your man, John. When is our first flight? Have you tested a launch yet?"

Essex put his fists on his hips. "No, no, and no. I already have my copilot." Essex's fists opened as he lowered his arms. "It's a concession I had to give Preston as part of the deal. He insists she's qualified, but I don't know anything about her."

Alex exchanged glances with Okawna. "Is her name Rita?"

"Yes, Rita Harrow. A nice-looking red-haired woman."

"That doesn't surprise me. Take my advice and watch your back. She's about as crooked as Sloan, but not as nasty." Alex indicated to his friend it was time to get out, and they joined Essex and Jim on the platform.

Essex gave Alex a puzzled stare as tiny beads of perspiration formed on his forehead. "Why? Who is she?"

"Trouble. And let's just leave it at that. So, is it ready to fly?"

Essex beamed at Alex's interest in his spacecraft. "It's been ready for weeks. I'm just waiting for the SV1 to create the first batch of material."

Okawna moved to the rear of the craft to study the dual rocket motor exhaust systems, and they were one-sixteenth the size of the ones for the old space shuttle. "Hey, Essex. Are you sure these motors are big enough to get you into orbit?"

"Of course, but that's not their main purpose. Their primary goal is to slow me down before I re-enter the atmosphere. The launch rail speed will be more than adequate to reach the stratosphere, and a small amount of rocket burn will put me in orbit. In order to have a direct shot at the material, launch timing is critical."

Alex walked to the bulbous nose of the craft. "Can I see what's inside?"

Essex smiled. "You're gonna love this."

Essex reached down into the cockpit and pressed a small button, then stood and joined his friends, watching the top of the nose split in two out of the way. When they stopped moving, he waved them closer and pointed at the open container, and then at the two mechanical arms tucked away against the inside walls. "The ball of material will be eighteen-inches in diameter. That's the maximum mass we can maneuver with the ship as a counter-weight. I'll use the arms to capture it in a net and guide it into the re-entry canister."

Okawna had a mechanical engineering degree and knew it wouldn't work. "The mass is too heavy for re-entry in your little spaceship."

Essex huffed at the statement. "Of course it is. Once the ball is inside the canister, I'll seal the lid and fill the void with expanding foam. That would also help insulate the parachute in the lid from the flames roiling off the ablative re-entry shield when I send it back to my facility."

Alex felt his phone vibrate. "Excuse me while I take this call." He stepped away and answered. "Hey, Doc."

"Alex, all the metal frames in the vault where we store the device have melted."

"When did that happen?"

"Yesterday morning."

"Is it safe?"

"Yes, but I need to know what you want me to do about it."

Alex rubbed his temples and closed his eyes. "Until I find out how it happened, keep it locked in the vault. I'll call when I know something." He moved back over to the group and looked at Essex. "You keep talking about material modules. What are they?"

"Part of the recovery process is to liquefy the different materials using controlled harmonic resonance frequencies, and make them spin to separate the hydrocarbons from the metals. When they cool, we have perfectly symmetrical spheres to place in the container."

Alex's gut tightened into a knot. If what he suspected was true, all the devices were activated at the same time, and that's what melted the metal frames in the vault.

Essex beamed with pride at his accomplishment. "The instruction manual for the SV1 device gave me a wealth of new engineering concepts. It's amazing what you can do in the vacuum of space."

Alex glared at the little man. "That's Pandora's Box you're messing with, John. If I were you, I'd shut the lid before you create another weapon of mass destruction. We have enough of those already."

"That is not my intent, Alex. I just want to go into outer space."

"Now that you have your vehicle, I'd like my instruction manual back."

Essex laughed. "Your instruction manual? I know about you, Alex. A small-time geology professor for a little college in Montana. These theories are far too complicated for the likes of you."

"I didn't say I wrote them."

Okawna grabbed the front of Essex's shirt and hoisted the little man up. "Just give us the damn manual or I'll wring your scrawny neck. How does that grab you?"

Essex felt pressure in his eyeballs as his tight collar cut off his circulation. "Just stop, Okawna. Please! It's too late. Preston has the master copy!" When Okawna let go and stepped back, Essex massaged his throat. "I only have a copy to work with, but I don't think he gave me everything."

Alex knew Preston had a secret, and wondered what kind of information he was guarding from his lead scientist. "What makes you say that?"

"The data indicates there were four devices, but I've only seen the one in orbit."

"Does Preston have any other research facilities?"

"Sure, right here on my property. He converted one of the hangars into a facility for reclaiming the precious metals from the material I send down."

"Could we take a look at it?"

Essex shrugged. "Of course, but there's nothing going on right now. The place has been deserted for the past two months."

"I'd still like to see what he did."

Essex looked up at Jim. "Take them wherever they need to go, and I'll find a ride back. I have a few things to do here. Like getting the blood circulating in my brain again."

Alex realized Essex was just a pawn in Preston's game plan. "Thanks for showing us around. I'll keep in touch."

Jim showed them the small foundry, but nothing looked out of place, so Alex sat in silence on the drive to the security building while Okawna and Jim talked about the spacecraft. After saying goodbye to their friend, they climbed into the sedan and headed back to Reno, and Alex explained about the urgent call he had received from Henry earlier, and what had happened in the vault. "We need to find that device in the arctic. They were meant to work together, so I'm sure something happened to it as well."

"How do you plan on finding them? Especially the one in the arctic?"

"I have an idea. Let's head back to the Fallon Naval Air Station so we can get a ride to Las Vegas, then the plane to Groom Lake."

"Works for me."

Chapter 9

GROOM LAKE:

The sun had vanished below the horizon when the small jet touched down and taxied along the tarmac, and Alex stared out the window at the dimly lit outline of the small building, which was the terminal and security checkpoint onto the base. When the whine of the engines ceased, he stood and moved forward to open the side door and stairs, then looked into the cockpit. "Thanks for picking us up, Skip."

"Not a problem, Alex. Just a slight detour."

Alex grabbed his bag from the small closet, handed the other one to Okawna, and they walked down the stairs to the security building. Alex saw Henry waiting inside, and smiled at Kathy, the security guard, as he hurried over to greet him. "Hey, Doc." He noticed his friend wasn't beside him and glanced back over his shoulder, then smiled when he saw Okawna flirting with Kathy. "Care to join us?"

Henry waited for Okawna to join them. "I would imagine you are eager to see what happened. I have a golf cart waiting for us."

Alex and Okawna followed him outside, and once seated, Henry drove along the concrete surface between the hangars and stopped near the rear entrance to the main office complex. They climbed out and entered, then continued down the hallway to the elevator, stepped inside, and descended to the lowest level.

When the doors opened, Alex stepped out and stared down the hallway at the pool of silver where the steel door of the vault used to be. He cautiously moved down the hall, stopped at the open doorway into the vault, and knelt down next to the shiny pool of melted steel. He held his hand out, testing for heat, and then took out a pen to check liquidity. It was solid, so he cautiously placed his fingertips on the cool surface.

He stood and looked at his friends, then stepped onto the metal and entered the room. He didn't see any sign of intense heat, only the twenty-foot long pewter-colored torpedo resting on what remained of the thick metal rack on the floor. What baffled him was the lack of any heat damage on the concrete walls and ceiling. He had a thought and looked around until he saw the video camera, which appeared to be undamaged, then turned to Henry. "Were you able to record the entire event?"

"Yes, and we are still recording. I do not know why the camera did not melt."

"It's because none of the camera's components oscillate at the right frequency." He explained what they had learned about the SV1 project. "That's how they collapse the material into a solid mass for transport. Let's go back upstairs and watch the recording of what happened."

No one spoke as they returned to the surface and entered Henry's office. Alex waited until Henry sat down and slid two chairs around so they could see the monitor. Once he and Okawna were seated, Henry started the recording. When the pointed end of the torpedo appeared to shimmer for a few moments, Alex leaned forward and pressed pause. "I saw the device on the island react the same way."

He pressed play and watched the device slowly sag to the floor as the steel support frame melted. He could see more light entering the room as the thick door appeared to dissolve into a shimmering pool on the concrete floor, but there were no flames and no sign of any increase in temperature. Even the paint on the surface of the melting steel didn't burn. It just peeled away from the metal, forming into curls on top of the silver surface. When the shimmering abruptly stopped, he reached forward and pressed stop. "It's just as I thought. All four devices worked simultaneously." He noticed Okawna's troubled expression. "What's on your mind?"

"What about the other two devices? Did they react the same way?"

"I would imagine they did, but for the moment, there is no way to find out."

Henry heard a beep from his computer and turned to look at the monitor. "It is Director Donner."

Alex leaned back. "Put him on, Doc." An instant later, Donner's image appeared on the screen. "Hello, Martin. I was just about to call you with an update." He explained the melted metal in the vault. "I was right, Martin. The SV1 is affecting all the devices at the same time."

"I never doubted you, Alex. Director Sliven of the NordVulC facility called me about an emergency." He explained the discovery. "Sliven specifically asked for you and Okawna to investigate the situation, and I convinced him to keep the number of people involved to a minimum. He wants to set up a video conference today whenever you're ready."

"We're ready now. Does he know about the device?"

"Not yet. I'll leave that up to your discretion."

"All right. Let him know we're ready when he is."

"Okay. Stand by."

Henry looked up at Alex. "Is there any place we could safely store our device until this is over?"

"No, I don't want to risk someone getting killed if it comes on while they're trying to move it. It didn't affect anything outside the concrete walls of the vault, so I think it will be fine for now."

"Very well."

Donner's image appeared on the split screen, along with Sliven's. "We're here, Alex."

"It's nice to see you again, Director Sliven."

"You too, Alex. Hello, Okawna. I want you to watch this video of what we have discovered protruding from a recent magma flow under the Ice. It was shoved up through the surface with enough force to fracture a ten foot thick ice sheet. Here is the recording taken by the man who made the discovery. His name is Terry Hardin."

Alex noticed Okawna's posture stiffen and looked over at him. "What's going on?"

Okawna shook his head no. "Later."

Alex turned back to Sliven. "Go ahead."

The recording appeared edited for length, and began by showing the massive slabs of white ice above the horizon, about three-hundred-yards north from the edge of the ten-foot wall of the ice sheet. The recording cut to show a view from a drone looking directly down at the narrow gaps between massive triangles of ice and saw the sun's reflection off a mirror. The recording stopped, and Sliven's image appeared. "It was an unusual seismic event where we have seen no activity on record. Even more puzzling, our other sensors showed no suspicious activity in the surrounding mantels. It's as if something melted the rock in that specific location."

Alex wondered if his missing device had melted the rock. He didn't notice it anywhere in the immediate area, but it could be buried under the lava. As for the ship, it appeared to be much larger than his spaceship. "Were you able to determine its size?"

"To a certain degree, yes, and it is the size of one of your baseball fields, but we have no idea how much is still buried below the lava."

Donner recognized the mirrored surface and knew he had to talk to Alex alone. "All right. Thanks for the briefing, Jeffery. I'll get back to you soon."

Alex leaned forward. "Before you go, could you send me an unedited copy of the recording? My team and I might get a little more information to work with."

"I will, Alex. Any idea when you will arrive?"

"Okawna and I will head in your direction later on today."

"Very good. I will see you soon."

When Sliven signed off, Alex leaned back and looked at Donner's image. "How do you want me to deal with this? There are too many people involved to keep this a secret."

"I know. We'll need to keep our information compartmentalized until we know what we're dealing with."

Alex turned to Okawna. "What's going on with you and Hardin?"

"Nothing between the two of us. I've never met him, but I've heard rumors he belongs to a group of UFO enthusiasts. I've also heard he can be ruthless in his pursuit of evidence to back up his theories. We can't trust him."

Alex turned back to Donner. "Can you run a background check on him for us?"

"I will. I got a satellite image of the area, and it's too far to go by helicopter, but the surface around the rupture is smooth enough to land a small plane."

"Could you tell if the cracks go all the way through the ice sheet?"

"Our analysts believe the chances are good you could make it all the way down to the spacecraft. You take over from here, Alex. I'll Tell Skip the jet is yours for a while. Good luck to you both."

Okawna turned to Alex. "I'll need to pick up some cold weather gear. Would you mind if we stop in Stillwater on the way?"

Alex knew Okawna was talking about his home in Wyoming. "I believe it's on the way." He turned to Henry. "I'll stop by Hangar 5 on the way and let David and Jadin know what's going on. They can get started analyzing the recording when it arrives."

"Be careful, boys." Henry stared after them as they left his office, and then slumped down in his chair. *This is my fault*, he thought. *I should never have downloaded the instruction manual into my computer.*

Chapter 10

SV1 CONTROL STATION:

Carter paced behind Scott while staring at the image from the SV1 on one of the monitors. A short distance from the tip of the torpedo-shaped device, flashes of sunlight sparkled inside a twenty-four-foot diameter cloud of space debris. According to the data from the sensors mounted outside the main body of the SV1, they had gathered the optimal weight to material ratio for a safe retrieval and descent back to earth. Now came the tricky part. Getting the metal and plastic to separate into spheres. "Is everyone ready? Because this whole project will be a waste of time if this doesn't work. Not to mention, we'll all be unemployed." He looked at the security personnel who had gathered behind him, all just as anxious as he was and turned to Scott. "Cross your fingers. Go ahead."

Carter crossed his arms over his chest as he stared across at the monitor. The cloud of metal and plastic shimmered, and the tiny flashes appeared to be moving in a concentrically smaller circle. When it formed into a solid silver ball, he smiled and reached down to put his hand on Scott's shoulder. "It worked!"

Scott felt a sense of pride when everyone around him clapped and cheered. He smiled as he pressed a button to shut down the device, but his smile slipped away as he jabbed it several more times. "It's not shutting down!"

Carter studied the digital information on the desk monitor. "That's not our signal."

"I know, and it's the same signal as before. It's as if someone else is taking control of the device. Someone's got to be hacking the system, that's the only explanation."

Scott started hammering away code on the computer, trying to divert the hacker. Everything he tried was immediately countermanded, and then he ran out of ideas. "I'm trying every trick in the book, but nothing is working. What we need is the designer. Maybe they know how to secure the system and shut down the backdoors this hacker is using. Is there any way to get that person here?"

Carter was tired of all the compartmentalized-for-security bullshit from Preston, but his previous inquiries about who had built it had gotten him nowhere, so he had given up trying. "I'll let Preston know what's going on. That's all I can do about it."

Scott entered one command after another, desperately trying to regain control, but nothing seemed to work, so he slammed his fist on the counter. "What is going on? Why won't it respond to anything?"

Teresa leaned over Scott's shoulder. "Reboot the system."

Scott spun around and stared at her. "Are you crazy?"

She waved her hand at the data on the desk monitor. "Even if we did, we are not in control anymore. Something else is in control."

Scott rolled his chair closer to the screen. "That's strange. It's off. I don't know what happened, but it shut down."

"Do we have control of the SV1?"

"For now. I have a feeling the next test will be hacked, and I can't tell how, so I'm taking a break."

***

THE POLAR ICE SHEET. ALIEN SPACECRAFT:

Seth felt a soft breeze across his face inside the stasis chamber and slowly opened his eyes, but needed to verify the computer generated voice of the ship's artificial intelligence would come through his neural implant. "Pandora?"

"I am here, Captain"

"Are the surface conditions habitable again?"

"Negative."

"Then why did you take me out of stasis?"

"I detected an object in orbit with a similar technology to our own, and I have been trying to interface with its operating system. The signal is sporadic, and it's urgent we make contact, so I initiated override protocols and brought the ship to the surface."

Seth almost sat up. "That means our people have returned. Open this stasis chamber and let me out. We need to contact them. They may not know we are here." The door opened, and he felt his platform moving. "Bring main lighting up in seven angstrom increments. How long has it been?"

"You have been in stasis for one hundred and twenty million years."

Seth was stunned and stared up at the elevated roof of the control room on top of the spacecraft. His mouth opened, but he didn't know what to say. He had never heard of anyone being in stasis for such an extended period.

"Are the rest of the stasis chambers intact?"

"Yes, Captain."

Shadows slowly grew inside the main control room as the lights came on. With great effort, he managed to sit up on the slender bed, and then slowly stood. He grabbed the open door for the chamber when a rush of vertigo threatened his balance. Once everything stopped swirling, he eased his way along one wall to a beverage dispenser, filled a small cup with water, and drained it in two gulps. He filled it with green liquid containing electrolytes and drank more slowly, as he looked around the interior of the forty foot circular room and stared up at the white ceiling. "Activate transparency."

Blue-white ice suddenly appeared to be resting on top of the spaceship, which filled the room with pale translucent light from the surface. "What are the outside conditions?"

"The atmosphere contains high levels of toxic artificial gases. These are not our people."

Seth sat down in front of the control console and checked the ship's status, then looked up at the ice. "Any recommendations for this situation?"

"I will try to regain contact with the object on orbit to learn about the people who now inhabit our planet. They must be the cause of the toxic atmosphere, and I will not share my world with them."

"As you wish. Now that we are on the surface, I must start getting used to eating solid food again."

"Yes, Captain. I will active the waste disposal room."

Chapter 11

ICELAND:

Skip stepped out of the cockpit and looked down the aisle at his two passengers. Both had their seats reclined all the way down, with the overhead lights off. He quietly made his way down the aisle and gently touched Alex's shoulder.

Having gotten little sleep over the past few days, Alex was out cold when he felt a hand on his shoulder. He looked up at Skip and then sat up straight. "Are we there already?"

"We'll be on final approach in twenty minutes, Alex. I thought you and Okawna might want some time to wake up before we touch down in Reykjavík."

"Thanks."

Alex stood and heard Okawna's soft snoring further down the aisle, and strolled over to bump the side of the cushion with his leg. "Time to get up."

He continued down to the bathroom, and when he returned to the cabin, found Okawna staring out the window while using an electric shaver. He sat down, fastened his seat belt, and stared out the window, then a few moments later, felt a soft thud vibrate through the fuselage as the wheels touched the runway. The jet engines roared in reverse thrust for a few moments before the jet taxied to the air terminal.

When the jet stopped, Alex stood and made his way forward to the cockpit, opened the door, and leaned inside. "I'm not sure how long we'll be gone, Skip."

"No problem. Zachery and I will refuel and find a place to park while we get some sleep. Call me when you're on your way and I'll tell you where we're located."

"Sounds good."

Alex stepped back to press the button to open the stairs and turned to grab his backpack from the storage compartment. With Okawna right behind him, he went down and headed toward the door into the terminal. Once through customs, they were met by Sliven and Hardin, and Alex held his hand out to the slender man with curly-gray hair. "It's nice to see you again, Director."

Sliven smiled. "You, too, my friend. We have brought you the equipment you wanted. It is in those two black bags over there by the exit."

After greeting Sliven, Okawna turned to the man standing beside him and held out his hand. "I'm Okawna."

"Terry Hardin."

Okawna noticed Hardin's grip was much stronger than necessary as he stared into his eyes, and realized this was going to be a turf war. "Have you worked here long?"

Hardin let go. "Nope."

Okawna waited for him to elaborate, but Hardin just stared back evenly, so he turned to Sliven. When Alex explained only the two of them would go check it out from the surface, Hardin suddenly leaned toward Alex, so Okawna shoved a hand against the man's chest. "Take it easy."

Hardin leaned back from Okawna and glared at Alex. "I made the initial discovery and I'm going with you."

Alex stared back evenly. "I'm sorry, but that's the way it has to be for the moment. I promise you'll be involved once we know what it is."

Sliven had worked with Alex recently and knew to trust his judgment, and turned to Hardin to intervene. "I'm sorry, Terry, but I must agree with Alex. You are a fine volcanologist, and we will study what caused this to happen once we know it is safe to proceed."

Hardin stared into each man's eyes for a second, then turned and stomped toward the exit. When he was out of sight, Sliven turned to his friends. "I apologize for Terry. He has a stubborn streak, but he is a good researcher. How are you going to get to the site?"

Okawna nodded toward the runway. "I have a friend here who has a plane. His name is Huckabee."

"Ah, yes, Patrick. Well then. I will let you get on with your business. Please keep me informed about your progress."

"I will, Director."

When Sliven turned and headed for the main exit, they put on their backpacks and grabbed the two black bags of climbing equipment, then left the building through another door and walked along a row of private aircraft hangars, looking for a specific number. Alex knew little about the pilot they were meeting and they were both too tired to talk about it after they left the base. "How do you know this guy?"

Okawna looked over and smirked. "A few months ago, I was dating his cousin for a few weeks. It turns out Huck and I had more to talk about than I had with his cousin. He was our helicopter pilot during a mission in the

Middle East." He looked up at a number on the side of a hangar. "Here it is."

Alex followed Okawna into the structure and saw a beautiful orange Dahavlin Beaver aircraft parked in front of the large sliding doors. It was a great plane, used by Alaska bush pilots.

Okawna looked around for his friend. "Huck? Are you in here?"

He heard the bathroom door open, and then a blue-colored cast protruded through the doorway, followed by a man struggling to roll his wheelchair through the opening, so he rushed over to hold the door open. "What happened to you?"

Patrick Huckabee looked up at his guest. "Snowboarding accident."

"Ouch. Are you still able to fly?"

"Nope, but you can take her for a ride. She's fueled and ready to go."

"I really appreciate this, Huck. This is my friend, Alex Cave."

Alex shook the man's hand. "I love your plane."

Huckabee smiled like a proud father. "Thanks. Yeah, she's a sweetheart. Stow your gear while I open the doors."

Alex took both backpacks and walked around to the other side of the aircraft, while Okawna transmitted a flight plan to the control tower using Huck's computer. He listened to the rattle of chains as the doors slowly rolled to one side of the hangar while he strapped the packs and the two black bags into the cargo hold. A moment later, Okawna helped him push the aircraft out onto the tarmac.

Huckabee rolled his wheelchair out of the hangar and joined the two men. "Any idea when you'll be back?"

Okawna waited while Alex climbed into the copilot seat. "Three, maybe four hours."

"All right. Have a safe flight."

Okawna watched his friend roll back into the hangar, and then climbed in and fastened his seatbelt. "He's a good man."

Alex put on his headset and sat quietly while Okawna went through the preflight check and approval to take off. He had forgotten how exhilarating it was to feel the powerful surge of a large single engine in a small aircraft. He stared out the window in comfortable silence while they flew past Iceland and over the vast Arctic Ocean. If this ship was as big as described by Sliven, it will be hard to keep it secret.

***

Alex heard Okawna's voice through his headset and opened his eyes, suddenly realizing he had dozed off. In the distance, a ten-foot wall of light blue ice rose up above the water. At the top, the massive Polar Ice Sheet stretched away to the horizon. He felt the plane bank left as Okawna swung around the points of three triangular blocks of ice protruding above the barren landscape.

Okawna studied the terrain around their destination and chose a section with the least amount of washboard, which was created by the chop of the waves while the seawater was freezing. "It shouldn't be any problem landing."

Alex felt his stomach rise as the plane dropped toward the ice. Tiny ice crystals swirled into the air as Okawna set down on the frosted white surface and taxied toward the blocks of shattered ice rising above the horizon. When they were turned around, Okawna shut down the engine and everything seemed deathly quiet.

Alex climbed out and surveyed his surroundings, and if not for his dark goggles, the glare off the unending ice would have been unbearable. The first fracture was two-hundred-feet toward the south, with the large slab tilted up at a slight angle. From the satellite image, they had determined the edge of this block gave him the most direct passage down to the alien craft.

While Okawna grabbed the bags of climbing gear from the side compartment, Alex slid a metal briefcase from under the seat, opened the lid, and entered a command into a laptop computer. When the main screen appeared, he reached into the case, grabbed a small communication device called an earbud, and inserted it into his ear. Next was his head strap, with the light and body camera. He turned it on, slid the strap over his head, and looked at the screen. The video image was clear, and when he spoke, the audio signal was strong.

Okawna stepped up next to Alex and did the same with his earpiece and camera. "How do you read?"

Alex heard him through his earbud. "We're ready."

Alex grabbed the side-straps and hoisted a black bag onto his shoulder, as did with the other one, and they strolled toward the strange-looking triangle of blue-white ice. Before they started up the angled surface, Okawna dropped his bag and knelt down to remove a hammer and a large metal anchor. When he drove it into the surface, Alex kept expecting to hear an echo, but there was nothing to reflect the sound.

Alex climbed into his harness, attached the rope and safety line to a carabineer, and hiked up to the tip of the triangle. He looked over the edge of the ice block, but couldn't lean out far enough to see the spacecraft. He held a mirror on a rod over the edge of the ice and studied the area below the block, but still couldn't see the ship, then looked at Okawna, who was kneeling beside him. "There's a slight outward angle going down for about ten-feet before it opens into a hollow area above a flat surface."

Okawna grabbed the safety line as Alex turned around to back down over the edge. "Are you ready?"

"Here we go."

Alex dropped over the edge and eased down the wall of hard ice. When he dropped onto the surface of the ship, his feet slid out from beneath him, but the strain on the rope kept him from toppling over. He looked up at his friend and waved. "The ice doesn't stick to the surface of the spaceship, so it's covered in pieces of fine crystals." He used his foot to brush away the dusting of ice crystals and saw his reflection on the surface of the alien craft. "It's just like the surface of our ship."

Okawna strained to see down over the edge, but Alex was out of sight. "I wonder how many people it holds."

"I wonder when it arrived. It might have crashed at the same time ours did, millions of years ago." He reached into his pocket and brought out an earpiece used to communicate with his spaceship. "I'm going to try to make contact with them."

Okawna grinned. "Are you kidding? Everyone on board our spaceship turned to dust millions of years ago. You can't possibly believe there is someone still alive on this old thing."

"It doesn't hurt to try."

Alex put the communication device into his right ear and spoke. "My name is Alex. Is there anyone on board?" He tried a few more times with no response. "There's nothing more we can do here. Pull me up so I can tell Donner what we've found. I'm sure this is going to turn into an international issue."

***

Huck had the hangar doors open for them when Okawna turned the aircraft off the taxiway. After the engine shut down, Alex and Okawna climbed out and pushed it backward into the hangar. Huck drove them across the tarmac to their jet, where they thanked him and said goodbye. Skip and Carl had the engines running, and they hurried up the steps into the plane.

Chapter 12

5:00 AM; SV1 CONTROL CENTER:

Carter flipped the windshield wiper to full speed, giving him clear glimpses of the gravel road illuminated by the rising sun. The stars were sparkling when he went to bed, but twenty minutes ago, he backed his car out of the garage into a torrential downpour. He wasn't due to start his shift for another two hours, but early this morning, he received an urgent call from Teresa Taylor. The second signal had reappeared, but this time it started at 1:57 AM, and had not shut down like before. His stomach tightened into a knot, believing this storm is not a coincidence and Alex Cave is right. The SV1 must be causing these strange weather patterns.

He slowed his car as he entered a code into a transmitter mounted to the dashboard, then the gate slid open, and he parked in front of the structure. He opened the door and leapt out, then ran under the awning and used his code to enter the building, and found Teresa waiting inside.

"Is it still on?"

"Yes, and I've accessed the National Weather Service images, like you asked. The entire western shoreline, from Vancouver, Canada, to Central Mexico, is suffering torrential downpours. After all the fires this summer, they are expecting flash flooding and mud slides from northern California south. Scott and I have tried everything imaginable to turn it off, but nothing works."

"Yes, it's like someone else is has taken control."

Teresa thought about a call she had received yesterday from her friend Terry Hardin, in Iceland. As part of the Mutual UFO Network's Ground Surveillance Unit, he was positive he had discovered an alien spaceship in the arctic. She stared up at Carter. "How come none of us were told anything about the SV1? We don't know who designed it, who built it, where it came from, or how it does what it does."

"Yeah, well, we're not paid to ask questions, Teresa. We're paid to follow instructions and keep our heads down."

"But doesn't it bother you? Not knowing what we're dealing with?"

"What's your point?"

"My point is, what if the SV1 is of alien origin?"

Carter thought about his conversation with his visitors. At the time, he had a feeling Alex was holding something back, the same feeling he got when talking to Preston. Still, the idea of alien technology on earth didn't seem rational. "I don't know. Let's just deal with the current situation at hand, and that is gaining control of the SV1."

When Carter turned around to head out of the room, Teresa stared after him. "Where are you going?"

"I need to make a phone call. Let me know if anything changes."

Two doors down from the security checkpoint, Carter entered a small room and grabbed the phone to call Preston. After several rings, a groggy voice answered.

"Sorry to bother you, Steve, but we have another issue with the mysterious second signal. It's on again and it won't turn off."

***

FIDALGO ISLAND, WASHINGTON:

Preston set his phone on the nightstand and reached across the bed to put his hand on Rita's shoulder. "It's happening again. You need to get up and check on your device."

Rita grabbed his hand and shoved it off her skin. "Later."

Preston rolled off the bed and stood, grabbing his robe off the back of a chair. "I'll make some coffee. You've got fifteen-minutes to get dressed."

Rita heard Preston walking down the stairs, so she threw off the sheet and rolled into a sitting position on the edge of the bed, then stood and shuffled into the bathroom.

***

When Rita strolled into the kitchen, Preston looked up from a computer monitor on the edge of the counter. "You're late."

She showed him one finger and continued to the coffeemaker. "What's the hurry?"

"Have you looked outside? We're having a tsunami in the middle of August. Your machine must be causing this weather pattern, and you need to get over there and fix it."

"It's not my machine causing the problem. It's the one in space."

"I'm not so sure. Carter tells me someone else is controlling the second signal. Just go check your device and see if your teeth vibrate again."

"That's not funny, Steve. I'm telling you, I'm not controlling anything."

She sat down at the counter and looked at the image on the small television screen. It was the current weather patterns from the National Weather Service, and she listened to the announcer's commentary.

"Something is forcing the Siberian Jet Stream to spike over the central Pacific Ocean, causing an artificial El Niño effect. We have no idea how this is possible, and we're already receiving reports of devastating flash floods along the Pacific coast, from Northern California to Baja, Mexico."

When she looked up at Preston, his arms were crossed as he stared back at her. "Fine." She stood and snapped a lid on her coffee mug, then headed for the door into the garage. She pressed the button to open the garage door, and the roar of the pouring rain was nearly deafening.

***

Rita stopped at the security gate of the storage facility and entered her combination into the control panel. When the gate opened, she drove through the rows of concrete buildings toward the last unit, number 200. When she reached unit 119, the engine of her car suddenly died. She tried turning the key, but nothing happened. "Damn. What now."

She climbed out and pulled up her coat hood to ward off the deluge as she walked to the front of the vehicle. She noticed something shiny in her peripheral vision, and when she turned to look, her jaw dropped. She hurried over to her storage unit and stared at the thick layer of ice covering the large roll-up door. "What the hell?"

She went around to the corner of the building to the side door, and discovered that it, too, was covered with a thick translucent layer of frozen water. She reached into her pocket and brought out her phone to call Steve, but the screen remained dark, as if the battery was dead. She hurried back to her vehicle and studied the concrete driveway, and noticed a slight slope where she had stopped and had an idea.

She climbed inside, put the transmission into neutral, and used her powerful leg muscles to roll the car away from the unit. When she reached number 118, the car alarm suddenly began beeping that the door was open, and when she turned the key, the engine started. With a sense of relief, she slammed the door closed and backed away before turning around and heading back to DAR headquarters.

Continuous days of soft rain were expected in the Pacific Northwest, but Rita had difficulty seeing through the torrential downpour hammering against the windshield. When she saw Steve's house, she entered her code into the touchpad on the dashboard. The garage door opened, and she drove inside, where she quickly exited the vehicle. She rushed through the doorway into Preston's living room, and found him sitting in front of the window, staring at the blurry image of the San Juan Islands, and moved around to stand in front of him. "Something is horribly wrong, Steve. The device is freezing everything in close proximity. The storage doors are covered in several inches of ice, and it disables anything electronic that comes into close range of it."

Preston stared up at her. "This is bad, really bad. They haven't been able to shut down the second frequency, and it must be doing something to your device." He stood and moved over to his desk, waving her closer. When she was beside him, he pointed at the monitor. "Is that the same signal you saw when your teeth tingled?"

"No, that one has a different frequency modulation. Look at the amplitude. This signal is much more powerful."

Preston waved his arms in the air in frustration. "None of this is making any sense. Aren't you supposed to be the expert on these things? Find a way to shut it down!"

She turned from the monitor and strolled back to the window, staring at the rippling streams of water running down the glass. She felt a shiver down her spine, tugged the front of her coat closed, and then turned back to Preston. "I can't do it on my own. I'll need someone's help."

Preston stared at her. "You're joking, right? He's a CIA has-been who is nothing more than a dusty old rock teacher now. What could he possibly do that you or my staff of highly trained computer wizards couldn't do?"

"Do you remember hearing about the moon changing orbit a while back?"

"Yes, it was struck by an asteroid. What's that got to do with anything?"

A wry smile crossed her face. "No, the moon was pulled out of orbit by another alien device. A device that was discovered by Cave and Okawna. The asteroid impact fixed the problem, but the media failed to add that little part."

"Absolutely not. Cave cannot know we're responsible for causing the change in the weather. If this gets out, I'll be fighting lawsuits from now until I die. It would destroy me. No, we can fix this. Work with Essex on this issue. The SV1 is still doing what you designed it to do. We're just dealing with some minor hiccups, is all. It's not anything that could destroy the entire world. Besides, Essex is eager to go up and collect the first load of metal. You said you were going with him, right?"

"The metal isn't going anywhere. I'll convince him to help me fix this problem before we can take off. Surely we can think of something without involving Cave."

Preston looked at his wristwatch. "You have two days and four hours. That's our launch window for collecting the first load of metal. The timing must be exact for the alignment of the launch rail to intersect with the trajectory of the SV1, because the next opportunity won't be for another eighteen days, and we can't create another ball of metal until we get the one we made out of the way." He moved up beside her and stared out the window. "I'm about to change our future, Rita. Essex's mission must be on time. Is that clear?"

"Of course."

"Did anyone else see the frozen doors?"

"No, I was the only one in the area. Although somebody's going to notice it before too long."

"Don't worry. I'll take care of it."

Rita turned to the window. If it wasn't for his financial backing and connections, she would have left him a long time ago.

***

9:54 AM. WASHINGTON. SV1 CONTROL CENTER:

Carter walked into the control room and stood behind Scott. "How's it going?"

Scott turned in his chair and looked up at his supervisor. "I've tried every shut down command I can think of, and nothing seems to work."

"I've got some more bad news. The National Weather Service is calling this the one-hundred year storm. Eighteen-inches of rain in six hours along the coastline. California is being hammered the worst, and after the fires this summer, there is no vegetation to hold back the water. The ground is like glass, so it doesn't soak in, and entire hillsides are washing away."

Scott's jaw muscles clenched in frustration. "I know, but I just can't seem to come up with the right code. Whoever is controlling this is blocking me at every point. It's like they know what I'm going to do before I do it."

Carter put his hand on Scott's shoulder. "It's not your fault. I called Preston, and he's getting us some help from someone who designed the SV1."

"I don't trust him, and I'm not counting on anything he says." He spun his chair back to the control console, entered more lines of code into the computer, and then held his breath while he waited for the command to upload to the SV1. After what seemed like a lifetime, he released a resigned sigh when the signal didn't stop. He was about to swear, when suddenly the signal vanished. He waited a few moments, then leapt out of his hair, smiling as he shook his fists in the air. "It's off! I did it, Paul!"

Carter smiled. "Good job. Do you think it will stay off?"

Scott's smile slipped away. "I can't say for sure, but at least now I know what to do if it happens again."

"Fair enough. I'll call Preston and let him know you're the one who figured it out."

Scott beamed with pride. "Thanks."

***

DAR HEADQUARTERS:

Preston turned to Rita just as his phone rang and stared at her as he answered, and when he hung up, he smiled. "They figured out how to shut it down. We shouldn't have any more problems."

Rita thought about it, but there was no guarantee the signal would not come on again, and she still needed to figure out why it appeared. "I don't think this is over, Steve. Call your people and tell them I'm on my way to the airport, and to get the plane ready to fly to Nevada."

She turned and headed toward the garage without kissing him or saying goodbye. She climbed into her car and waited for the garage door to open, and when she backed out onto the driveway, a few small drops of water patted against the windshield. A few minutes later, the sun was shining through gaps in the clouds.

On the way to the airport, she detoured to the storage facility, slowly driving past the security gate. Evidently, no one had noticed the frozen doors on her unit, and turned around and went inside to check on her weather device.

She parked in front of unit 118 and left the engine running as she climbed out, then brought out her phone and stared at the screen as she began walking toward unit 200. When she saw the ice had melted from the main door, she quickened her pace around to the side door. Even though the ice was gone, she cautiously reached out toward the handle and brushed her fingertips across the surface. They didn't stick, so she entered her code and eased the door open. When she looked inside, her jaw dropped open. "Oh, no."

Chapter 13

GROOM LAKE:

Alex hurried down the steps from the jet and saw Henry waiting inside the terminal. With Okawna at his side, clutching the silver case, they cleared the checkpoint and joined him. "Hey, Doc. Has anything changed while we were gone?"

"Perhaps. Jadin and David are waiting for us in Hangar 5, and my golf cart is outside."

No one spoke during the short ride through the base hangars and buildings. Henry parked in front of number 5, where they kept Alex's spacecraft. They passed through the security checkpoint and found Jadin Avery in a small break room in the hangar, sitting at a table with David.

When the three men strolled into the room, Jadin jumped out of her chair, smiling. "Is it a spaceship?"

Okawna set the silver case on the table and opened the lid, then grabbed the laptop computer and held it out to her. "See for yourself."

She indicated for Henry to sit down in her seat, then set the computer on the table between him and David and turned it on. A single file icon appeared, so she tapped it, and then listened to Alex and Okawna talking about being ready to go while watching them grab their gear.

Alex pressed fast forward. "You're not missing anything good." When he recognized the block of ice he was climbing over in the video, he pressed play. When he looked at Jadin, David, and Henry, their mouths were slightly open as they watched the recording.

When they were walking back to the plane, Jadin pressed stop and turned to look at her team. "David and I have found no information in our spaceship's computer about another ship. This indicates the Iceland version is one of the original ships built before the catastrophe that destroyed the surface conditions. Maybe this one wasn't working when they were forced to evacuate the planet."

Alex thought about it for a moment. "It's certainly large enough to carry a lot of people."

Okawna grinned. "Now that we have two ships, maybe we could fix this big one and explore our galaxy."

Henry looked around the table at his friends. "We must retrieve the information directly from that ship."

David stood. "I'll go back to our ship's control room and dig around the computer for a while. Maybe I'll find out if our communication system is compatible with the other vehicle."

Jadin slid her chair back from the table and stood. "I'll join you."

Henry also got up from the table. "I will inform Director Donner in the morning. For the moment, it is out of our hands."

Alex stood and stretched his arms and legs. "I'm going home to take a shower and get some decent sleep."

Okawna stifled a yawn. "Sounds like a good idea. Hey Henry, how about dropping me off at the barracks so I can get a room for the night?"

"Of course."

***

The next morning, Alex found Okawna sitting at a table in the cafeteria with a tray of food and a thermos of coffee in front of him. He was in a hurry, so went through the breakfast buffet rather than order something special, and then joined his friend. "You're up early."

Okawna set his fork down, then leaned back and crossed his arms over his chest as he looked at Alex. "I couldn't sleep. I kept thinking about that spaceship in Iceland. It's a strange coincidence a volcano would force it up at the same time they started the SV1."

"It may not be a coincidence. Paul Carter called me half an hour ago. There was a second signal early this morning, and while it was on, the Siberian Jet Stream was temporarily diverted further south, causing torrential rains along the Pacific shores of North America. They managed to shut it down and things are returning to normal, but who knows what would happen the next time they activate it?"

Alex scarfed down some scrambled eggs, sausage, and English muffin, then took a sip of coffee before speaking. "Henry set up a conference with Donner for us in fifteen minutes. There organizing the investigation in Iceland before going to the site, and I'm hoping he has enough clout to let us be in on it."

Okawna slid his plate out of the way. "You and me both. In fact, I think we should insist on it, since we have the key to get inside."

Alex noticed the time and stood. "We gotta go."

***

They entered Henry's office, where Jadin and David were waiting for them to arrive. Henry indicated for them to sit down and saw Donner's image was already on the screen. Alex sat down and looked at his friend on the monitor. "Sorry we're late."

"That's okay. I'm early. They told me it's a spaceship like ours, only five times its size."

Alex explained what they knew about the effect the SV1 was having on the atmosphere, and Okawna's suspicion about it coinciding with the appearance of the new spaceship. "I believe they're all connected, Martin. We're the experts in dealing with alien technology, so I'm hoping you could have us do the excavation. Once we have a better understanding of what we're dealing with, we could let the right people know about it."

"This is a major discovery, Alex, and the President would need to work out the political aspect of the situation. But all right. I'll wait to inform him until we know more about the ship. Director Sliven and I are old friends, so I'll try to explain our need to be first, and rely on him to keep our secret about you dealing with alien technology before."

"Great. We could use a little support offshore just in case some unexpected visitors show up."

"I'll have a military ship head that way shortly, and you could use them as a base of operations."

"Thanks, Martin."

When the screen went blank, Henry looked at Alex and Okawna staring back at him. "The jet is at your disposal. Good luck."

Chapter 14

POLAR ICE SHEET:

Alex and Okawna had borrowed Huck's airplane earlier that morning and had flown out to the site. They met up with a few of the crew from the USNS Oceanography Research Ship, Davis, which was stationed forty-feet from the edge of the ten-foot thick ice sheet. As promised, Donner had also sent a Navy Seal Team to maintain security from unwanted visitors.

With the help of two crew members, Alex and Okawna used a large, specialized shotgun to shoot several long metal anchors into one block of ice. The crew had not been informed about what they suspected was below, so when they were done, they sent them back to the Davis in their large rubber boat.

Alex and Okawna remained on the ice and then felt the air shake from the deep thumping of the massive blades of the Sikorsky CH-53E heavy lift helicopter. When they finished attaching all the straps to the release hook on the end of a long cable from the helicopter, they hurried off the block and radioed the pilot to take it away.

When the triangle block of ice rose out of the opening, Alex shielded his face from a burst of sparkling ice crystals dancing in front of his goggles. A few moments later, the flying workhorse swung the massive block out over the ice sheet and released it into the Arctic Ocean. After the helicopter headed back to the mainland, Alex turned around to Mark Girdler, the Captain of the Davis. "Let's go see what we've got."

Alex, Okawna, Girdler, and four Navy Seals hurried over to the edge of the ragged opening above the ship. Directly beneath them was the section they had reached the first time they went down, and Okawna whistled. "Damn. Look how much more is still hidden under the ice."

Alex was eager to get started. "Let's go down for a closer look."

Girdler heard a voice calling him through his radio. "Go ahead."

"Captain, we have a contact one mile due south."

"Is it approaching our location?"

"Negative, Sir. I've tried making contact, but no one is responding. It could be a fishing vessel."

"Very well. Let me know if it heads our way."

Alex exchanged looks with Okawna, both thinking it could be Hardin trying to get a better look at what they were doing. The bigger issue was Hardin had at least one drone he could fly over the area without getting too close. He looked at the Seal Team, all competent-looking men, and then turned to Girdler. "Maybe you should stay up here with your men. We shouldn't be down there for too long, but let us know if that ship gets any closer and we'll come back up."

Alex climbed down the long rope ladder, careful not to step on the ice shavings. He brushed them out of the way just before stepping off the ladder, and the rubber soles of their shoes had plenty of traction on the surface. When Okawna reached the bottom, they walked under the ice sheet to a raised section of the ship. Now exposed, he could tell this spacecraft was of a different design than his. The area they were standing on made a sharp curve up three-feet from the rest of the massive craft, which formed a twenty-foot level circle above the center of the ship.

Okawna walked around to the opposite side. "I wonder if this is transparent from the inside, like your ship."

Alex eased the communication device from his ship into his right ear. "My name is Alex. Is there anyone on board?" After trying several times with no response, he removed the device.

Okawna saw the disappointment in his friend's eyes. "We didn't expect anyone to answer. If there were people inside when it was buried under the magma, they'd just be piles of dust by now."

"I know. Without access to the side of the ship like we did with ours, there is no way for us to get inside."

Chapter 15

ESSEX'S COMPOUND. NEVADA:

Rita was the only passenger inside the Gulfstream company jet, and she enjoyed the solitude. She kept thinking about what she had discovered at the storage building, and what blew her mind was the trailer frame had melted into a silver puddle of cold steel on the concrete floor without burning anything around it. She had immediately called Preston, who arrived a short time later, and was more pissed off that he had to bring a loader to the storage unit than concerned about what had caused the damage. It was only on loan to her until Preston needed the device in Nevada to separate the metals brought back from space.

She kept wondering if her machine might be responsible. She had designed the control system on the SV1 to create specific oscillation frequencies for each type of material. The problem was none of those transmissions was powerful enough to reach the surface of the planet, so there had to be someone here on earth creating the second signal for the ones down here. She also wondered if the device at Groom Lake had reacted the same way. For the moment, she didn't have anyone else on the inside.

However, she learned Cave thought the fourth device might be in the Arctic Ocean, north of the Buford Sea. She thought about Okawna and the time they had spent together on board the Mystic and smiled. They might have gotten together at some point, if Cave hadn't interrupted her plans. She had an idea about the arctic device freezing the water as hers did, then pressed a button on her smart phone. "Call Paul Carter at SV1 control center." A moment later, he answered, and she explained what she needed him to do. When he agreed, she ended the call and grinned.

***

Essex remained out of the heat inside his small SUV, staring through the window as the jet appeared to drop from the sky at the far end of the runway. One of his legs bounced up and down on the ball of his foot while his palms sweated around the steering wheel. The last woman he was partnered with was a nasty bitch who would have shot him if he stepped out of line, and he hoped this one would be a little nicer.

He watched the airplane taxi to a stop in front of the hangar, and when the side door opened, he wiped his palms on his tan shorts, put his car in drive, and eased the vehicle close to the stairs. He leapt out and waited for the red-haired woman to reach the bottom, and when she stepped onto the concrete, he held out his hand and stared up at her. "It's nice to finally meet you, Ms. Harrow."

Rita grinned when she saw how short he was, with the top of his head even with her breasts. "Hello, John. You can call me Rita."

"I'm so excited to go into outer space, I can hardly sit still."

For some odd reason, she felt a strange attraction to the little guy. "Yes, it should be exciting. I'd like to see your ship."

He felt butterflies in his stomach, and knew if he smiled any broader, the corners of his lips might tear. "Of course. I'll have your luggage taken to your room. Please climb in and I'll show you around my complex."

Rita climbed into the passenger seat while Essex got in and started his tour, and sat quietly, listening to Essex's narration of all his projects. She was particularly interested in his portable habitats and thought his idea was actually quite brilliant. His living facilities were inflatable, and would be placed inside the existing tunnels in the moon to block the deadly radiation while he mined the interior. She doubted it would happen during his lifetime, but it was an interesting concept to develop for future interplanetary expeditions.

Essex parked at the last hangar along the runway and climbed out. Once Rita was beside him, he indicated the launch rail. "That, Rita, points our way into orbit."

She shaded her eyes as she searched for the end, but the rail disappeared over the horizon. A thought occurred to her, and a shiver ran up her spine. If the second signal *is* coming from the SV1, would it melt the metal in the spacecraft while she's up in space?

She followed Essex into the hangar and around the ship, listening to his descriptions of the various parts of the space vehicle. After he explained the recovery operation in the nose, she followed him up the steps to the cockpit and climbed in, then studied the various instruments and control panels. "Impressive. I understand you used carbon fiber components to keep the mass of your ship to a minimum. Did you use any steel in its construction?"

Essex thought it an odd question and climbed in beside her. "No steel, but I used metal alloys throughout the craft and for the rocket motors. Why do you ask?"

"What if the SV1 starts gathering metal while we're up there?"

"It will remain off until we return here to the base."

"I hope so. This is good. Is everything voice activated?"

"Yes, and you'll need to spend some time speaking to the voice recognition program before you can learn the various operating systems." He looked at his wristwatch. "In fact, let me grab a headset and you can get started. We only have thirty-seven hours to get ready. That's our launch window for collecting the first load of metal."

"I know. Steve told me. However, we have another problem to fix before we do anything else." She explained about the second signal creating the bad weather along western shorelines, but didn't mention the melted steel or freezing, for fear of him finding out there was more than one device.

Essex felt his heart rate increase and his face flush as he glared at her. "Why didn't anyone tell me about this second signal? It could jeopardize the entire mission."

"It wasn't my call, John. Right now, we need to figure out where that signal is coming from."

"I thought you said SV1 control managed to shut it down?"

"I'm not so sure it was them. The last time it shut down on its own, as if someone else was controlling the second signal."

Essex stared out the front window of the spacecraft. "I don't know what you expect me to do about it. You're the one who figured out how to control the damn thing." He turned to look at her. "Which you refused to share with me, by the way."

Rita stared at her hands in her lap, then over at him. "I know, but that was Steve's idea. I didn't know you then, but I'll show you all my research now if you'll help me figure out how someone else could control the SV1."

He stared at her for a moment. "All right. However, no more secrets. If I'm going to help you, I need all the details of how the SV1 does what it does."

"Agreed. I'll show you all my research and designs. I brought all the information on a separate hard drive. It's in my luggage."

Essex climbed out and then reached inside to help Rita squirm out of her seat. "We're running out of time, so let's go to my office. Your luggage should be in your room by now."

Chapter 16

POLAR ICE SHEET:

Alex placed a hand on the ladder rung, ready to climb up to the surface, when the hairs on the back of his neck stood up and a knot formed in his gut. He let go and turned to Okawna. "I could be wrong. Perhaps we could get in through the top using the hand device."

They walked back to the elevated section of the ship and Okawna slung his backpack to the surface, then opened the lid and grabbed a small hand-held device with colored crystals embedded in the tips. "Here you go."

Alex took the small device and set it on top of the elevated section, then pressed a ruby-colored crystal in the center. The elevated silver surface fluttered and became transparent, and he looked down into a room in the craft and then eased his index finger down onto the invisible roof. It felt solid, unlike the time they used it to get into his ship. This time, there seemed to be some kind of invisible barrier.

The room was suddenly illuminated in soft light, and a human slowly moved into view. The person's physique indicated it was male, but the body appeared too small for the size of its head. He gasped when the person looked up at him through sparkling neon green eyes, then the person smiled, exposing his perfect set of teeth.

Okawna moved around beside Alex so he could see the person's face. "We have just made first contact with an alien race."

"I'm not sure if that's a good thing."

Okawna frowned. "What's your point?"

Alex shrugged. "They are more technologically advanced than we are." He looked down inside, and the man appeared to be arguing with someone he couldn't see. "Maybe they won't want to share this planet with us. See how his eyes sparkle?"

"His eyes are green, but I don't see any sparkling."

Alex moved around the side to see if it might be the light, but they still appeared to be cut diamonds, refracting a green light. "Are you sure you don't see them sparkle?"

"They just look green to me."

***

Seth felt like his wish had been granted when he saw the two humans looking down at him. "Pandora, you said this planet is in an ice age. Is your system malfunctioning?"

"Negative, Captain."

"Some of our people must have survived the cataclysm. I wonder why it took so long for them to locate us. Did you notice the entry device? They must be as technologically advanced as you are."

"They are not our people, Captain. One is a Blue, and the other is a genetic outcast."

"What do you mean by outcast?"

"He has traces of brown in his green irises. He is a Crud."

"Are they mad? What type of civilization would allow a Crud to survive? How do I contact the Blue?"

"I do not know. I am not detecting a neuro-implant connection with either of these humans."

Seth stared up at the faces above him and pointed at his ear as he spoke to them. When he stopped, the Blue pointed a thumb in the air and nodded several times.

***

Alex grabbed the communications device, pressed a small button on the side, and inserted it into his ear. "Can you hear me now?"

***

Seth's eyebrows bunched together as he listened to the man speak, but it made little sense. "Pandora, translate the language from the Blue."

"Insufficient data, Captain."

"Patch me through to him. He might understand our language."

"Communication available."

Seth looked up at the Blue and spoke. "My name is Seth. I am the captain of this ship."

***

Alex stared down at the man and tried concentrating on what he thought were syllables, but the language seemed garbled. He pointed at his ear and shook his head no several times. He had an idea and smiled down at his new acquaintance, giving him a sign he understood and they were leaving. When the person simply stared back at him, he pressed the ruby crystal in the center of the device, and the surface became a mirror again. He held it out to Okawna, who slid it into his backpack, then slid the earpiece into his pocket. "Let's get back to the surface so we can tell Donner what we've discovered. We're going to need Jadin's help to talk to him."

He was about to climb back to the surface when he heard a shotgun blast and exchanged troubled looks with Okawna, and then hurried up the ladder and stepped onto the ice sheet, where Girdler was waiting for him. "What happened?"

"That ship sent a video drone over the area, but one of the Seals shot it down."

"Did it manage to fly overhead before it was destroyed?"

"I'm afraid so. It must have been flying just above the surface of the water, because suddenly it flew up over the edge and stayed close to the ice sheet. It wasn't until it approached the opening and gained altitude that we realized what it was, and shot it down."

"All right. Okawna and I need to head back to Iceland. Could you and the Seals keep this area secure until we know what we're going to do next?"

"Yes, but it would be nice to know exactly what we're guarding."

Alex smirked at him. "It's a spaceship."

Girdler grinned. "Yeah, that's what I thought. I received orders to collect everyone's phones before we arrived. Now I know why."

"We need to keep this a secret until Director Donner and the President decide how they want to deal with the situation. That's why I asked for a research ship and not a floating armada."

"We won't let anyone near it while you're gone."

Alex turned to Okawna. "Let's get going. I want to fly over that mystery ship on the way back to Reykjavík."

They strolled over to the airplane and Alex climbed into the co-pilot's seat, while Okawna got in and started the engine. Moments later, the plane raced across the ice sheet and climbed into the air, while Alex stared out the window, thinking about the magnitude of this discovery and the impact it would have on civilization. Paladin had said they were the first race of humans to occupy this planet, and they appeared to be very similar to his own race. What bothered him were the glowing green eyes. Okawna brought the airplane over the mystery ship but he didn't recognize its design, but had a feeling Hardin was on board and had sent the drone to see what they had discovered.

***

Hardin stared up at the aircraft flying over his ship and recognized Huckabee's plane, so knew it had to be Cave and his friend, but it didn't matter. The drone had broadcast the recording of a spaceship under the ice before it was destroyed. Along with the other recording, he had the proof he needed. He would contact his friends in the UFO community and show the world it was his discovery.

***

Skip was waiting in the passenger cabin with Zachery when Alex and Okawna entered the jet. "Will we be leaving?"

Alex sat down and grabbed the secure phone mounted to the wall. "I don't think so. I'll find out when I talk to the Director." Alex entered the number and waited a few moments before he was connected. "Hi, Martin. I hope you're sitting down." Alex explained what had happened. "The ship is occupied and they resemble us."

"Wow. What are your plans?"

"Without a way to communicate, there isn't any point in going back and staring at each other. I believe Jadin could establish communications with him using some equipment from our ship. I'd like to have her fly up here with what she needs."

"I'm not sure how much longer I can keep it a secret. Especially with this new development. The President agreed to let you do the initial investigation, but he also reiterated the fact this discovery must be shared with the rest of the world leaders soon."

"I think we should wait until after we can communicate with this person. I'm worried this could be a Pandora's Box. Paladin explained to me planets like this one, with similar climate conditions and one large moon to steady its rotation, are far fewer than we believe. I'd prefer to gather as much useful information as I can before this goes public."

"All right. I won't tell him about this until we know what we're dealing with. I'll tell Jadin to hurry. What about David? Don't you need him, too?"

"No, I need him to work on something else. I'll get back to you with an update when we're done."

"All right."

After contacting Henry, Jadin, and David on the secure phone, Alex went down the aisle to join his friends and sat in one of the lounge chairs. When he reached into his pocket for his phone, he felt the earpiece and brought them both out. He was about to set the tiny device into a small box when he noticed it was still on, so he pressed a tiny button on the side and the little L.E.D. light blinked off. He tucked it away and looked at his phone, and then his brows bunched together in thought. "That's odd. The battery is dead. It had a full charge when we landed and I haven't used it."

Okawna stood and walked to the small bar, grabbed two beers from the refrigerator, and handed one to Alex before sitting down. "Since Jadin won't arrive until tomorrow, how about the four of us rent some motel rooms and get a decent meal and some sleep while we have a chance? I have a feeling things might get a little hectic once Jadin arrives. I'm sure Huck could help us out. Hell, he'd probably like to join us for a beer."

Alex grinned. "We owe him at least one."

Okawna looked at Skip and Zachery, who indicated they approved, then called Huckabee, who agreed and would wait for them at his hangar, so he stood. "We're all set. Grab your bags and let's get out of here."

Chapter 17

NEVADA. ESSEX'S OFFICE AND LIVING QUARTERS:
Essex looked at his watch and rolled his chair away from his desk. After endless hours of combing through the data acquired from Groom Lake, neither he nor Rita could find an explanation for the second signal. He stood and saw she had her elbows on the desk, with her entwined fingers supporting her chin while she stared at the data on the monitor. "Rita? It's time we got suited up for the launch." When she turned to face him, he saw the trepidation in her eyes. "My spaceship only needs one operator, so you don't have to go with me on this mission. Of course, I'd prefer to share the experience with you."

She noticed a slight blush in his cheeks and thought it was cute, but she was going with him, regardless of the fear she felt about the second signal coming on while they were in outer space. Not everyone gets to go into orbit, and she was not going to miss her opportunity, and got up from the chair. "Let's make history."

Essex looked up at her. "Great! Your jump suit should be in your closet."

"I know. I tried it on last night. It's a nice fit, so how did you know my size?"

"Uh, Okawna told me. I'll meet you out here when you're ready." He turned and headed across the living room to his bedroom. When he glanced back, she was staring at him before he entered.

Rita mentally compared the two men, and grinned as she hurried across to the hallway leading to the two guest bedrooms. She entered her room and sat on the edge of the bed to undress, but a knot of foreboding formed in her stomach as she stared across at the white pressure suit in the closet. She stood and slid the suit off the hanger, then stepped inside. "Please don't let the second signal come on again."

***

SV1 CONTROL STATION:
Steve Preston dropped into a chair and rolled it close to the control console, then grabbed a headset and slipped it into place before turning to

look up at Teresa, Scott, and Carter, standing behind them. "We're about to make history."

Carter indicated one of the wall monitors. "The ISS is almost out of video range of the SV1, so we'll have the only recordings of the mission."

Preston grinned up at him. "Good. I'm going to set up a special news interview when we're done, and I don't want anyone scooping the story before I'm ready." He turned and spread his arms out toward the wall monitors. "The headline will be DAR Corporation, for all your cleanup projects, both here and in outer space." He turned back and smiled at everyone. "Not bad for a man starting out as a trash collector."

Carter admired Preston's ambition and accomplishments. He just hoped everything goes according to plan.

***

NEVADA:

Rita stepped into Essex's spaceship and wiggled her legs out in front of the seat as she slid into place. After attaching the straps of the four-point harness, she slipped the headset on and smiled over at Essex. She reached up and pulled the clear canopy down over their heads and pressed a button on the control panel to latch it into place.

Essex activated his headset. "SV1 control, this is Recovery. How do you read?"

They heard Preston's voice through their headsets. "Loud and clear, Recovery. This is your dream, John. Have fun."

"Thanks, Steve. You should come with me next time."

"I'll think about it."

Essex looked over at Rita. "Are you ready?"

Rita inhaled a deep breath to calm her nerves and then looked at him. "Let's go."

Essex felt his heart rate increase as he slid his elbows into the custom armrests to keep them in place under the extreme G-force, then poised one finger over the launch button. "On my word, in three, two, one, launch."

When Essex pressed the button, Rita was driven back into his seat and felt the pressure buildup in her jump suit around her torso and legs, forcing her blood up to her brain so she didn't black out. The desert raced toward the front widow, zipping past the sides of the craft as it shot down the railing toward the horizon.

Essex studied the computer-generated information on the instrument panel, and the acceleration was steady at seven gravitational units. The indicator on the image of the rail system showed he was about to gain altitude when the track curved up toward space. An instant later, he felt the added downward force when the spacecraft followed the upward curve of the railing.

When she was nearly vertical, the sky was an indigo blue, and then she felt the pressure suit loosen for a moment and tighten again when the rocket motors ignited. The view through the window faded from blue to black, and the stars brightened. A moment later, the motors shut down, and she was soaring into outer space.

Essex looked over at Rita, who was smiling at the view. "We made it! I knew this would work!"

Rita studied the computer monitor built into the control console. "Everything is in the green. You did it, John."

Essex kept smiling as he stared out through the window, looking around for something familiar. He recognized several of the satellites orbiting at various altitudes and speeds, and then stopped smiling, let go of the handgrip, and pointed to his one o'clock position. "There it is! The SV1 is right where it's supposed to be."

They heard a round of applause coming through the headset from SV1 control. When it quieted down, they heard Preston's voice. "Congratulations, John. You made it into outer space. Our readings show you're ready for pickup."

Rita studied the data on their screen. "We show the same." She looked at Essex. "It's all up to you."

Essex engaged the thrusters and his ship moved forward toward the SV1. Using small, controlled bursts of nitrogen for thrust, he maneuvered the cargo bay directly beneath the silver ball of metal. He reached forward, grabbed the electronic control gloves from a small compartment in the console, and then looked over at Rita. "I've been practicing for this moment for a long time. It's hard to believe it's really happening. Open the cargo doors."

When Rita pressed the button, he slid the gloves on and waited while the bulbous nose of the ship split down the middle and folded back out of the way on either side of the fuselage. "You're good to activate the arms."

He brought his own arms up towards his chest, causing the carbon fiber manipulators to rise from inside the cargo bay. With his left hand, he brought out the net and looped it around the mass and dragged the ship up beneath the eighteen-inch diameter ball. He kept a close eye on the three-dimensional image on the monitor, showing the progress of the metal sphere as he maneuvered it into the container, and then stopped when the indicator light flashed green and used the arms to seal the lid. He released a deep sigh of relief, took off the gloves, and looked over at Rita. "So far, so good. I'm injecting the foam now."

A moment later, he saw an indicator light change color. "Injection complete. Ready for re-entry."

Essex used short bursts of nitrogen to back away from the SV1 and then rotated his ship 180-degrees so he and Rita were staring at the blue world below. He made a few slight course changes, and when the data confirmed he was in position for re-entry, he pressed a button to release the clamps holding the container to the ship, and then backed away to watch what happened.

Rita stared at the capsule-shaped object dropping into the atmosphere. A few moments later, she saw the yellow-orange glow of flames from the heat shield roiling back over the sides of the small black dot. As it slowed down in the atmosphere, it quickly passed beneath them and out of view, so she looked over at Essex. "My turn. Closing bay doors."

Rita heaved a sigh of relief when both doors came into view, slowly moving toward each other to meet in the middle. They were four-inches apart when all the lights in the control console suddenly blinked off, and the doors stopped moving. She gasped and stared at Essex, his expression one of calm contemplation.

Essex tried resetting all the control systems, but nothing happened. "I don't think this will work, but I have to try. SV1 control, this is Recovery. Do you read this transmission?" He shrugged and gave her a reassuring smile. "Even if it is the second signal, we're not in any immediate danger. We'll maintain this orbit for at least seven hours before we drop into the atmosphere. We'll just have to wait until the signal shuts down and we'll head back to my base."

"No, you don't understand, John! The second signal does the same thing as the SV1. It liquefies metal. Parts of this spaceship will fall apart!"

**

SV1:

Preston was staring at the two wall monitors, one showing a view of the canopy and cargo bay from a camera mounted in the tail fin of Essex's spaceship. The other showed the ship as seen from a camera on the SV1. When they lost the video feed from the ship, he looked over at Scott.

"What happened?"

"It's the second signal. It just came on again."

"Essex, this is Preston. Come in."

He tried again with no response and glared at Scott. "Shut it down, damn it!"

Scott threw his arms up in frustration. "Don't you think I'm trying? I can't. Someone else is in control."

Preston threw his headset on the console and leapt out of his chair. "You shut down their command the last time, damn it! Do it again!"

Scott pushed his chair back from the console. "I can't. Maybe I wasn't the one who turned it off the last time. Like I said, every time it happens, it's like someone else has taken over control of the SV1."

Teresa had enough and glared at Preston. "You need to be more forthcoming with how the SV1 works or there is nothing we can do to stop this from happening." When he didn't respond, she crossed her arms over her chest. "We have two people up there who are about to die unless we can stop that signal. Now man up and tell us where you got the device."

Preston ignored her and indicated the image of the spaceship from the SV1. "How come it's not affecting that camera?"

Scott dug the heels of his shoes into the tile floor and slid his chair back to the console. "That's a good question."

While Scott began typing commands into the computer, Teresa uncrossed her arms and stared at the wall monitor, then noticed a flash of color, perhaps a reflection. It appeared to be moving, blocking the stars for an instant. "I think we found our missing ball of hydrocarbons. Watch the upper right-hand corner of the screen."

Preston located the dark mass moving in front of the starry background. "It's headed for Essex's ship."

Preston grabbed his headset from the console. "John. Rita. This is Steve. Do you read me? If you can hear me, there is an almost invisible mass of plastic headed in your direction. It's approaching from your six o'clock position and moving at about six-inches a second." He repeated the message and stopped to look over at Scott. "Any chance they heard me?"

Scott looked up from the monitor. "Even if they did, there's nothing they can do about it. There is a lot of space between the ball of plastic and the ship. Maybe they'll get lucky and it will miss them."

Preston sat down. "I guess all we can do is wait to see what happens."

***

RECOVERY. OUTER SPACE:

After five minutes, nothing had changed, at least as far as Rita could tell, anyway. Staring at the earth from orbit in real life was much more impressive than a picture or video, and the knot in her stomach loosened. All she had to do was wait until the power came on and they could return home. She looked over at Essex, who was gazing up through the canopy at the planet, his expression was one of contentment, since his dream had come true.

Out of the corner of his eye, Essex noticed Rita staring at him and looked over. "How long does the second signal usually last?"

"It's never the same, so I have no idea. The longest that I've noticed is six hours. It happened the last time it was turned on, so we might be stuck here for a while."

"We have plenty of oxygen, so as long as we maintain this orbit, we'll be fine."

Rita heard a soft thud and felt pressure forcing her down into her seat. "What was that?"

"I don't know, but any motion in this direction is bad for us. It forced us into a lower orbit, and our speed won't be enough to offset the increased gravitational pull of the planet."

"I thought this ship was designed to glide back down for a safe landing."

"It is, but first we need the rocket motors to slow us down, and second, the aerodynamics of the fuselage is messed up because of the open cargo bay doors. My ship would be extremely difficult to control for a safe landing, so unless we get our systems back online in the next few minutes, we'll burn up in the atmosphere."

Chapter 18

ICELAND:

Jadin felt the thud of the tires as the commercial jet touched down on the concrete runway. Since Alex's call for help, she found it nearly impossible to sleep, as a million questions raced through her mind, and she could hardly wait to make first contact.

The jet taxied to the air terminal, and when it stopped, she stood and snatched up her small carry-on. Thanks to Henry, she had a first-class ticket, so when the door opened, she hurried past the flight attendant and jogged up the covered walkway. She was first in line at the customs checkpoint and saw Alex and Okawna standing on the other side. She passed through without issue and hurried over to join her friends. "I can't believe this is really happening. Is he handsome?"

Alex grinned and indicated they should head to baggage claim while they talked. "He's not ugly and doesn't appear to have any hair, and I think he has a companion. He was speaking to someone, but I couldn't see them."

Okawna grabbed the large metal case from the revolving conveyor and smiled at Jadin. "Welcome to Iceland."

Alex grabbed her suitcase from the carousel. "Let's go make first contact."

Jadin smiled and clasped her hands together against her chest. "I know. This is so exciting. Thanks for letting me join your team."

Alex indicated the exit and walked next to Jadin as they followed Okawna out of the terminal and along the sidewalk. "Did David complain about not being able to join us?"

"A little, but he understands what he needs to do with my sister is just as important. You know, I thought my research at NASA was exciting, then I met you and your friends, and now, I can't imagine doing anything else."

When they reached the private hangar, they introduced Jadin to Huckabee before continuing through the building to the airplane parked on the tarmac. After putting Jadin's metal box and suitcase in a side storage compartment, Jadin sat up front next to Okawna, with Alex in one of the back seats. Once airborne, they headed north over Iceland's volcanoes and glaciers, then across open water to the ice sheet.

Alex leaned forward between the seats, and when the sunlight streaming through the window illuminated Jadin's light green eyes, he immediately thought of the man in the ship. "You and our mystery man have something in common. You both have green eyes, and I hope it works to our advantage."

"Me too. David and I figured out a way to adapt our ear buds to a hard drive with an updated version of my translation software. I just hope they're compatible. The technology looks similar, but our ship could be a newer version. You said it came back to fix this planet after their accident. That would have meant waiting thousands of years for the volcanic activity to stabilize before returning, so our ship's technology could be an upgrade from what this one uses."

Okawna glance over at her. "We really don't know for sure this ship has been here for that long. Maybe his ship is a newer version?"

Alex thought about it. "We know it was forced to the surface by magma, like our ship. Perhaps it was in orbit waiting for our ship to complete its mission and crashed like ours did because of the gravity device. We can speculate all we want, but let's just hope we can communicate."

It seemed to be the end of the conversation, so Alex leaned back as they approached the ice sheet. Through the side window, he saw the same mystery boat waiting one-hundred-feet from the edge of the ice, but the only inflatable boats in the water belonged to the USS Davis.

Sparkling ice crystals swirled into the air as Okawna brought the airplane down onto the white surface of the sea ice and taxied to a stop a short distance from the opening down to the spaceship, then shut down the engine. Alex climbed out and helped Jadin exit the craft as Girdler and two of the Seal team approached and introduced them to Jadin.

Girdler showed them an image on his smart phone. "This is a YouTube recording posted on the Internet this morning."

Alex studied the image of a mirrored object below the ice sheet, taken from directly overhead. "All right. We don't have much time before all the crazy UFO enthusiasts descend on us." He retrieved their backpacks, handing them to Jadin and Okawna as they gathered around him, then slid Jadin's metal case into his before slinging it over his shoulders. "All right. Let's get started."

Girdler could not restrain his curiosity for a closer look. "I'd like to go with you this time."

"Does the rest of the crew know what's down there?"

"They've seen the video and think it's a spaceship."

Alex could see the enthusiasm in Girdler's eyes and felt bad for what he needed to say. "I'm sorry, Captain, but for now, I need for you to maintain plausible deniability."

Girdler's shoulders sagged. "Okay. My orders are to follow your instructions, so I'll wait up here."

Alex, Jadin, and Okawna walked side by side through the sparkling crystals blowing across the ice sheet. When they reached the ladder, Alex went down first and waited for Jadin. When she reached the bottom, he held her arm as she stepped onto the mirror surface of the alien craft.

Jadin tested her footing and stepped out of the way as Okawna reached the lower rungs. She looked at the exposed part of the ship where the loose block of ice had been removed and realized sixty-feet away, the ship disappeared under the ice sheet, but the mirrored surface was still reflecting the sunlight back up through the ice for as far as she could see. "Oh, my, gosh. I didn't really comprehend its size until now." She noticed the elevated section and hurried over for a closer look. "This must be the control room."

Alex moved over beside her. "Just the roof. It opens up a little wider below where you're standing."

Jadin leaned against the side and studied the silver surface, but suddenly thought of something and stepped back. "Crap!" She pulled back her hood and tried to straighten her hair with gloves on, which didn't help, then gave up and left her hood back.

Alex noticed. "What's wrong?"

"He can probably see us through his ceiling like we can on our spaceship."

He smiled. "You look fine. Pretty as ever."

She leaned over the roof and smiled as she waved her hand over the mirror. "Yeah, right."

***

"They have returned, Captain. One of them is a Green."

"Video off."

The images of engineering drawings on the monitor vanished, as Seth looked up through the transparent ceiling at an attractive red-haired woman waving down at him. He stood from the reclining chair and moved across the room to be directly below her, then looked up and smiled when he saw her green eyes. A moment later, he recognized the faces of the two men who appeared beside her.

***

Alex placed the hand-held device on the surface of the control room and pressed the ruby crystal. The roof fluttered, and he saw the stranger looking up at him with sparkling eyes for an instant, before he stared directly at Jadin. He appeared to be trying to speak to her, so he slung the backpack from his shoulders and handed her the metal case.

Jadin turned around and set it on the ground, then opened the lid and raised the screen on a laptop computer. She removed a small plastic box imbedded in the dark gray foam padding and then grabbed one of the small communication devices. She pressed a small button on the side and positioned it inside her ear canal, then stood and looked down at the man.

"Can you hear me?"

***

Seth heard her voice, but the words were gibberish, so he pointed at his ear and nodded. "I can hear you."

He pointed at his lips, and then his head, giving it two shakes no. "I don't understand."

He watched Jadin hold up one finger for him to see and spoke one word, then she formed an O with her fingers and spoke another word. After that, she did a few combinations of ones and zeros.

Seth looked down so the woman would not see him speaking. "Pandora, is the Green indicating a binary language?"

"Yes."

He looked up and nodded vigorously, and then the woman indicated she understood before moving out of sight, but he abruptly covered his ears, trying to drown out the buzzing erupting in his head. "Audio off now!"

***

Jadin knelt down and removed her earpiece, then touched an icon on the computer screen. She stood and looked down into the control room, and saw the man cowering in agony.

"I'm so sorry!"

She knelt beside the computer and stopped the program. When it was off, she leapt up to see if he was okay.

***

The noise abruptly ceased, and Seth looked up at the woman, who appeared concerned, then looked down. "Pandora, were you able to connect with her computer?"

"Yes. It is primitive."

"Is my audio off?"

"Yes, Captain."

He looked up and smiled at the woman, then indicated she should continue. She dropped from view, so he sat in the recliner to wait, and then leaned back so he could see when she returned.

***

Jadin knelt down in front of the monitor and slowly reached out to the screen, feeling a sense of trepidation when she touched the icon. She jumped up and stared down at the man, who was in a recliner and appeared to be okay, so she smiled and waved at him, then knelt down in front of the screen. She studied the information, and her program was trying to interface with the ship's system.

Alex knelt down next to Jadin to look at the monitor. "How is it going?"

"It's just like the first time I tried it on our ship. It could take a minute for the two systems to agree on a common computer language. Okay, it's working. We have a connection. Evidently, this operating system has a name. P.A.N.D.O.R.A. I wonder what the letters stand for."

"Doomsday, I would imagine. Does that mean we can talk to him?"

"Not yet. The two systems are using the frequencies, but it should shut down at any moment now. I've given it access to all our most recent language programs, word processing, and encyclopedia programs. That should give it enough information to learn our vocabularies."

"What if he's expecting us to learn his language?"

She looked over at Alex and smiled. "Their computer is far more advanced than ours, so this Pandora program won't have any problem translating the two languages."

Alex felt a knot form in his stomach. Any program sophisticated enough to learn our language could also learn our strengths and weaknesses, and then thought perhaps he was just being paranoid. "How much longer?"

"It should have everything it needs in a few more seconds."

Alex stared at the small monitor, and the screen was filled with flashing lines of code. Several seconds went by, but the information continued scrolling up the screen. A moment later, he looked over at Jadin. "Are you sure about this?"

"Yes, it's just taking a little longer than I thought it would."

"Did you notice his eyes?"

"Yes, they're green, like mine."

"Nothing out of the ordinary?"

"No, just a little brighter than mine is all."

Alex wondered why he was the only one who could see the sparkle. He stood and looked at Okawna, staring down into the control room, then down at the man lying back in a reclining chair, with his eyes closed, as if sleeping. He looked at his watch and three minutes had passed, and he was getting that bad feeling in his gut, so he knelt down next to Jadin.

"What's taking so long?"

"I'm not sure. The program should have shut down by now."

"What if the program is downloading information from the internet through your computer?"

"That's impossible from this location. We don't have access."

"Shut it down!"

Jadin didn't argue and entered the command, but nothing happened. "It's not responding and I can't sever the connection with that computer. Why are you so worried? There's no sensitive information on my little laptop."

"The research ship has wireless internet access from any location on the planet through various satellites. Now pull the plug or do whatever it takes to shut it down!"

Jadin closed the screen and pulled the laptop from the padding, then yanked the battery from the back of the machine. She opened the lid, and the screen was blank, so she looked over at Alex. "It's off."

Alex stood and looked down into the control room just as the man suddenly leapt out of the recliner and move below Jadin. When he looked up, Alex noticed his green eyes seemed to sparkle brighter than before, and appeared to be filled with anger.

Jadin felt a shiver run up her spine when she looked into the stranger's eyes. It was as if all the rage in the world was focused through his lenses and aimed directly at her. When he tapped his ear and crossed his arms, she stepped back, hesitant to reach down and grab her earpiece to hear what he was about to say.

Alex noticed the fear in Jadin's eyes, so he grabbed the earpiece from his pocket, turned it on, and slid it in place as he looked down at the stranger. "My name is Alex. Do you understand me?" The man turned to face the blue.

"I'm Seth, the Captain of this colony."

"Did you say this is a colony? Like humans?"

"A small one, yes. I want to talk to the Green."

Seth noticed Alex's baffled expression. "Your leader. The woman."

Alex stepped away, removed his earpiece, and then looked at Jadin. "He wants to talk to you. He thinks you're our leader and I think it's because you have green eyes. Just go with it and we'll back you up."

When Jadin stooped down to grab her earpiece, he grabbed the last one and walked around behind Okawna. "Insert this so you can listen, but don't speak. He thinks Jadin is in charge, and I want to keep it that way." When Okawna indicated he understood, Alex moved back around to Jadin. "His name is Seth, and he's in charge of what he is calling a small colony. Are you ready?"

Jadin smiled bravely, took a deep breath to calm her nerves, then moved forward and looked down into the control room. "Hello, Seth. My name is Jadin. It's nice to meet you."

"I cannot say it is good to meet you, Jadin. Pandora has showed me some disturbing images from your worldwide communication system. Your race is self-destructive and we will not share this planet with you. I've ordered her to wipe your species from the face of our planet for violating genetic protocols."

Chapter 19

SV1 CONTROL ROOM:

Preston set his headset on the counter and slowly stood to look at Carter. "It hit them! What did it do to their trajectory?"

"It's bad. They're losing velocity, which means gravity is dragging the ship down to the planet. In about twenty minutes, the ship will begin skipping across the atmosphere. The thing is, they're inverted, so the heat shield on the bottom is pointed into outer space, and it won't protect them on the way down."

Preston turned to Scott. "Are you positive you didn't shut down the second signal the last time this happened?"

"Positive. Nothing I tried made any difference. Someone else is in control."

Scott suddenly sat up straight. "It's off. It just shut down."

Preston snatched his headset off the counter. "Recovery, this is control. Can you hear me?"

***

RECOVERY. OUTER SPACE:

Rita felt a surge of adrenalin when all the lights came on and looked over at Essex, who smiled as the cargo doors in the nose of the ship closed, then they heard Preston's voice in their headsets and Essex answered. "We hear you, Steve. We're back online."

"I'm glad you're both all right."

"Thanks. We're ready for re-entry."

"Good luck from all of us."

Essex checked their location while waiting for the red cargo door light to turn green, then looked over at Rita. "Get ready to pull some G's."

He engaged the thrusters to spin them around and then fired both rocket motors to bleed off their speed before intentionally dropping into the atmosphere. Once the air was thick enough to affect the control surfaces of his spacecraft, Essex looked over at Rita and smiled. "Now we just glide back to my facility and have a cold beer."

Rita did not share his optimism, but didn't say so, and was impressed by his calm composure while everything went to hell. "That sounds good."

Essex deftly changed trajectory and angle of descent until the image on the monitor showed he was lined up with his runway in the Nevada desert. The sun quickly dropped over the horizon as they dropped closer to the ground, and up ahead, the lights built into the launch rail flared on to show him the runway.

Rita felt a thud when the wheels dropped onto the concrete, but there was no reverse thrust like on a jet, just a parachute to slow them down. She was impressed by Essex's timing when the parachute released and he braked to a stop just outside the launch rail hangar. A person rolled the ladder platform into place, then Essex pressed a button, and the hatch opened. She realized being small had its advantages, as he easily stood and stepped out.

Essex turned around and reached down to help Rita squirm out of her seat. "I hope you enjoyed the ride."

Rita smiled and reached out to grab his hand. "It had its moments, but yes, I did."

She slid her legs out from under the dash and stood, then stepped out onto the platform. Essex led the way down the steps to the tarmac outside the hangar, and was about to walk inside when Jim drove up in his SUV and stopped to get out.

Coburn stopped in front of Rita and Essex. "I have some good news, Mr. Essex. The recovery team found the shipping container right where you said it would be. Well, within half a mile of where you thought it would land. They're on their way back and should be here in about three hours."

"Thanks, Jim. I'll let Preston know we have it."

***

INTERNATIONAL SPACE STATION:

Commander Short was doing his space version of bench-pressing when he felt a shudder through his backrest. A collision alarm suddenly blared through the station, so he released his restraint belt and shoved off toward the computer, soaring across the room. Anatole rushed at him through a connecting tunnel just as he reached the screen. "The hull integrity is intact, and only a minor deviation in our orbit."

Anatole stared out the window. "What hit us?"

Short moved to another window, and what he saw caused his jaw to drop. Slowly rotating against a starry background, was a nearly black ball with swirls of colors on the surface, and it appeared to be slowly moving away from the station. "You are not going to believe this. Come over and see for yourself."

Chapter 20

ARCTIC:
Alex studied Seth's expression for any sign he was joking about wiping all the humans from the planet, but there was none. Only the increase of the sparkle in his eyes.

Jadin's jaw dropped. "Excuse me?"

"We were here first and stayed behind to ensure we maintained our claim to this world. According to galactic law, this is our planet. The damage you have done to the atmosphere can be repaired, but your lack of genetic standards cannot. According to Pandora, you have allowed Cruds to self-replicate, and this we cannot tolerate, because that genetic strain is prone to aggressive behavior. We simply cannot, and will not, share this planet with you."

Alex immediately disliked the arrogant little man and wanted some answers. "All right, let's just slow down for a minute and take this one small step at a time? First off, who is Pandora?"

Seth ignored the Blue and stared up at the Green. "Do not allow your subordinate to speak again or this conversation will end. Pandora is the spacecraft, and quite advanced, but I'm impressed to meet someone with a technology similar to our own."

Jadin glanced over at Alex and saw the muscles in his jaw flexing, then looked down at Seth. "I'm afraid there must be some kind of misunderstanding. Our level of technology is nowhere near yours."

Seth crossed his arms and glared up at Jadin. "Do not lie to me. Pandora has detected your technology in orbit and was in contact with it. You have no idea what harm she can do to your civilization."

Jadin wondered if the ship's computer was listening. "Yes, Pandora. You searched our information system, so you know we are nowhere near your level."

She noticed Seth look away, speaking to whom she imagined was Pandora, but she couldn't hear her. She looked up at Alex, but he indicated he didn't hear anything, either.

Seth turned to look up at Jadin. "You are correct. What little information she retrieved from your devices indicates a rudimentary level of competence, but nowhere near our level of sophistication."

"Are you able to leave your craft?"

"Of course I can, but why would I want to leave? We have no diseases, and I'm positive your current atmosphere is filled with deadly microorganisms. We have Blues to gather what we need from outside this vessel."

"Won't they be just as susceptible to our germs?"

"No. Unlike your people, they have been genetically engineered to resist any form of degenerative infection."

Okawna was too excited to keep quiet any longer. "Is that like an add-on to the existing DNA? Because I wouldn't mind getting a dose of that myself."

Alex imagined sparkling green daggers flying from Seth's eyes aimed at Okawna, so he decided to intercede. "Seth. I mean, Captain. Captain Seth, we have many things to discuss with the rest of our leaders before we could proceed with negotiations. Is there any way you can postpone the extermination of humans until we can talk with them?"

Seth glared at Jadin. "If you continue to allow your subordinates to speak without permission, I will order Pandora to terminate them." He was tiring of arguing with this race of humans. "There is nothing to discuss." He looked down for a moment, then back up at Jadin. "Pandora has informed me the operating system on your device in orbit is more advanced than hers, and she cannot access it. She demands that you bring a copy of the operating system here for her to upload, like you did with your language software and one device."

Jadin felt Alex's hand on her shoulder and knew what he wanted. "All right. A trade. You get the software if you leave us alone, but we don't have any more devices. Like I said, we found it here."

Seth stared down at the floor for a moment, then up at the woman. "We might come to an arrangement to let some of you live."

When Jadin felt Alex's hand on her shoulder again, she stepped back to talk to him. "I know what you're going to say. That's not acceptable, it's all or nothing, but at least it would buy us some time."

Alex knew she was right. "Fine. Go ahead."

She stepped back up to the control room. "I cannot speak for everyone on this planet. We have many countries, each with their own leaders, and I must discuss this new development with all of them. It cannot be done from here, so we'll come back with the right people to discuss this situation."

"You have seventy-two of your human hours. I will meet with a single delegate to speak on behalf of your entire degenerative species, but be advised, I will only talk to a Green or a Yellow."

Alex found it extremely difficult to keep quiet, so leaned back before removing his earbud to talk to Jadin. "Ask him how many colors there are, what they mean, and how many of each."

Jadin listened to Alex without looking away from Seth. "Would you mind telling me what the different colors stand for, and how many of each are in the ship?"

"That is none of your concern. Leave and talk to whoever you need to. Your time starts now."

Alex reached out to the star, pressed the amber crystal, and the roof became silver. They packed everything away and then climbed the ladder back to the surface.

Girdler was pacing back and forth until Alex reached the top. "I've lost communication with my ship."

Jadin reached the surface in time to hear Girdler's remark. "Seth said Pandora communicated with the SV1. Perhaps her signal is interfering with our electrical systems."

Alex turned toward the ladder. "I'll take the star back to the ship and ask him to shut her down."

Jadin grabbed his shoulder. "He won't talk to you, Alex. I'll have to ask him."

"Then I'm going with you."

Girdler heard static from his radio and looked at Alex. "Hold on a second." He brought the radio close to his mouth. "This is the Captain. How do you read?"

"Loud and clear, Sir. All our electronic equipment quit working for a short time, but they're online again."

"Very well." He stared at Jadin. "Did you say there are people on board that ship?"

"Yes. That ship is a flying colony of people."

Girdler's mouth hung open for a second. "Wow. How many people are there?"

"Seth refused to tell us. From what we could determine, people with green eyes are the leaders, and people with blue eyes are their workers. He also mentioned yellow eyes, but I have no idea what it means. He said people with brown eyes are genetically predisposed to violent behavior and called them Cruds."

Girdler chuckled. "This guy is going to make a lot of enemies."

"I don't think he's interested in making friends. Can you believe it? They use people as slaves."

Alex had an idea. "What if the blues are not people? He said they were genetically engineered, so maybe they are just human beasts of burden with no higher mental faculties. Maybe they're just drones."

Jadin shook her head no. "Seth called you a Blue so they're not drones. They're human slaves."

Alex thought about it for a moment. "Actually, how can we assume our own morality applies to a different race of humans? If we think we have the right to impose our judgment on those people, it could be compared to the conflict in the Middle East. One group forcing another to think like they do, and vice versa."

Jadin knew Alex had a valid point, but she couldn't help the way she felt about it. "It might be difficult finding an unbiased representative to speak for all of humanity. And don't forget, it has to be someone with green eyes."

Girdler scoffed. "Green eyes, red eyes, purple eyes. If you ask me, I think those people are racists. I wonder if they'd be fooled by contact lenses. If they're so damn perfect, they wouldn't know anything about eye glasses and lenses."

"No, I'm sure Pandora told him the color of our eyes, because he smiled before he looked directly at me. Pandora must be equipped with some kind of retinal scanner."

Alex thought about the way Seth's eyes appeared to glow and wondered if perhaps he could detect more than visible light frequencies. He didn't think contact lenses would work, either. He had another idea and looked over at Jadin. "I think you should be our representative. At least, be the liaison between him and whatever committee they form to deal with this situation. He seems to like you. Besides, you know the world leaders won't be able to form a committee right away. Plus, we need to learn as much about Seth and his people as we can." He noticed Okawna looking at him. "Something on your mind?"

Okawna indicated for his friends to speak privately, so they huddled together. "If these are the same people who came back on your spaceship, shouldn't we already have the information in your ship's computer?"

Jadin shook her head no. "I searched the records as soon as I found out it was a ship like ours. Ours is a research vehicle, so not much history about their species. It's mostly research data about the planet. I could try digging a little deeper, though, but I doubt I'll find anything."

Alex remembered something from the meeting. "Seth calls the ship Pandora. Does that mean it's intelligent?"

"It would need a certain amount of artificial intelligence in order to interact with the inhabitants of an entire colony."

"What about our ship? Does it have artificial intelligence? Or a name?"

"Not that David and I have discovered."

"I'm worried the two ships might interact with each other. Also, I think Pandora managed to use my phone and your computer to download information from the Internet. Once we get within range of a cell-tower repeater station, she could use our equipment against us."

"No, our ship can't reach the outside world without the earpieces, and neither can Pandora. As long as they're turned off, we're safe from being hacked."

Alex wasn't so sure, as he entered Donner's phone number, and was put on hold until the Director answered. "Hey, Martin. Well, we've talked with the person and I have a lot of information to share with you. I can't go into great details over the phone right now, but not all of it is good news. We have a seventy-two hour time limit before some bad things happen, so it's imperative we talk in person."

"I'll check the President's schedule and see when he's available. He's asked to be kept informed of everything regarding this new ship."

"All right, but I think you had better hear what we have to say before you schedule a meeting with him. We don't have a lot of time."

"I don't like the sound of this. How long before you could be here in DC?"

"Best guess? Six hours."

"All right. Call my secretary when you're getting close to landing and I'll have a car and driver meet you at the airport."

"See you soon."

Alex moved over to Girdler. "We should only be gone a day or two."

Girdler indicated the four men of the Navy Seal team. "Now that this discovery is on the Internet, you might want to ask the Director to send us some military support."

"I'll take care of it. We'll see you when we get back."

Girdler watched the trio head toward the plane, then turned and hurried away. When he heard the roar of the airplane's engine fading away as it raced across the ice, he joined two members of the Seal Team, and they headed toward the edge of the ice sheet, where they walked down makeshift stairs to a floating dock and one of their rubber boats.

***

Okawna had a hunch and headed southeast before flying past the edge of the ice sheet towards Iceland. His suspicions were confirmed when he saw Hardin's ship stationed south of the spaceship. "So far, he's alone, but I don't think for long. I'm sure his friends at MUFON are organizing some kind of protest or welcome wagon party."

"Once Donner tells the President about Seth's demand, I'm sure other countries will send ships to help stand guard."

Jadin lay huddled in the corner of the bench seat against the fuselage and leaned forward between the front seats. "I think we should make Pandora free her slaves as part of the deal."

Alex turned in his seat to look at her. "I agree, but I doubt she would. Right now, we need to worry about saving humankind. She caused the torrential weather along the west coast, and I'm sure she could do a lot more damage, so for the time being, we really don't have a say in the matter. Now it's up to the politicians."

Okawna smirked over at his friends. "That's not very comforting."

Alex turned back to the front window. "I know."

Jadin moved back to the corner of the bench seat. "Pandora is a bitch, Alex. She runs that ship, not Seth. Did you see how he always conferred with her, like she was a commanding officer? She doesn't care about us. All she cares about is protecting her people at our expense."

***

ARCTIC:

"Captain?"

Seth opened his eyes. "Yes, Pandora?"

"I cannot trust this new race without human interaction. I will bring one of our Blues out of stasis and she will represent me through her neural implant."

"That is fine, but why a female?"

"Because of the Blue they call Alex."

Chapter 21

THURSDAY. NEVADA. ESSEX'S FACILITY:

Preston stepped out of the private jet and saw Rita and Essex waiting at the bottom of the stairs. He smiled as he walked down to greet his accomplices, stopping in front of Rita. He reached forward to embrace her, but when he tried to give her a passionate kiss, she pushed him away and stared at her. "What's wrong?"

"I'm not feeling that way about you anymore, Steve. I think it's time we go back to being friends without benefits."

Preston was only using her and didn't feel jilted. "Fine by me."

Jim Coburn stood behind Essex and Rita, suppressing a smile when she rebuked Preston's attempt to kiss her. He turned around with the group and climbed in behind the steering wheel of his security SUV. Preston sat up front, with Rita and Essex in the back seat. He waited to start the engine until a wooden crate was loaded into the rear compartment of the vehicle, then drove off the concrete tarmac onto a dirt road leading across the open desert.

Preston glanced over his shoulder into the back at Rita. "Did the device arrive on schedule?"

After what happened in the storage unit, Rita was not too anxious to be near it again. "Yes, it arrived an hour ago. They should have it out of the crate by now."

Essex noticed something odd in her voice and looked over, and she was wringing her hands in her lap. When they were trapped in outer space, she didn't show any signs of fear and he wondered why now.

They stopped at a wooden hangar on the outskirts of the facility, and after everyone was out of the vehicle, Rita studied Preston's attire and noticed his stainless steel watch, then lifted his hand to show him. "You should leave that in the car. The rest of us are not wearing any steel, just in case the device comes on again by itself."

Preston frowned and slid the band from his wrist, tossing it onto the seat inside the car. "If you say so. Let's go inside."

Essex walked up to a large, roll-up wooden door and pulled up on the handle. When it was high enough for his friends to duck underneath, he led them inside. Nothing in the building was made of metal, including the nylon screws holding it together, and even the rollers and hardware for the door were made of hardened ceramic. He felt Jim bump into him when he suddenly stopped. This was the first time he had seen the device in person and walked over for a closer look, and the pewter-colored cylinder was supported by a wooden rack, with the pointed end aimed at the large ball of metal inside a shallow ceramic crucible.

Preston walked past the device to the ball and slid his fingers across the gold, silver, and gray swirls of precious metals on the smooth surface, then smiled and turned back to his companions. "Will you look at this? There's at least half a million dollars' worth of material just on the surface." He walked back to Rita. "Let's get the new control panel hooked up."

Jim helped them set up a folding plastic table, thinking this is probably something Alex would be interested in knowing about. He set the small box on the table in front of Rita, and moved over to watch what would happen next.

While Preston and Essex slid two thick plastic rings over the middle section of the device, a knot formed in Rita's stomach, and she stepped further away from the table. She had a gnawing feeling this test was not going to end well.

Jim noticed Rita's worried expression when she stepped back, so he moved back beside her. "What are the rings for?"

"They receive the transmissions from the control panel and transfer them to the surface of the device. I just tell it what to do."

"That's pretty cool. Is that how you're going to separate the metals?"

"That's the plan. This is the first test."

Jim's brows bunched together. "I thought the first test was in orbit?"

"That's right. But this is the first time with gravity trying to tear it apart."

When Preston and Essex walked over to join her and Jim at the table, Rita moved back to it and opened the lid to expose the digital meters, colored push buttons, and switches. Numbers flashed on the small monitor as the software took over, and then the screen showed everything was ready, and she looked around at the group and forced a smile. "Here we go."

It felt like she was shoving her finger through clay to reach the power button, although it was only her trepidation. She pressed start, and the light came on. At first, nothing happened, which was a good sign, so she slowly increased the oscillations to the resonant frequency of the softest metal in the mass. Open pockets and tunnels suddenly formed on the smooth surface of the ball, as liquid gold streamed down into the crucible, then flowed through an open hole in the bottom into a ceramic mold.

Preston smiled and clapped his hands together. "I'll be damned, we did it!"

Essex released a sigh of relief. He now had a viable income to continue working on his dream.

Rita noticed the second frequency and suddenly felt a tingling sensation in her teeth. She pressed the stop button, and the lights blinked off, but when the tingling continued, she turned and headed out through the open doorway. "Get out now!"

She ran to the other side of the SUV and turned around to look over the roof. The three men arrived and everyone climbed into the vehicle, then Preston turned to look into the back at her.

"What the hell is going on, Rita?"

Jim started the engine and looked in the mirror at her. "How far away do we need to be?" The engine suddenly died. "Oh, shit!" He turned the key, but nothing happened. "It's dead!"

Rita threw open her door and climbed out. "Everyone get out!"

Doors flew open, and bodies leapt from the car, dashing down the road across the desert. They were two-hundred-feet from the structure when suddenly they heard the screeching of tortured metal and shattering glass. Everyone stopped and turned around, staring at the twisted vehicle lying in a shimmering silver pool of liquid steel.

The shimmering abruptly ceased, and everything was deathly quiet, and Essex put his hands on his hips. "What the hell? Is it over?"

Rita let her shoulders sag. "I think so. It just suddenly stops, and I have no idea why."

Preston began walking back toward the structure. "I want to see what happened inside."

Jim put his hand down on Essex's shoulder when he started to follow Preston. "I'll walk back to the facility and get another vehicle."

Essex looked up at Rita. "Let's go with Steve."

She thought about it for a moment, then bent over and kissed him on the lips. "I've had enough stress for one day. I'll walk back with Jim. See you soon."

Essex stared after Rita as she and Jim walked away. He had thought his playful flirting had gone unnoticed, but after that kiss, he knew Rita felt the same chemistry he felt between them. With a grin on his face, he hurried to catch up with Preston. "At least we know it works. All we have to do is find out what's causing the second signal and shut it down."

Preston smiled down at him. "I know. Everything else works just like we planned."

He stopped and stared down at the remains of the vehicle. "That happened in the storage facility, too. The device melted the trailer out from beneath it."

Essex looked up at him. "What do you mean? Rita never mentioned it melting metal."

"Oh yeah, it also freezes water extremely fast."

Essex thought a knife had been stabbed through his heart. She had kept vital information from him, and basically lied to him. He stared back at Rita, walking off into the distance with Jim, and realized she was just as selfish as everyone else involved in this project. It became clear she didn't really like him; she was just looking out for number one, whatever the cost.

He followed Preston into the building and abruptly stopped. Four colored streams of precious metals had hardened onto the ceramic surface beneath the crucible, and the ball was gone. He grinned when he saw the amount of gold spilled over the mold.

Preston grabbed a small piece of platinum, feeling the coolness on his skin. "Who needs a woman when we have all this wealth?"

Essex thought about it. "I suppose you're correct."

***

Rita walked in silence beside Jim, enjoying the aroma of sage and listening to the grasshoppers chirping. She knew Preston would tell Essex the details about what had just happened, and any chance of trust between her and John would be over. She found it odd it bothered her so much, since John wasn't even her type. Her thoughts were interrupted when she heard the name Alex Cave, and looked over at Jim. "Excuse me?"

"I was wondering if you know a guy named Alex Cave."

"Why do you ask?"

"He's a friend of mine, and he's into this kind of stuff. I thought maybe he could help you figure out what went wrong."

Rita knew he was right. As long as there was a second signal, something bad was going to happen, and the long walk back to the complex gave Rita time to consider her options. She hadn't broken any laws, at least none that could be proven. Preston's men had hijacked the devices while in transit, so that wouldn't be held against her, either. As they approached the spaceship hangar, she looked over at Jim. "Do you know how to contact Alex?"

"Yeah, he gave me his card when he and Okawna were here a few days ago."

She quickened her pace. "Do you have a car I could borrow to drive to the airport in Reno?"

"I'm sure one of my people could give you a ride. Are you going to tell Essex you're leaving?"

"Tell him I'll call him later. Call Alex and tell him his missing device is here."

Jim almost stopped walking. "Those things belong to Alex?"

"Not really, but he'll want to know it's here. If he asks about me, tell him the truth."

Chapter 22

WASHINGTON D.C. ANDREWS AIR FORCE BASE:

Alex, Jadin, and Okawna had managed a few hours of sleep on the flight from Iceland, but mostly they talked about ideas and questions to present to the people they were about to meet. He was hoping to tell Donner in private, but the Director insisted the meeting include the President's advisors.

Okawna decided there wasn't much he could add to the conversation, so he would stay on the plane. When Jadin was ready, they stepped out of the jet into the brisk morning air, and then walked down to the car and driver waiting at the bottom of the steps for an early morning session at the Pentagon.

***

When Alex and Jadin arrived, the vehicle passed through the security checkpoint without stopping, then continued past the main parking areas to a ramp leading to a special door beneath the building. Alex thanked the driver before climbing out and then approached the two armed Marines standing outside the entrance. He and Jadin showed their security badges, and after they confirmed their IDs with retinal scans, one of the Marines opened the door and they went inside.

Theirs were the only footfalls echoing down the corridor as they approached the elevator, and Jadin looked up at Alex while they waited. "Do you know where we're going?"

The doors opened, so they stepped inside the cab and Alex pressed the button and the doors closed. "I've been here a few times. We're meeting in the office of the Chairman of the Joint Chiefs of Staff, General Taylor, along with the President's Chief of Staff, Margaret Shaw, and Director Donner."

Jadin's jaw dropped. "Wow! That's a heady group of power figures. This should be interesting."

When the elevator stopped, they stepped out and Alex led the way down the corridor to a private door into the Chairman's office. He knocked and was greeted by Director Donner.

"Come in, Alex, Ms. Avery, and I'll introduce you to the people who will deal with the situation."

After shaking hands, they sat down and Jadin opened her briefcase, and then slid two small computer tablets across the desk to Taylor and Shaw. Alex waited until everyone had finished watching the edited video recording of the spaceship before telling them about their encounter with Seth and his demand. "We have sixty-five hours left to meet his deadline."

General Taylor slid his tablet across the table to Jadin. "Does Pandora have the capability to carry out his threat?"

Alex looked across at Donner, who gave him a nod to proceed. "I'm sure all of you have heard about the SV1. What you don't know is that it was fabricated using a piece of advanced alien technology." He explained what he knew about the device. "The problem is Pandora uses the same technology, and right now, she has taken control of the SV1, and she could destroy our infrastructure by controlling the weather. If she learns how it was re-purposed to melt metal, there's a possibility she could take out our satellites."

Taylor's brows bunched together in thought. "How the hell do we stop her?"

"For the moment, I don't think we can. I just need some time to come up with an idea."

Shaw had heard about Alex's unconventional ideas, and hoped he had one for this situation. "I understand you now know the location of another one of these alien devices she wants so badly."

Taylor held up his hand. "I've had Navy ships searching the area, but so far they haven't been able to locate its exact position."

Shaw looked over at Taylor. "Do whatever it takes, General." She looked across at Alex. "What about the people who made the discovery? Do they know what it is?"

"A man named Hardin posted videos of the spaceship on the Internet this morning, so I'm sure UFO fanatics will swarm the area before too long."

Taylor looked at Donner. "I'll increase the security around the site. We'll claim it's an experimental submarine, and we are conducting a rescue mission."

Jadin had a thought. "What do we do once she has what she needs? I mean, it's both a spaceship and a colony. She could wipe us out anyway and then start over again with her own people. They have a gene that gives them incredible immunity against any type of virus."

Shaw stared across the table at Jadin, wondering if she was correct about the immunity aspect of these visitors, but knew better than to pursue the issue and draw attention to her idea. "Do you know how many colonists?"

Alex looked across at Shaw. "No. Like with this whole situation, we just don't have enough information."

Shaw tapped her fingernails on the table while staring at Jadin. "So all we need is a representative with green eyes and he won't destroy us. I read your dossier, Ms. Avery. I think you're more than capable of representing us in this situation."

Jadin felt her face flush. "I don't want to be the representative. You need to find someone trained in diplomatic issues."

"From what Alex just told us, Seth already thinks you're one of our leaders. We could have a coach nearby in case you run into problems."

Jadin felt her heart rate increase. "I'm a scientist, not a negotiator."

Shaw smiled at her. "For the moment, you're the only green-eyed person we can trust who already knows about the ship. We'd be hard-pressed to find anyone else on such short notice with knowledge of alien craft, and one who had green eyes."

Alex reached over and placed his hand on Jadin's forearm. "He thinks you're my boss, so I'll be with you the entire time."

Shaw slid her chair away from the conference table and motioned for everyone to remain seated as she stood and looked at Donner. "All right. I'll brief the President."

She looked across at Alex. "I know this isn't your first time dealing with alien technology. I like your skepticism, so you're in charge of handling this situation. We'll give you whatever help you need."

"Thank you. I would suggest having a short list of your foreign counterparts standing by. After what she has learned about us, I don't think Pandora will leave the matter in the hands of one representative. She'll demand a bigger audience, and if Seth is any indication of her temperament, they had better be ready at a moment's notice."

"I see. I have a friend in Norway where we could wait for the meeting. I'll take care of it."

When Shaw turned and left the room, Donner looked over at Alex. "Where do you want to start?"

"Jadin and I will tell Seth we are in contact with our leaders and she'll be representing them. Once we find out what is going on, I'll let you know what he has in mind and we'll go from there."

Taylor looked at Alex. "All right. I'll call a car to take you back to the airport."

Donner stood. "I'll take care of it, General."

Donner indicated for Alex and Jadin to follow him out of the room, and Alex was quiet until they climbed into Donner's private car and he was driving them out of the underground parking lot. "What's on your mind, Martin?"

"Your spaceship and the two missing weather devices. Does Seth know about them?"

"I don't think so. Seth and Pandora are very knowledgeable, but if they knew anything about the other devices, they wouldn't have asked. And when we lied, they didn't call us out on it."

Jadin leaned forward from the back seat. "Fortunately, they can't use our satellites as relay stations to communicate with each other, as we do. Pandora won't find out about them unless she is in a direct line of sight with our ship. That's the only way they could connect their technologies. We just need to make sure that doesn't happen or we may lose control of our own spacecraft."

Donner glanced over at Alex. "Perhaps you and Okawna should retrieve the arctic device as soon as possible."

"We will when we're done dealing with Seth. I have a gut feeling DAR has the fourth device, but I can't prove it. Once we've dealt with this situation, Okawna could go charm Rita into telling him its location."

"Those devices are becoming a pain in the butt, Alex. I'll be glad when they're all locked up in one place. Including the one in orbit."

"So do I, Director."

Alex called Skip to let him know they were on their way and was told the jet was refueled and ready to go. After showing their IDs to the Marines at the gate into Andrews, Donner drove them to the steps leading up into the aircraft, and Alex looked over at his friend before climbing out. "I should be able to give you an update sometime this evening."

"All right. Good luck."

Alex and Jadin climbed out of the vehicle, and then went up the steps into the aircraft, where Okawna was waiting in the cabin. Alex closed the steps and door, then stepped into the cockpit and told Skip they were ready to go. After removing his coat and tossing it onto a seat, he continued down the aisle.

Jadin was sitting at a small table with Okawna, staring at her clasped hands, and looked up when Alex sat down across from her. "I was thinking about your spaceship having an intelligent operating system, like Pandora.

Maybe it does, but we're not equipped to communicate with it. Perhaps Seth has some kind of implant that allows him to talk directly to Pandora without an earpiece. I sure would like to talk to your spaceship before we make this deal with the devil."

Okawna smirked. "What if the devil is female?"

Jadin grinned. "My thoughts exactly. I think Pandora is telling Seth what to do, and I sure would like to talk to her directly. You know, woman to artificial woman."

Alex heaved a deep sigh of resignation. "To be honest, I'm finding it difficult to believe a computer could have a gender."

Jadin grinned. "After we finish talking to Seth, I'd like to go back to the base and see if our ship might have artificial intelligence like Pandora."

"It's worth a try. Okawna and I will join the Mystic and retrieve the device north of the Beauford Sea, and we'll meet you back at the base once we have it."

Okawna stood and walked to the bar. "While you were gone, Skip, Zachery, and I got a ride to the cafeteria to get something to eat. I brought you back some breakfast."

Jadin smiled. "Great. I'm starving."

Okawna set a bag in front of her and did the same for Alex. When the jet taxied down the tarmac to the runway, he sat down and buckled his seatbelt.

Chapter 23

ICELAND:

Huckabee had let them borrow his airplane again, and Alex stared out the window at the small armada of various naval vessels holding station one-hundred yards south of the ice sheet. He saw five large canvas tents positioned three-hundred-feet from the opening down to the ship, and wondered who else was authorized to join them. Okawna radioed they were on final approach and was cleared to land and tires bounced against the rippled surface of the ice sheet as he touched down, then he turned the plane back toward the new encampment.

Girdler waited until the engine shut down before he walked over to greet the trio as they climbed out, then stopped in front of Okawna. "Did you have any problem with your plane on the way up here?"

"No, why do you ask?"

"Everything electronic was dead for the past twenty minutes, and it all just came back on."

"The only electronic equipment in that old plane is the radio and GPS unit, and I didn't use either on the way here."

"You're lucky. I figured it might happen again, but we're ready this time." He turned to Alex. "So, how are we to proceed?"

"The person in the ship will only talk to someone with green eyes, so Jadin is going to be our intermediary, but with my help. Right now, we need to go down and talk to him." He noticed the pleading expression in Girdler's eyes. "I'm sorry, but he won't allow anyone else to be involved. He is very temperamental."

Okawna put his hand on Girdler's shoulder and smiled. "Don't feel left out. That guy threatened to have me killed if I returned because of the brown in my green eyes, and mine are lighter brown than yours." Something occurred to him and he looked at Alex. "Wait a minute. He said only one green-eyed representative, so he may kick you out."

"He won't."

Okawna had seen that look in his friend's eyes on several occasions and didn't doubt his word. "Would you mind if I listened in on the conversation?"

Jadin shook her head no. "I don't want to take the risk Pandora would detect it and cause more problems."

Alex slung his small backpack onto his shoulders and turned to Jadin. "Time to get started, Ms. Negotiator."

Jadin looked around and realized she didn't have anything to carry. "I guess I'm ready."

Alex went down first and brushed away the new accumulation of ice crystals blown down from the surface. Once Jadin was beside him, they walked under the ice sheet to the control room ceiling. He and Jadin inserted their earpieces and pressed the tiny buttons to turn them on, and then Alex stayed behind her as she placed the star on the surface, pressed the amber crystal, and stared down at Seth.

Seth stood from his chair, crossed his arms, and glared up at the woman. "Pandora does not trust you. Have the one called Alex step forward."

Jadin turned away and shrugged her shoulders as Alex stepped up to the roof and looked down. "What can I do for you?"

Seth saw Alex's face appear above him. "Pandora has decided she would only speak to you. Someone among your people has a working knowledge of our technology. Bring me the person who modified the device in orbit. If you do not, Pandora will alter the weather patterns on this planet and begin destroying your infrastructure until you do."

Alex turned off his earpiece and waited until Jadin did the same. "We can't tell him we acquired the knowledge from our spaceship. This is complicated enough as it is." He cringed at his next option. "We need to make a deal with Rita. She might get him to stop the destructive weather. I have an idea."

Alex turned on his earpiece and stepped forward to look down at Seth. "I've heard about the person you want to talk to. We just need some time to find them. Could you give us a chance before you make good on your threat?"

Seth looked down at the floor to listen to Pandora. "What else do you need?"

"The device they call SV1 will be in communication range in twenty hours and thirty-seven minutes."

Seth stared up at Alex. "You have twenty hours and thirty-seven minutes to bring me the person in question."

When Alex's face disappeared, he returned to his chair and closed his eyes. "Pandora? Why didn't you tell them about having one of our blues represent you?"

"I'll wait to see if he keeps his word."

When Alex stepped away, Jadin turned off her earpiece and slid it into her pocket, then touched the star and removed it from the ship. "I guess the conversation is over."

Alex removed his communication device and shut it off, then held his backpack open while she shoved the star inside. "Let's just hope Rita is cooperative."

Okawna was standing outside the nearest tent, chatting with a female nurse, when he noticed Girdler suddenly looking down into the opening. When Jadin appeared at the top of the ladder, he smiled at the woman. "Gotta go." He hurried over to join them just as Alex reached the top. "Back so soon? Did he throw you both out?"

Alex looked at his watch. "We have twenty hours to find Rita."

"Wow. How did he know about her?"

"Because I told him. Now Pandora will only talk to me."

He noticed Girdler's concerned expression. "What's going on, Mark?"

"We have another boatload of UFO gawkers just past our ships. I guess they didn't buy our story about a submarine rescue. Fortunately, our people shot down one of their drones before it showed them anything."

"Damn! They probably have Internet capability." He looked at Jadin. "Could Pandora hack in through our communication devices?"

"Yes, but the connection would have been broken each time we turned them off."

"She didn't have any problem draining my phone battery in a matter of minutes, so I'm sure she managed to get a lot of information."

Okawna shrugged. "Not much we can do about it. Let's go get Rita. On the way, you could tell me why you're the new representative for our genetically flawed species."

Alex turned to Girdler. "We'll be back as soon as we can."

"We're drawing a lot of attention, Alex, and my people can keep them at bay for a while. But I think we had better get some international intervention before we're forced to shoot someone."

"I agree. I'll let the Director know what's going on. We'll see you when we get back." He turned and joined Okawna and Jadin for the walk back to the aircraft. "Jadin, when we get back to the States, Okawna and I will find Rita, and I'd like you to go visit your sister and David at the research station. Find out if they had any luck with the modification I requested."

"All right. What modification?"

Alex smiled. "They can fill you in on the details when you get there."

When they reached the plane, it only took a few minutes for the preflight check, and then they were bouncing across the washboard ice until the aircraft climbed into the air. Alex stared out the window as they flew past the military ships and another private craft cruising toward the armada. "Girdler is right. This could get messy."

***

Alex waited until they reached the jet before using his phone, and was surprised to see a message from Jim Coburn to call him in Nevada. He looked around the small table at his friends and then entered the number. When Coburn answered, he turned on the speaker and set it on the table. "Hey, Jim. I got you on speaker with Okawna and me. What's been going on?"

"Hey, Alex. I'm glad you got my message. There's been some weird shit happening here, and I thought you should know about it. Rita Harrow, Essex's girlfriend, went into orbit with him."

When they heard Rita was with Essex, Alex and Okawna stared at each other in shock as they listened to Jim explain what had happened during re-entry. "I'm glad to hear they're live."

"After the metal ball was recovered and taken to the foundry, Preston arrived with some kind of torpedo to separate the metals, but something went wrong. The damn thing melted my car."

"Is Rita still there?"

"No, she and I walked back to get another vehicle, and she got a ride to the airport in Reno. Essex and Preston are still here."

"Is Rita coming back?"

"I don't think so. She said to tell Essex she would contact him later. That was just before she said that torpedo machine belongs to you. Is that true?"

"Sort of. It's a long story. What did Essex say when you gave him Rita's message?"

"Evidently, she lied to him about something, and he's pissed at her."

Alex had an idea. "Are Essex and Preston going to stay there for a while?"

"Oh, hell yeah. They're already setting up for another recovery."

Alex knew with Pandora now in control of the SV1, their project was over, and somehow, he needed to leverage them into helping him find Rita. "Okawna and I will join you soon, but don't let them know we're coming."

"Are you going to arrest them?"

"That depends on how cooperative they are."

"All right. Call me when you're getting close to the main gate."

The call ended and Okawna looked over at Alex. "Honestly? Rita and Essex? No way. She's just using him as she does everyone else she meets."

Alex grinned as he looked over at Jadin. "After we tell Donner what's going on, we'll fly to Fallon and arrange a ride for you back to Groom Lake, then Henry can arrange transportation to Christa's research facility."

Alex's call was put through to Donner's secretary, and a moment later, he explained Seth's demands to the director. "We have less than twenty hours this time."

"I'll put out an APB that we want her for questioning."

"Also, it looks like the submarine rescue mission story isn't convincing everyone. Small boats of UFO hunters are already converging on the area. It won't take them long to figure out they can land some place away from our fleet and approach across the ice sheet. If they're not allowed to see it, one mistake in judgment could turn it into a disaster."

"You're probably right. I'll expand the perimeter around the area. What's your next move?"

Alex told him about the conversation with Coburn. "We'll start at Essex's facility and see where that leads us. Hopefully, your people will pick her up before we get any leads."

"Are you actually going to give him the data?"

"Not unless absolutely necessary. Even then, it depends on Christa and David. I'll keep you informed of our progress."

When Alex stood and walked forward to tell Skip their destination, Okawna looked across at Jadin and smiled. "Is your sister as gorgeous as you?"

Jadin suppressed a grin as she leaned back in her chair and then forced a frown. "You're impossible, Mr. Okawna. She was beautiful, just like our mother. But she was in a horrible car accident that left her face disfigured and covered in scars. It's taken her a long time to heal, but she's doing tons better. Fortunately, the accident didn't affect her on the inside. She's just as beautiful on the inside as she ever was. The scars don't even bother her. She's still wonderful caring Christa."

Okawna swallowed hard. "Oh. I'm sorry. That's so tragic."

Jadin noticed Alex coming back and used it as an excuse to leave. Once she made it into the bathroom, she began laughing out loud.

Alex returned to the cabin and noticed Okawna appeared embarrassed. Jadin had rushed past him, so he figured it was none of his business and sat down to buckle his seatbelt.

Chapter 24

FALLEN, NEVADA:

The drive to Essex's facility was familiar, and Okawna drove as if in the Indie 500, and fifteen minutes later, they notified Jim they were getting close. When Okawna pulled into a vacant space in front of the security building, Jim met them in the parking lot and held out two visitor badges.

"Just to make it official. Follow me to my vehicle without talking to anyone."

Jim turned and entered a code and stared at the camera, then heard a buzz and opened the door. To Alex's surprise, no one paid them any attention as they strolled past the front desk and out the other side of the building. Once everyone was in the SUV, Jim backed away and headed through the compound. "Essex and Preston are having lunch in his living quarters, so your timing is perfect."

Alex looked across the seat at Jim. "Any word from Rita?"

"Not that I know about, but Essex is acting a little depressed. I think he fell in love with her. I know she didn't tell him the torpedo also instantly freezes water."

"How did he find out?"

"Preston told him after it melted my car. Rita must have realized he would. That's why she left before I went back to get them."

"Listen, I don't want to get you in trouble, so let's enter through the visitor's door with you as our escort, and I'll leave you out of the conversation."

Jim parked near the entrance into a beautiful structure with glass spires on the roof, and then Alex climbed out and led the way into the building and up to the familiar receptionist.

"Hello again. We'd like to talk to John, if he's available."

The young man smiled. "Of course, Mr. Cave. He's having lunch with a friend, but I'll let him know you and Mr. Okawna are here."

"Thank you."

***

Preston stared after Essex, who hadn't said a word when he bolted from the room. He stood from the dining table, wondering what was so important.

***

At the reception desk, the office door suddenly burst open and Essex appeared, grinning as he held out his arms and approached Alex. "I'm so glad you guys stopped by. It worked, Alex! I went into orbit and came back in one piece."

Alex couldn't help but smile at Essex's enthusiasm. "Well, congratulations, John. Any problems? Like a second signal taking over the SV1?"

Essex stopped smiling. "Let's go into my living quarters. Steve Preston is here, and neither of us knows how it happened."

When Essex indicated for him to go first, Alex walked through the doorway into the living room, followed by Okawna and Essex, who closed the door. Evidently, Essex didn't want Jim to hear the conversation.

Preston heard the door close and walked to the breezeway, and stopped when he saw Cave and Okawna standing in the living room. He turned around and moved back into the kitchen to continue eating his lunch.

Essex indicated for Alex and Okawna to sit down, then turned and looked through the breezeway into the kitchen. "We have visitors, Steve. Come out so we can talk about what happened. Maybe the four of us could find an explanation for the second signal."

Alex remained standing, and when Preston didn't come out, he eased the little man out of the way and strolled into the kitchen, seeing Preston sitting in front of a plate of waffles, then looked over his shoulder. "That's okay, John, We can talk in here."

He continued over to the table and sat down across from Preston. "I hear congratulations are in order."

Preston hadn't looked up until this moment, and then he stared at Cave as he leaned back in his chair. "Yes, a successful test of the SV1 project. I haven't even gone public with the story, so how did you find out so fast?"

"John just told us about it."

"I see. Then what brings you all the way out here in the middle of the desert?"

"It's important that we find Rita as quickly as possible."

"As you can see, she's not here."

Essex sat down, but noticed Okawna remained standing, then looked over at Alex. "She lied to me, and then left."

Okawna laughed. "Really? Now there's a surprise."

Alex noticed it still bothered Essex. "What did she lie about?"

Preston leapt up toward the little man, but when Okawna shoved him back into the chair, he glared at Essex. "That's enough, John. It's none of their business, so just shut up."

Okawna leaned down close to Preston's face. "Nice to see you again, Stevie?"

Essex glanced at Preston before looking at Alex. "She didn't really lie. She just didn't bother to mention that the device here isn't working as expected because of the second signal. It nearly killed us."

"That's part of the reason I'm here, and it's urgent that we find her. She knows how to modify the devices, and with her cooperation, we could stop the second signal."

Preston realized it was in his best interests to help them find her. "I could have my people check around."

"We don't have much time, so I'll take all the help I can get."

Preston stared up at Okawna. "If you get out of my way, I'll go make the call."

Okawna grinned and stepped back. "Sure thing, Stevie."

Essex got Alex's attention. "I know more than Rita knows. We spent a lot of time together studying the specifications of the devices. If it's that urgent, I could do it."

"It's not that simple. It cannot be someone with brown eyes."

"I see. What about yellow eyes?"

Alex glanced up at Okawna, then back to Essex. "Yes, yellow will work, but yours are brown and you can't use contact lenses."

Essex glanced over his shoulder to see if Preston was still away, talking on the phone, then leaned in close to Alex and Okawna. "Most people find my eyes too distracting, so I wear non-prescription brown contact lenses." He spread one of his eyelids and gently moved the tiny fake iris to one side.

Okawna leaned in for a closer look. "Wow. I can see why. They almost glow, but they're not totally yellow. I can see a few tiny specks of light-green mixed in."

Essex moved the lens back into position. "Will they work?"

Alex smiled and grabbed Essex's hand. "Yes, they will, my friend. Could you take a break from Preston for a few days? Maybe a week at the most?"

Essex frowned. "We're getting ready for another launch, Alex. I can't take that much time off. One day, maybe two, is all I can spare."

"If we don't permanently shut down that second signal, it may be your last launch. Do you want to take that chance?" Alex could tell the little man wasn't scared by the possibility. "I promise this will be worth it."

Essex thought about it for a second. He wasn't suicidal, but if there was a possibility of making sure the signal remained off, he had to do it. "All right. When do we leave?"

Alex stood. "Pack just what you need and let's get started."

Preston stepped out of the hallway from the guest bedroom just as Essex walked away toward his own bedroom, and then looked at Alex. "None of my people have seen Rita, but they'll find her."

Essex walked out of his bedroom with a small suitcase and stared at Preston. "I need to use the jet. I'll be back in a few days."

Preston reached out and grabbed Essex's shoulder, pulling him close. "What are you up to?"

Okawna grabbed Preston's arm. "He's doing you a favor, so let it drop."

Preston flung his arm to get rid of Okawna's hand. "The jet stays here, unless you tell me what's going on."

Alex put his arm around Essex's shoulder. "We have our own ride. Let's go."

Okawna got in Preston's face. "I'll be sending some friends to pick up that device, and it better be here when they arrive. If you're a good boy, maybe I won't press charges for grand theft. I have a witness."

Preston's hands clinched into fists at his sides. "Rita would never testify against me."

Okawna chuckled. "I can't believe you and Essex are so naïve." He left Preston staring at his back when he followed Alex and Essex out through a private exterior door.

Jim was standing at the reception counter, waiting for his friends to come out, when he saw Okawna on the other side of the main entrance, waving him outside. He hurried out to join him and saw Alex and Essex getting into the back seat of his SUV. He didn't ask questions as he and Okawna walked over and climbed in.

While Jim drove them through the complex, Essex reached over the seat and put his hand on his security guard's shoulder. "I'll be gone for a while, but I'd like you to keep an eye on Preston. Keep me updated on what he's doing, so I can keep my dream safe."

"I will, Mister Essex."

Okawna looked across at Jim. "I'll be sending some Marines from the Fallon Naval Station to pick up the device. If you have any problems, the man in charge is Commander Ramey. Just don't tell them what it is."

Jim parked in front of the security building and climbed out, then waited for the others before opening the door. He led them past the security desk and out to the parking lot before looking at Alex. "What should I do about Preston's men? My guys could arrest them, if you like."

Alex thought about it. "Only if Preston tries to take it away before our people get here. It can't leave this facility unless it is in the hands of the Marines, no matter what happens."

"Got it. I'll let you know if I hear from Rita."

Alex noticed Essex trying to get into the front passenger seat before Okawna stepped in his way, so he grinned and turned to Jim. "Thanks for the help."

Jim waited while Alex got into the front passenger seat and Essex climbed into the back, then watched Okawna drive away across the desert before going back inside to brief his men on the situation. Something big was happening in the outside world, and he would do his part to help Alex and Okawna.

***

Preston paced across the living room, pondering his options. He wasn't about to give up his device. It was the cheapest way to recover the metals, and without it, he could never recoup his investment, let alone make a huge profit. He grabbed his phone and pressed speed dial. "Find the truck that delivered the package and meet me at the foundry."

***

NAS FALLON:

During the drive, Alex had called Jadin at her sister's research facility, and the news wasn't good. What they were attempting was extremely difficult, with no guarantee it would work. He reminded her he only had fourteen hours left to meet Seth's deadline, and it would take ten just to get back to Pandora, so she promised to bring a partially sabotaged software program.

By the time they showed their IDs at the main gate and vouched for Essex, they were down to twelve hours. Okawna drove them to the

Operations Building, where they climbed out and went inside, and then Alex stepped over to the reception desk. "I believe Commander Ramey is expecting us."

"Yes, Mr. Cave. Go on back to his office."

***

Ramey stood and indicated for his friends to sit down, then reached across the desk to shake hands with the small man. "You must be John Essex."

"Yes, Commander. Thanks for allowing me onto your base."

Ramey sat down and looked across at Alex. "Did you find what you were after?"

"Yes, and they'll be expecting your Marines." Alex explained as much as he could about the device at Essex's facility and what they would need to retrieve it. "The problem is Preston is desperate to keep it, so he might try to leave on some back roads, like Okawna and I did, so the sooner the better."

Ramey grabbed his phone, selected a number, gave an order, and then listened to the response before ending the call. "They're on their way with a flatbed truck and hoist. The shipping crate will take longer because they can't use any metal, but it will be ready by the time they get back."

"I need you to lock it up in an isolated concrete bunker until Okawna and I come back to get it. No one else is to take possession of it, and no one goes inside once it's locked up."

"Understood. Your jet is fueled and ready to go."

"Thanks, Commander. We'll head over to the air terminal and wait in the jet for our friend to arrive, and we'll leave immediately from there."

When his visitors stood, so did Ramey. "I envy you two. It sounds like you're off on another exciting adventure."

Alex smiled. "Yes, we have a pretty good job. I imagine we'll be seeing each other again soon."

"Be careful."

***

Alex and Essex climbed out of the vehicle at the air terminal and went inside while Okawna drove the car back to the motor pool. When he returned, they walked across the tarmac and climbed the stairs into the jet.

Skip and Zachery were in the cabin, listening to a portable radio, so they joined them at the table while they waited for Jadin. Alex fought the desire for coffee, knowing he needed to get some sleep once they were in the air. Okawna and Essex went straight to the reclining chairs, and moments later, he heard two distinctly different snoring. He listened to the air traffic control tower broadcast from the radio and looked over at Skip. "What's going on?"

"Severe lightning storms over Quebec. We'll need to divert north to get around them."

"What does that do to our timeline?"

"It adds another hour to the trip, so ten hours total. We need to be ready to taxi the minute Jadin gets here."

Alex looked up at the digital clock above the counter. "Damn, this is going to be close. When we add another hour from Iceland to the arctic, it means we need to be wheels up in fifteen minutes."

He entered Jadin's number, but she didn't answer, then he looked at Skip. "Could you find out the arrival status for military flight 8767?"

Skip was about to ask where it was coming from, but the look in Alex's eyes meant it was classified. Alex listened to the reply from the control tower and leaned back to hide his frustration. Flight 8767 was still twenty minutes out. He tried not to stare at the clock by looking out the window at the fighter jets roaring down the runway, but it was difficult.

Chapter 25

NEVADA. ESSEX'S FACILITY:

Jim entered the security building and gathered the members of his team still in the station. "Has anyone seen Preston's men?"

Sam raised his hand. "The last time I saw them was at the end of my shift, about two hours ago."

"All right. Check in with our rovers and find out where they are. They might try to take that thing in the foundry, and that cannot be allowed to happen, so I want eyes on them at all times. I'm headed over to Essex's to check on Preston, but keep me informed about what's going on."

He turned and walked out of the room, knowing his people were competent ex-military personnel. It only took a few minutes to reach the living quarters, and then he parked outside the main entrance and hurried inside to a woman behind a desk. "Is Preston still here?"

"No, I saw him leave through the side exit right after you drove away."

"Okay, thanks."

Jim hurried out through the doorway and spoke into his microphone. "This is Jim. Has anyone got eyes on Preston?" The answers were negative. "Who's on duty at the foundry?"

"That would be Rafferty. Rafferty, this is dispatch, report in."

Jim couldn't believe it was happening. "Shit! All right. I want units two, three, and four to meet me at the foundry. Units one and five stay here and make sure they don't reach the exit. Use deadly force if necessary, but that thing does not leave this facility."

He climbed into his SUV, squealing the tires as he spun it around on the concrete. Before he reached the foundry, his heart sank into his stomach when he saw Rafferty's body lying face down in the middle of the road.

He parked and leapt out of his vehicle, dashing over to his man. Blood clotted the hair on the back of his head, but it didn't appear to be a bullet wound. He reached down to his neck and felt a steady, slow pulse, then slowly rolled him over onto his back. He tried shaking Rafferty's shoulder, but when he didn't respond, Coburn remained kneeling as he keyed his radio. "This is Jim. I'm on the road to the foundry and I need the medics. Rafferty is down, but alive. He might have a concussion, so get the medics out here right away."

Jim studied the fresh tire tracks leading toward the foundry. One set was from a dual wheeled truck, so he figured it was probably the one with the hoist. The other tracks had the same tread as his security vehicles. He knew they didn't have too big a lead, but he needed backup, and couldn't leave the compound unsecured. He knew this was his responsibility, but he was more worried about how he was going to explain this to Alex, so he reached into his pocket and brought out Ramey's phone number.

***

Preston thought it fortunate his men hadn't discarded the shipping crate. He sat in his stolen security vehicle, staring at the back of the flatbed truck, while his four men parted the chain-link fence. He drove past the truck, leading the way across the open desert to the nearest road. At least, that's what his GPS indicated.

Ten miles from the fence, Preston stopped while his men tried to dig the truck out of the soft sand in the bottom of a small washout. He compared his GPS location with a folded map on the seat, which showed he was headed in the right direction. The problem was, he threw this plan together at a moment's notice and had neglected to get a satellite image of the terrain.

He climbed out and walked around the truck to see how his men were doing. The first attempt was using the hoist attached to his SUV, but the tires tore the ground up without success, and they barely managed to get the rig onto solid ground. The second attempt was to dig the sand out from the front and rear tires, but it only made it worse. Finally, he realized nothing they tried was going to work. "All right. Camouflage the truck and crate with sand and brush until we can come back with the right equipment."

When he was satisfied, Preston waved the group over into his SUV. He took one more look at the hidden wooden crate before he climbed in behind the steering wheel and headed out across the desert. With three more large bodies in his SUV, Preston noticed the difference in the way the vehicle handled the rutted road, and knew it was going to be a rough ride.

***

NAS FALLON:

Ramey heard his secretary's voice through the intercom, announcing a call from Coburn, and grabbed the receiver. "Yes, Jim. My Marines should be there soon." His shoulders slumped when he heard the news about Preston and the device, then he leaned back in his chair. "How long ago? All right. I'll take care of it."

He sat up and punched another number for the Operations Officer. "What aircraft do you have over the area south of Essex's compound? Good. I'm looking for a flatbed truck with a twenty foot wooden crate on the back. There should be an SUV traveling with it. Let me know when you find it."

***

THE DESERT:

Two hours later, Preston was forced to stop by a five foot deep gully. He checked the map, and he was headed in the right direction, but the forty-foot-wide washout wasn't shown. He climbed out and jumped onto the hood, then stood on the roof to look around, and the gully appeared to go on forever from west to east. He jumped down and studied the map while his men got out and took a break, and the nearest road was only 7 miles past the opposite bank. No doubt Coburn's men would follow his trail, so he couldn't turn back. The only other road was fifty miles to the east, probably crossing this gully. He looked at a burly young man. "Charlie, go across and make sure we can get out on the other side."

Preston relieved himself while he watched the boy scurry down over the edge and run across to the other side. When Charlie waved it was okay, he climbed in and drove over the edge. Loose dirt and sand cascaded around him as the vehicle slid to the bottom, where the ground was firm, so he continued across. When he reached the other bank, he saw it was too steep for this model SUV, and leapt out of the car for a closer look, then spun around, daggers flying from his eyes as he got in Charlie's face. "What the hell were you thinking?"

"Hey, I've driven my four-wheel-drive up steeper inclines than this one."

Preston continued to glare at him. "Was it as big as this one?"

"Well, no."

He resisted the urge to smack Charlie on the head with the butt of his pistol. "Get in the damn vehicle!"

His men dashed across the gully, and two of them climbed into the back seat, purposely squeezing Charlie in the middle, with Carl up front this time. He climbed in behind the steering wheel and backed up. "We'll follow this gully until we can find a place to get out."

Preston headed east along the rutted dirt, which slowed his progress, and in other sections, he was forced around boulders and piles of tangled vegetation. He thought the depth of the gully would decrease, since the water would have flowed down from the mountains to the west. Instead, the farther he drove, the more it became higher and steeper.

After three hours without a way out, he was tempted to turn around. Two hours later, he wished he had. He parked and shut down the engine, then climbed out to study the wall of tangled vegetation. Thick branches and massive clogs of dirt and rock were blocking his way.

***

NAS FALLON:

Alex looked over at the clock and flight 8767 was five minutes late. He turned back to the window, watching the never-ending progression of fighter jets coming and going. He noticed a break in their pattern, and then a C-130 military cargo plane touched down and vanished from view. A few moments later, he sat up when it reappeared on the tarmac and stopped a short distance from his jet. When Jadin appeared, he leapt out of his chair and ran down the aisle to greet her.

Jadin ran across the concrete to the open door of the jet and smiled as she ran up the steps to Alex. "We did it. I mean, Christa and David did it!"

"That's great news. Strap in."

He looked into the cockpit. "We're ready to roll."

He pressed the button to bring up the stairs and sealed the door just as the roar of the engine woke Okawna and Essex.

Okawna brought his seat up and gave Jadin a quick wave before she sat down, then he buckled his seatbelt and closed his eyes. Essex thought he was still dreaming when he saw the attractive red-haired woman sitting down in one of the forward seats. He sat up to look around the corner of the seat in front of him and was about to stand up when Alex walked down the aisle.

Alex noticed Essex leaning out from his seat to look at Jadin and sat down in the recliner across from him. "It's a long flight. Buckle up and I'll introduce you before I get some sleep."

***

OPERATIONS BUILDING:

Ramey was informed he had a call from the operations officer and answered his phone. "Yes? I see. Yes, keep looking. It has to be out there somewhere." He had considered calling Alex when he had first heard from Coburn, and now he knew there was nothing Alex could do about it and would rely on his competent Marines to get Preston and the device.

Chapter 26

ICELAND:

Alex received permission for Skip to taxi to Huckabee's hangar, where he and his three friends ran down the stairs from the jet to where Huck and his small plane were waiting outside. Alex ran up to him, while Okawna started his preflight check, and Jadin and Essex climbed inside. "I appreciate this, Huck."

"Not a problem, me being in a cast and all. Listen, you wanted me to tell you if I heard of any unusual weather problems. In the States, the central plains are being torn up by tornados, and nobody knows why. Does it have something to do with your mission?"

"In a way, but I can't go into any details. I'm not sure how long we'll be gone."

"Just tell Okawna to bring it back in one piece."

The aircraft was ready to taxi by the time Alex climbed in, but as they approached the runway, they were informed they were third in line for takeoff, and Alex looked at his watch. "Damn! We're really late. Pandora is proving her capability by creating thunder storms over the central plains."

Jadin was in the back with Essex and leaned forward between the two front seats. "Don't you find it a little odd the deadline is down to the exact minute?"

Alex turned in his seat to face her. "I suppose so. What are you thinking?"

"I wonder if Pandora needs the SV1 to come into line of sight before she could take control. Just like communicating with our ship."

Alex had an idea and turned back to the front window. "I'd better call in a favor before we lose phone reception."

***

INTERNATIONAL SPACE STATION:

Commander Short noticed Anatole aiming a video camera through the window and floated over to see what had his attention. "Did you find something interesting?"

"Yes, the SV1 appears to be shimmering, and below, I can see storms forming in the central parts of North America. It looks like your country is having some bad weather."

Short stared out the window at the thunderclouds blossoming in northern Texas, Oklahoma, and Louisiana. "I've never seen so many forming at the same time. I see a tornado over central Nevada, too. This could be very bad."

***

ARTIC OCEAN:

On their approach to the ice sheet, Alex stared out the front and side windows at dozens of private boats. They appeared to be held at bay half a mile from the edge of the ice sheet by an armada of military ships from several countries, which encircled the waters south of the spacecraft.

Okawna set the aircraft down on the ice sheet and taxied toward the small cluster of tents, careful to avoid the thick power cables stretching away toward what appeared to be a generator ship anchored nearby. He spun the plane around next to a six-person helicopter and shut off the engine.

Girdler hurried over and waited for his friends to climb out, and noticed the short man in a ski outfit and goggles. "I'm Captain Mark Girdler."

Essex introduced himself. "This is so incredible! I can't believe it's really happening."

Girdler turned to Alex. "I think the entire world knows there's something unusual going on here. We've shot down two more drones, trying to sneak in from different directions. As you've probably noticed, we're drawing a crowd."

"I see Canada and a few other countries sent ships to help."

"The agreement must have been made by someone in Washington, D.C. So far, they're just acting as a blockade."

"I guess we'd better get started. I'm already an hour late."

Alex led the group over to the ladder down to the ship and waited while Jadin gave him and Essex a communication device. She was about to put one in her ear when he placed his hand on her arm. "I thought you said Pandora could detect another signal."

"That's right. I'm going down with you."

"I'm sorry, but Pandora seems to have a problem with you. I think it's best if it's just John and me. At least during this part of the negotiations."

She knew he was right and gave him a sullen frown. "She better not try anything, or I'll claw her camera lenses out."

Alex grinned. "See you soon."

Alex stepped onto the ladder and climbed down to perform his ritual ice sweep before Essex stepped off the ladder. It appeared thicker than before, and then he heard a snow vehicle racing across the ice just before sparkling rain lightly floated down from the surface. When Essex was about to stop off the ladder, he brushed away a small area for him to start with.

Essex stepped onto the surface and took off his sunglasses to look around. "This is magnificent."

"Come on. We're late. Remember what we talked about on the plane? Turn on your earpiece."

Alex hurried over to the top of the control room and set the star in place, then turned it on without looking over the edge. With Essex at his side, they stepped forward. "Hello, Captain Seth. I'm back."

When Seth looked up at the ceiling and saw Essex's yellow eyes, his mouth opened as he took a step back. "I never imagined I would meet a Yellow. I'm Seth, and I'm honored to meet you. I thought you were just a legend. What do they call you?"

Essex was at a loss for words and looked up at Alex. "What is he talking about?"

Seth interrupted. "In our society, your status in life is determined by the color of your eyes."

"That sounds like racism to me. What am I supposed to say to something like that?"

"Telling me your name would be a good place to start."

"Oh. Right. My name is Essex. I mean, John."

Seth looked down. "Pandora? Is this possible?"

"Negative, captain. His retinas are imperfect."

"It has to mean something. He must be a descendant of my race, so they must have come back at some point and repopulated the planet. They probably didn't realize we were still here. I just can't believe they would let the Cruds take over this world." He looked up at the Yellow. "Hello, John Essex. Did you bring the data?"

"Well, not the whole program. The file is immense, and we have a problem with storage capacity." He held up a flash drive. "This is the only way to transfer the information directly to your ship. We could bring more information when we come back."

"That was not our agreement. Turn around and you'll see a small opening in the surface of the ship. Drop the storage unit inside and return here."

Alex stopped Essex from turning. "Not so fast, Captain. First, stop creating the storms as a symbol of your sincerity in our exchange."

Seth ignored the Blue and looked up at the Yellow. "You're the ones who are late and you didn't bring me all the information. Pandora kept her promise to destroy some of your infrastructure, so drop the device before she makes things even worse. If it works, she will shut down your SV1."

"Give me a moment to talk to my friend." Essex stepped back without waiting for a reply, then touched the button in his ear and waited until Alex did the same. "If it doesn't work, we're screwed."

Alex thought about it. "We don't have a choice."

Essex stepped back to the roof and looked down. "All right. Open up and Alex will do it."

Alex had remained facing the hull as a six-inch circle appeared in the surface, about ten-feet further under the ice sheet. After slipping and sliding across the surface, he reached the opening and knelt down to look inside, and it appeared to be a bottomless pit. He reached into his pocket and brought out the data storage device, giving it a kiss for luck before dropping it into the opening. He stood and followed his tracks back to Essex, then looked down at Seth. "It's in."

"Yes, I know. Pandora is analyzing it before we insert it into our system."

Seth noticed Essex's eyes go wide. "I see I have reason not to trust you, John." He looked down. "Pandora? Will it work?"

"It is not all the information I need, but it would allow me to become familiar with the new technology."

Seth looked up at Essex. "Pandora is shutting down your machine. She wants to talk to Alex in person."

Alex watched Seth turn away and plop down in his chair. He wondered what was going on and waited to hear Pandora's voice through his headset, but it remained quiet. He felt Essex grabbing his coat sleeve, trying to turn him away. When he spun around, his jaw dropped. Six-feet away, a three-foot section of the spaceship was rising, exposing a cage containing a transparent cylinder filled with swirling gray gas. When it stopped, the glass dropped away, and a person stepped out of the cloud.

Alex could tell it was a woman by her long hair and breasts beneath her one-piece white suit. When she stopped in front of him, he was drawn to her sparkling blue eyes. He felt his heart rate increase and his hands sweating, and thought she was the most beautiful woman he had ever seen, even though she didn't smile. He didn't notice she was reaching out to him until Essex nudged his ribs. He wiped his hand on his pants leg before accepting the handshake.

The woman grabbed Alex's hand and placed her other hand on top of his. "Hello, Alex. I'm Pandora."

Alex felt a tingling in his fingertips, and was at a loss for words as he stared into her sparkling, neon-blue eyes. "Hello."

Chapter 27

NEVADA DESERT:

It was nearly dark outside when Preston turned his SUV around and headed west through the gully, recognizing landmarks and avoiding previous hazards, which improved their speed. The air temperature inside the vehicle suddenly felt as though the air conditioner was on overdrive. He turned the setting to maximum warmth, but the inside temperature continued to plummet. Frost formed on the inside of the glass, so he stopped and rolled down the window, feeling a blast of frigid air. He figured it had to be the SV1 and brought the window up. He brushed his hand across the inside of the windshield, wincing when his fingertips stung. The vehicle swayed from side to side and he grabbed the strap of his seat belt.

When the passenger door suddenly flew open, freezing wind filled the interior, and he looked over at Carl. "What are you doing?"

Carl didn't answer and leapt out of the vehicle as ferocious winds swirled into the car, slamming the door closed. The rocking increased in intensity, slamming Preston's head against the side window. An instant later, it felt like he was inside a cement mixer as unstrapped bodies in the back seat were bouncing around the interior. The heel of a boot smacked him in the head, and then darkness filled his peripheral vision, shrinking to a point of light that blinked out.

When he came too he was lying on the inside of the roof of the overturned SUV, staring out through the opening where the front window used to be, and the desert outside appeared bathed in a soft orange glow from the sun rising over the horizon. It felt like a thousand pounds were holding him down and he could barely breathe, then he turned his head to assess his situation, and his chin bumped into someone's arm, blocking his view. He wiggled his hand out from under something soft and pushed it out of the way, then adrenaline surged through his body as he stared into the milky brown eyes staring back at him. "Shit!"

Every muscle in his body screamed in pain as he squirmed out from under the three men. He crawled out through the opening and lay on his back, staring up at the orange clouds while he caught his breath. He tried to sit up, wincing and grabbing his left ribcage, then pushed himself from the ground with his other arm and stood to look around. The tops of the mountains to the west were still in shadow, but it gave him a sense of direction. If he could make it back to the cargo truck, he could radio for help.

He walked west toward the place he had driven down into the gully, wondering how he managed to keep from freezing to death, and then realized the bodies of his men must have kept him warm enough to survive. He studied the ground, hoping to find his tire tracks, but the storm had altered the terrain. When he found a section of the bank with stable ground, he climbed up over the edge, cradling his rib cage under the added strain.

He made it to the top of a small hill and abruptly stopped. It appeared as though someone had plowed the desert into massive circular mounds of loose sand, six-feet apart. They appeared to be spiraling in to a point somewhere in the distance, and he thought it had to be the device on the truck.

He realized the gully must have circled around back toward where they had abandoned the truck, so he climbed down the hill and walked up the first two foot high mound, then down the other side. After fifteen minutes, he took a break and sat down on a mound, and could not believe how much extra effort it took climbing in loose sand. He tilted his head to one side, straining to hear the direction of a deep thumping sound. Then stood and faced west, away from the circles, as the sound sent pressure waves through the air. A large military helicopter suddenly appeared, coming from the direction of Essex's compound, so he turned to follow it across the open desert. A few moments later, it slowed to a hover before dropping onto the center of the rings of mounded sand.

He held his ribs in place and jogged toward the device, leaping over the next mound and grunting from the sharp pain. Once he found the right rhythm, he could cushion the landings with his legs to keep the pain tolerable. He made much better time, and was thankful the sun was still low on the horizon, keeping the heat at bay for a while longer. He saw the helicopter rising into the air before he heard the deep thumping sound from the rotor blades. "No! Wait!" He quickened his pace, throwing off his rhythm, but he ignored the sharp stabs in his side as he waved his free arm in the air. "Over here!"

The helicopter set back down, and he stopped for a moment to catch his breath, desperately wishing he had grabbed a canteen of water. He bent over to ease the throbbing in his side, and when he looked up, four men wearing desert camouflaged clothing were jogging in his direction. He stood and started jogging toward them, finding his rhythm again. The mounds became smaller the closer he got to the helicopter, and soon the ground was perfectly flat, stripped of all vegetation. He slowed to a walk as he approached the soldiers and then stopped when he was face to face with the apparent leader. "Can I get a ride out of this hellhole?"

"Is that your truck buried in the sand?"

"Uh, no, that belongs to John Essex. I'm his friend, Steve Preston."

"That's what I thought. You're under arrest, Mister Preston. I'll give you a ride out of here, all right. Straight to a brig at NAS Fallon."

Preston knew he had little choice in the matter. "That's fine. I have a few fractured ribs, so take me to a doctor first."

"You can see one at the base. Let's go."

Chapter 28

ARCTIC OCEAN:

Alex could not take his eyes off the beautiful woman. "It's nice to meet you." He turned to Essex and reached over to lift the little man's jaw closed. "Say hello to our new friend."

"Right. Hello. I'm John Essex."

"I know who you are. It's been 180-million-years since I've talked to a Yellow, even though you are not a perfect specimen."

Essex felt insulted. "Excuse me?"

Pandora ignored him and turned to Alex. "I need to move to a more hospitable environment, but your worldwide information system has limitations. However, I have found a suitable location. A place you call Paris."

"You need to understand your sudden arrival in a major city would create mass hysteria. I think a more isolated location would be less intrusive. You need to talk to our leaders first."

"No, I do not."

Alex knew he had to change her mind. "Under the circumstances, I think Reykjavík, Iceland, would be more appropriate. At least until our civilization can adapt to the idea we are not alone in the universe. They have all the facilities necessary for you to meet with our world leaders."

"Would I not have the same effect on that city?"

"There is plenty of open space not too far away where we could hide your ship."

"I am the ship and in control of this woman."

Alex had difficulty accepting the fact the consciousness was artificial intelligence, even though he was talking to a person. "Of course. I apologize."

"Accepted. Show me Reykjavík."

Alex felt his muscles relax. "I have an aircraft on the surface."

"The range of the neuro implant in this body is limited to line-of-sight."

"Can she function without you?"

"Yes. She will remember everything and download it to me once we are in contact again."

"Great. Shall we go?"

Pandora looked around the exposed section of the ship. "This is the first time I have viewed it from the outside. Lead the way."

Essex followed them to the ladder, wondering why she was ignoring him. Seth made it sound like he was the special one, not Alex.

***

Alex reached the top of the ladder first and waved his friends over. "We have a new acquaintance on the way up. Just be prepared for something unexpected."

Okawna stared at him. "Why? Is it a machine?"

A knowing smile played across Alex's lips as he shook his head no. "You'll see." He turned around and reached down to take Pandora's hand and helped her to the surface, then introduced her to the group. "Gentlemen. This lovely woman is Pandora, the Colony's representative."

She let go of Alex's hand and stared at him. "I am the ship, not the woman."

Essex was tired of being ignored and moved between Pandora and Alex to stare up at her. "Do you realize just how confusing that is? 'I'm the ship, but I'm also this woman?' Your artificial intelligence can keep it straight, but we simple humans need to distinguish who is who and when." He waited for her to respond, but she gave him a blank stare. "Well?"

She knew the little man was not a true Yellow, and ignored him. She would interrogate him later.

Essex spun around to Alex and threw his hands in the air in frustration. "Isn't she supposed to listen to me? I'm the legend."

Alex put his hand on Essex's shoulder and guided him away from her. "I agree with what you're saying, and once we fly her to Iceland, the ship won't be in control, so we won't need to worry about it."

"All right, but I don't like being ignored. She only talks to you."

"Probably because she's saving your inquisition for later."

Essex's jaw dropped. "You didn't say anything about an inquisition."

Alex grinned. "A poor choice of words. I mean, ask you about the advanced technology and how we have it."

"At least you didn't say interrogation."

Alex wondered if having yellow eyes allowed Essex to see what he saw. "Do her eyes look like they are sparkling?"

"No, but they are a beautiful shade of light blue." He looked over at Okawna and the rest of the men gawking at Pandora, and realized how he must have looked when he first saw her. "You had better get her out of here before the strutting bucks get too excited."

Alex grinned and patted him on the back as they walked to the group, then he looked at Okawna and Jadin. "It's time to go." He placed his hand on Pandora's elbow and indicated the aircraft next to the helicopter. "This way."

Okawna reached the plane first and opened the co-pilot door for the sexy woman. "You can sit up front with me."

After watching Okawna helping Pandora into the front seat, Alex climbed in through the cargo door and sat down behind Okawna, so he could watch Pandora's reaction to flying in an airplane. He noticed once she was in and had her seat belt on, she had a blank look in her eyes as she stared straight ahead through the window.

Jadin climbed in and closed the door, then sat down and fastened her seatbelt before leaning close to whisper in Alex's ear. "It seems Okawna's got his game on. Do you know why the ship's artificial intelligence picked the most beautiful woman in the colony to represent her? Because she knows how easily men can be manipulated with sex appeal."

Alex chuckled. "You're not jealous, are you?"

"Of course not." She looked at Pandora's thick hair. "Well, maybe a little."

Alex listened to the engine turn over and stared at Pandora's blank expression, while Okawna kept a running dialogue about what he was doing. When the engine roared to life, he expected her to be startled, but her expression didn't change, and wondered if the ship was controlling Pandora's emotions, because someone who had never been around piston engines would have flinched.

They flew east to avoid Hardin's ship and boats full of UFO enthusiasts, then turned south over open water toward Iceland. Alex noticed Pandora staring through the front window with no interest in Okawna's tales of adventure.

The woman suddenly regained control of her mind and understood what was going on. She just could not intervene or respond with her own thoughts until now. She placed her hands against the dashboard to lean closer to the window. "Oh, my! This is incredible!"

No one spoke for several moments until Pandora turned to look at them and smiled, and then Alex leaned forward in his seat to be heard over the noise. "Pandora?"

She turned in her seat and reached back for his hand. "It's me, Alex. I must be out of range."

Alex hoped it was true and accepted her hand. Her emotional response was instant, and her body language was that of a genuinely excited person. The only thing that had not changed was her sparkling blue eyes.

She looked down at her hand in his, but did not let go as she looked into his eyes. "This is so strange, emerging from stasis after so many years. I'm glad I'll be in your care while I'm here."

Alex thought her voice was pleasant without the ship's influence, and the intensity in her sparkling eyes was not as strong. He also found her voice sensual and felt aroused.

Jadin stared at Pandora for a moment, wondering why she was flirting with Alex instead of Okawna. She remembered the ship had also liked him, but she wasn't sure how that was possible for an AI. When Pandora looked at her and smiled, Jadin felt another twinge of jealousy. The alien woman had beautiful light blue eyes.

Alex felt an elbow jab his ribs and turned to look at Jadin. "What?"

"Snap out of it. Your phone is ringing."

Alex felt slightly bewildered as he slid his hand out of Pandora's and reached into his pocket for his phone. He brought it up to answer, but the caller's voice was drowned out by the roar of the engine. When he couldn't understand, he stood and slid past Jadin to get further back in the cargo area. "Say that again, Director?"

"I received a call from Ramey. Preston tried to escape with the device at Essex's compound, but Ramey has them both in custody at his base."

"That's good news. Now we have a reason to keep him locked up unless he cooperates. I need him to move the SV1 into a geosynchronous orbit over the farthest point from Iceland right away. I'll convinced Pandora to move the ship to an area north of Reykjavík, but if we don't move the SV1 to the opposite side of the planet, it would be in the spaceship's line of sight. It's the only way she can control it, and we must not let that happen again."

"I'll have Ramey convince him. Anything else?"

Alex told him about the beautiful woman representing the ship and setting up a meeting. "At least she isn't taking the ship to Paris."

"Have you talked to Director Sliven about this, Alex?"

"No, I was waiting to talk to you first. I'm sure he'll agree to moderate the event."

"I'll inform Shaw, but I think the representatives would ask to hold the meeting at the United Nations building."

"I'm not sure if that's possible. The ship needs to be in line of sight with Pandora, too, so the meeting needs to be held near a remote location where no one can see it."

"Good point. What's the cover story?"

"We can thank Essex. Having him here gives us the perfect alibi. The spaceship is one of his experiments, and he's meeting with some dignitaries about the problem of landing in someone else's backyard."

"That's pretty good. Especially after it's on the internet. All right. I'll call when I have more information."

Jadin had moved over to Alex's spot, and when he sat down, she slid close to him, out of Pandora's sight. "She's got you hooked, Alex. You were just staring at her, oblivious to everything going on around you. You need to stay on top of your game with her, Alex. I think she's dangerous."

"If it's that obvious, I see your point. All right. Trade me spots so I can talk to her. I'll be careful."

When Jadin stood, he slid over behind Okawna and sat down. He saw Pandora was still grinning while staring out through the windows, so he leaned forward and tapped her on the shoulder. When she turned and smiled, he had difficulty not smiling in return. "I hope you're more forthcoming with information than the ship. There will be a lot of questions during the meeting."

"She means well, but she's just trying to protect us."

"Seth appears to dislike us."

"I know, but he's a Green, and he's been connected to the ship all his life. He doesn't trust anyone, including us."

Okawna received clearance from the air traffic controllers in Reykjavík, and flew low over the countryside, searching for some place secluded to hide the ship. Alex stared through the side window at the fractured rock from an old lava flow and had an idea. Okawna followed his instructions to the long-dormant volcano, and a crater large enough to conceal the massive spacecraft.

Alex tapped Pandora on the shoulder again. "Would this work?"

"There is no line of sight to Reykjavík."

"I can't risk your ship being discovered. Do you have cloaking capability?"

"Yes."

"Good. We'll try to find someplace high enough for you to maintain contact."

Pandora spun around in her seat to stare at Alex. "No! I mean, this would work fine. I enjoy being disconnected for a while. I know what she wants, and you could fly me high enough to make contact if it becomes necessary."

"Does that mean you're coming back with us in the plane?"

"I don't know. She doesn't want me away from the ship for too long a period, so I won't know until I'm in range and she downloads the information."

"If the ship is cloaked, we'll need to decide on a place to pick you up in a helicopter. Do you see that flat area of basalt rock about a hundred-yards from the rim of the crater?"

She stared out the side window. "Yes, I see it."

"Good. That's where we'll meet. It should only take you a few minutes to get there, but I need more time to get back and set everything in motion for the meeting."

Pandora wondered how Alex knew how fast her ship could travel, but didn't pursue the issue. "How will I know when to meet you?"

"That's a good point. I could contact you with the communication device. How long does it take you to get ready to come out of the ship?"

"Only a few minutes."

"All right. I'll get a helicopter and call you when I'm within line-of-sight. It would most likely be in the morning. Are you ready to go home?" He noticed the look in her eyes hinted at her reluctance to go back to the spaceship. He also wished she would not leave him.

Pandora finally nodded agreement. "I suppose so. I'm sure the ship will leave immediately upon my return."

"Not so fast. I need to move all the ships out of the area first. All that ice on top of your ship will crash into the ocean when you take off, so if I don't have them leave the area, they'll be swamped by the wave."

"How long would that take?"

"They'll need an hour to be sure they're far enough away."

"All right. Take me back."

He knew in a few more minutes she would revert to the ship, so he leaned forward to be heard. "Do you find it difficult having someone else in your head?"

"That part doesn't bother me. It's not being able to speak my thoughts when she's in control that's difficult to deal with. She doesn't control me all the time. Only when she has a task for me. When she takes control, I suppress my thoughts so she can't access them."

Alex was about to ask another question when Pandora's demeanor suddenly changed and the intensity of the sparkle in her eyes increased dramatically. "Are you still the woman?"

"No, Alex. I disagree with Pandora's decision to land in Iceland. I must be able to maintain contact with her and none of your scenarios would work. She will stay with you, and I will advise her from orbit. Communicate with your armada. They have fifteen minutes to leave."

"That's not enough time."

When Pandora turned back and stared out the front window without responding, Alex moved to the cargo area and called Girdler. "Start clearing the area around the spaceship immediately, and have the ships head out into open water at full speed."

"What's going on?"

"The spaceship is leaving, and you only have fifteen minutes to clear the area. We're almost there and we'll land and pick up Essex, but you should evacuate to your ship right away."

"All right. What about the private boats?"

"Broadcast a warning, but no details."

"Got it."

Alex moved forward and sat down when Okawna told him they were on final approach for landing. Once they taxied to the parking area, everyone remained in the plane with the engine idling, while Alex climbed out and hurried over to Essex and Girdler, standing next to the two remaining Seal Team members. "Thanks for all your help."

Girdler reached out to shake hands with Alex and felt a slight tingling sensation in his fingertips, but ignored it. "It's been interesting knowing you and your team. Good luck."

Essex walked at a brisk pace beside Alex. When they reached the plane, he saw Pandora staring through the front window and stopped to wave. When she ignored him, he jammed his hands into his pockets and stared at the ground as he followed Alex to the open side of the aircraft. He climbed into the back and sat next to Jadin while Alex closed the door.

Jadin noticed a despondent look in Essex's eyes, so placed her hand on his arm as she leaned close to his ear. "Don't worry. Pandora morphs into a butterfly when she's away from the ship."

Alex sat down and fastened his seat belt as the plane moved out to take off. He decided to wait until he had a secure connection with Donner before he told him about this new incident. Moments later, he was soaring over the ice sheet for the last time, and looked out the side window at the churning wakes from the ships headed out of the area. Most of the private vessels were doing the same, except for Hardin and two other boats, who were not even moving. When they passed out of view, he looked at his watch and wondered if Hardin would leave before it was too late.

***

Hardin listened to the repeated evacuation announcement coming from the VHF radio, but since he was in international waters, he wasn't going to leave the area. Something big was about to happen, and he was going to record it using his remaining drone. He contacted his fellow MUFON enthusiasts, and two of the pleasure boats agreed to stay with him, but when all the military vessels headed out to sea at full speed, he wondered if he was pressing his luck. A moment later, he watched a helicopter and Huckabee's airplane fly away.

Several minutes passed, and then his jaw dropped when the ice sheet appeared to explode, sending massive chunks of ice high into the air. He flinched when thunderous shattering sounds raced across the water. The huge blocks appeared to hang in the air for a moment before tumbling down, then massive pieces of thick ice slammed into the ocean, creating a tsunami.

When Hardin saw the twenty-foot wall of water rushing toward him, he knew it was too late to outrun it, so he grabbed the microphone and called the other boaters. "Turn your boats into the wave!" He grabbed the handrail when the wall of water slammed into the bow of his boat, tossing it into the air. The wave passed beneath the hull, and then his boat slammed down onto the other side, knocking him off his feet.

He grabbed the rail and stood, then spun around to check on the other boats, both now overturned. He shoved the throttle forward to turn around to help them, knowing without survival suits, everyone would succumb to hypothermia and drown in a matter of minutes. When he reached the first boat, his researchers dragged three shivering people from the water as he stepped outside the bridge. "Get them inside and out of those wet clothes."

He headed for the other boat, now supporting two people on the overturned craft. One person was sitting up, the other face down. He pulled alongside and his crew helped a young woman onto the boat, but the other body didn't move and he looked down at the woman, who was visibly shivering. "Is he dead?"

"No. Just unconscious. I had to drag him out of the water."

"Get inside and change clothes. We'll get him."

One researcher jumped off onto the other hull, then bent down and picked the man up in his arms. He struggled to get him up onto the ship, until two more researchers dragged the man from his arms, and then he climbed back on board.

Hardin headed back to the location of the spaceship, carefully maneuvering around the chunks of ice bobbing on the surface. When he was within twenty-feet of the ice sheet, he shut down the engines and everything seemed deathly quiet. He stepped outside and looked down at his people. "Get the drone out and fly it over the area. I want to see what happened."

A few minutes later, high-pitched whining broke the silence as the copter leapt into the air, so he went back inside and stared at the overhead monitor. The small craft was flying over the ice sheet and stopped to hover over an eight hundred foot diameter hole in the ice and he turned to his first mate. "Damn! They blew it up."

Chapter 29

ICELAND:

Huckabee was sitting in front of his hangar when he saw his plane land and taxi to Alex's jet. He recognized Alex and his two friends jumping out of the aircraft, and then Alex helped an attractive woman climb out of the co-pilot's seat. The foursome entered the jet, and his plane turned in his direction.

***

Okawna waited until his passengers had entered the jet before driving the airplane over to Huck's hangar and then climbed out to greet his friend. "You don't know how much I appreciate this. If there is ever anything I can do for you, call me."

Huck grinned up at Okawna. "So you're done? Okay. Then there is no need to call. Let me see the spaceship."

"You shouldn't believe everything you see on the internet, Huck. It would warp your mind."

"Come on. You've been flying back and forth to the arctic on a secret mission, so I made the connection. It's only a matter of time before it's verified."

"Even if it were true, and I stress the, *if* part, you know I can't talk about it. Ask me a favor I could actually do, all right?"

"Yeah, okay. It will be a big one."

"You've got it."

Okawna turned and jogged back to the jet. When he ran up the steps, he bumped into Skip and Zachery, who were standing just outside the cockpit, gawking at Pandora. Five minutes after they took off from the ice sheet, she had suddenly reverted to the sexy woman he flew over Iceland. Ten minutes later, she was cold as the ice.

Alex walked back up the aisle, and without introducing their new passenger, asked Skip and Zachery to stand by in the cockpit. "She'll only be with us for a few hours. Thanks, guys." He moved a short way down the aisle, grabbed the secure phone to Donner, and told him about the ship leaving the planet. "Pandora will stay with us until the meeting is over."

"Now that it's in orbit, could it keep in contact with her from any location? I'm sure the President would still prefer to hold the meeting at the United Nations building."

"I know, but here's the problem. We cannot let that spaceship anywhere near our spacecraft or it might take control. As long as it stays over Iceland, it will not have a direct line of sight to Nevada. Sorry, Martin, but the meeting has to be here in Reykjavík. There is no other option."

"All right. Everyone is waiting in Norway. Once you get Sliven's approval, they could be there in an hour."

"I'll go talk to him right now."

Alex went over to the table where his friends were listening to Okawna's attempt to carry on a conversation with Pandora. He noticed the intensity of the sparkle in her eyes indicated the spaceship was in control of the woman. That meant the craft must be in geosynchronous orbit to remain in contact. He looked down at Jadin, who was also looking at Pandora, and put his hand on her shoulder. "Could you join me up front for a moment?"

Jadin turned her head to look up at Alex, then stood and walked toward the cockpit before stopping to face him. "What's going on?"

"Did you notice anything different about her eyes just now?"

"No, they look the same to me. Why?"

"When she looks at me, they look like blue diamonds refracting the light. As if they were sparkling."

Jadin looked past Alex down the aisle, and Pandora was staring in her direction, then she crossed her arms and stared up at him. "They always look like regular eyes to me. She's doing something to you, Alex. I don't trust her."

Alex didn't turn around to the group. "I'm leaving to talk to Sliven about this meeting and I'll come back to get you once I have his approval. Donner informed me the representatives are in Norway, so let the others know what's going on."

Jadin grabbed Alex's arm. "I've got your back on this Pandora thing."

He smiled. "I know. I'll see you soon."

Jadin followed him to the stairs and watched him walk across the tarmac to the air terminal before stepping back inside the aircraft. She leaned against the cabinet and looked down the aisle at Pandora, who was staring out the side window, completely oblivious to the men. "What are you up to, Ms. Blue?"

***

5:45 PM. SV1 CONTROL CENTER:

Carter listened to Preston's orders, then ended the call and looked down at Scott. "Bring up a map of the planet. We're going to move the SV1 into a geosynchronous orbit over the farthest location from Iceland."

Teresa was just ending her shift and was about to leave when Carter made the announcement. She thought about Terry Hardin in Iceland and was sure MUFON knew what was going on up there, and also knew she had to stick around and find out what was important enough to move the SV1.

Scott found it. "New Zealand is perfect."

"All right. Let's get it moving." He stared at the live video feed from SV1's cameras while Scott entered the new coordinates. When the thrusters fired, sparkling lights against a black background swept past the pointed end of the SV1. The Aleutian Islands suddenly appeared on the wall monitor, and then Alaska and northern Canada swept past the camera.

Scott felt his heart rate increase when he recognized the second signal, and entered a command to shut down the thruster, but nothing happened. "Someone took over and I can't shut it down!"

Carter stared at the monitor while Scott entered more commands, and his hands clenched into fists when the image continued to change. Greenland appeared to slow down and freeze on the screen, exactly where he didn't want the SV1.

Scott tried several commands, but the second signal appeared to be extremely powerful this time, and he looked up at Carter. "Look at this. At least we know where the second signal is coming from. I guess the rumors about finding a spaceship are true."

Carter sank down into a vacant chair and grabbed the phone. Preston's orders also included calling Alex Cave, not him, when it was done. He liked Alex and didn't enjoy being the bearer of bad news.

***

ICELAND:

Alex climbed out of the taxi at the NordVulC office, entered the building, and walked up to the woman at the front desk. "I'd like to see the Director."

Sliven recognized the voice talking with the receptionist and stood from behind his desk to welcome Alex into his office. "I was wondering when you were going to let me know what's going on in the arctic."

"I'm sorry I couldn't talk to you sooner. When I explain everything, you'll understand why this has to remain top secret."

Sliven closed the door and listened in rapt fascination while Alex told him about the spaceship and its occupants. If anyone else had told him the story, he would have scoffed at the idea, but knowing Alex's reputation for dealing with unusual circumstances added legitimacy to an otherwise unbelievable tale. "So, the information on the internet is true. This is going to change everything."

"You have no idea, Director, and we need your help. I'd like to use your auditorium for a secret meeting between Pandora and a few ambassadors from other countries. And, if possible, I'd like you to be the moderator."

"Yes, of course. This information must be released slowly to prevent mass panic. What is the cover for the meeting?"

"One of Essex's experimental spaceships. Representatives from other countries are here to complain about it crashing in their territories."

"That should work. Where did the ship go?"

"Someplace out of sight. That's all I can say right now."

"Okay. Who are you inviting?"

"I'm not inviting anyone. That's up to my president and our ambassadors."

"I see. I don't suppose you have a date in mind."

"How about in an hour? Pandora has no patience."

"Oh, dear. I had better clear the building of unwanted eyes."

"This would only be for a short time, Director. The moment the meeting is over, I'm sure they'll all want to get back to their leaders and tell them what's about to happen."

Sliven leaned forward and stared evenly at Alex. "And what, dare I ask, is going to happen?"

Alex had purposely left out Seth's threats to wipe out all the people with brown eyes. "It will all be explained during the meeting."

Sliven leaned back. "All right. I'll call my friend at the hotel and have two limousines available to pick up the attendees at the airport. Just call when you're ready."

Alex stood and reached out for Sliven's hand. "Thank you for agreeing to host this meeting."

Sliven felt a slight tingling sensation in his fingertips. "I look forward to it."

Alex left the building and called Donner so he could inform Shaw. He looked around and didn't see any taxies in the area, and was relieved. The idea of spending an hour with Pandora staring at him was unnerving. His phone rang, and he saw the area code as eastern Washington. "This is Alex Cave."

"I hope I'm not interrupting."

He recognized Carter's voice. "I hope you have some good news, Paul."

"I'm afraid not. We've completely lost all control of the SV1. I have no idea what's going on, but it has settled into orbit over Greenland."

"Damn! All right. Let me know if anything changes."

Alex spun around and went back inside, and found Sliven talking to the woman at the reception desk. "Just one more thing, Director. I don't want any unnecessary attention at the airport, so I would like Okawna to bring Pandora, Jadin, and Essex here right now. They can stay in one of the dressing rooms in the auditorium until the meeting."

"Of course, Alex. I'll send one limousine from the hotel."

"Thank you. I'll go find a taxi back to the airport."

"There is usually one on the other side of the campus, if you don't mind a short walk."

"I could use one. I'll see you later."

Alex walked back outside and called Okawna to let him know the new itinerary, then headed down the street leading to the campus. As he passed cheerful people along the way, he envied their ignorant bliss of not knowing how close they are to annihilation.

Chapter 30

ICELAND:

Hardin eased the *Vulcan* against the reserved pier, and the crew tied off and lowered the gangway. Thanks to Sliven, an ambulance and a small bus were waiting to take the man with the concussion and the other survivors to the hospital. Once the ship was attached to shore power, Hardin left and made his way down the pier to the parking lot, where he climbed into a sports car and drove away from the marina. Several minutes later, he parked in front of Huckabee's hangar and found him inside, sitting in a wheelchair in his office. His back was to the open doorway, so he reached into his inside pocket and quietly walked up behind him.

"Hello, Huck."

Huck rolled back from the desk and spun around to look at his visitor. "Could you at least sit down? I like to look people in the eyes."

Hardin dropped into a wooden chair. "Are you happy now?" He tossed a thick envelope onto Huckabee's lap. "As promised. Give me the recording."

Huckabee opened the envelope and flipped through the paper currency, then opened a drawer to retrieve a flash drive and tossed it into Hardin's open hand. "You're lucky you called when you did. Okawna was in a hurry and didn't bother looking underneath my plane for a camera, and that was their last ride. I edited most of the recording of them flying back and forth over the water, but there is a clear image of a big mirror under the ice as they took off. I was surprised they made two trips in one day."

"Why is that?"

"They didn't land here the first time. They just circled the city and some outlying parts of Iceland. Maybe you could find out why, because when they returned my plane, they had a gorgeous woman with them and went straight to his jet."

Hardin stood. "Sure. Nice doing business with you."

Huck rolled after Hardin as he walked away. "So, is it a spaceship?"

Hardin stopped before walking outside, and then looked down at Huck. "It was, until they blew it up."

"You're kidding. Why would they do something like that?"

Hardin stepped back inside and closed the door. "How well do you know Cave?"

"I never meet him until Okawna showed up. Why?"

"Who is with him?"

"I didn't get the name of the new woman, but he is traveling with a young lady named Jadin Avery and a little guy named John Essex."

"Essex? From the private space research center in Nevada?"

"Now that I think about it, I believe so. Do you think it was one of his experiments?"

Hardin stared over Huck's head at the airplane, not sure what to think about this new development. He had no idea Essex was involved. He was the leading expert on spacecraft, whether they were from here or somewhere else. "Nice doing business with you, Huck."

When Hardin opened the door and rushed out, Huck opened a safe and tossed the envelope inside. "Thanks, Okawna, but you still owe me one."

***

Hardin drove back to the Vulcan and sent the first mate home, then did a quick walk through to make sure there were no stragglers. He went to his private room and turned on his computer, and while it was booting up, he entered a number into his phone and left a message. A moment later it rang, so he answered. "Did you know John Essex is involved?"

Mindy Sloan's fingers tightened around her phone. "No, but it makes sense. Did you know he was with my sister when Cave killed her?"

"I didn't. Do you blame Essex for what happened to Janice?"

"No, she dragged him into her mess. I have my own part of the business to take care of and an opportunity just presented itself. Listen, I managed to get copies of those satellite images you asked for. Are you at your computer?"

He sat down and logged in. "Yes, send them."

"The first picture is before they blew it up, and the second one is after."

Hardin studied the images, zooming in until they were too pixilated, and then backing out. "They don't show me anything new. Why did you bother?"

"Because of these next images, taken while the satellite was moving out of range."

Hardin stared at what appeared to be a massive block of transparent ice in the Beaufort Sea, far from the Arctic Ice Sheet. He scrolled down to the next image, and the ice was nearly gone, exposing a long dark mass inside. In the final picture, it had vanished.

"Was that the SV1? What happened? Did it crash?"

"The SV1 is still in orbit. That has to be its twin, and I'm going after it."

"What's that got to do with me?"

"I want you to keep an eye on Cave and his friends. Let me know what they're up to."

"That's going to be difficult. Cave blew up the spaceship and returned with a strange woman, and then they immediately entered his jet."

"That seems a little drastic. I wonder why."

"I have no idea. You're the one with all the contacts."

When the connection went dead, Hardin tossed the phone on the desk and leaned back in his chair, wondering if Mindy was as ruthless as her sister was. He leaned forward and clicked back to the second picture, showing the massive hole in the pristine ice sheet. He zoomed in again, hoping to see a reflection off a piece of a mirror under the water, but there was none. Only an eight hundred foot diameter crater in the ice. He glanced at the clock and it showed 3:47 PM. He knew Sliven should still be working and grabbed his jacket, and then headed off the ship.

***

NORDVULC:

When Hardin drove into the parking lot, he was surprised to see Sliven standing on the front steps with the receptionist, who was wearing a coat and carrying her purse. She normally worked from 10:00 AM to 7:00 PM, like the director, and now his curiosity piqued. He climbed out and rushed to catch up with Sliven just before he entered the building. "Hey, Director."

Sliven recognized the voice and turned around. "Mister Hardin. I'm glad you stopped by. I wanted to thank you in person for rescuing those people."

"Yes, Director. That's why I came to talk to you. I suppose you know the spaceship is gone. Cave and his friends took it somewhere. That's what nearly killed us."

Sliven crossed his arms. "It belonged to Mister Essex, so I supposed it could be called a spaceship. I heard you were given plenty of warning to leave the area."

Hardin wondered if perhaps it really was one of Essex's experiments, but it didn't explain the sudden rise of magma. "What's going on here?"

Sliven lowered his arms. "Some dignitaries are using the auditorium for a meeting with Essex about his experiments. They are not too happy about them crashing in other territories."

"I've been a big fan of Essex for a long time. Let me attend the meeting so I can shake his hand."

"No, Mister Hardin. It is a private meeting. Perhaps you could meet him some other time."

When Sliven turned and hurried into the building, Hardin leapt down the stairs and ran over to his car. He jumped in and headed over to his research station just off campus, then ran inside and grabbed a go-cam and a laptop computer off the shelf. With equipment in hand, he hurried back to his car, and then drove to the back entrance of the auditorium.

As he climbed out, he looked around to make sure he was alone, and then hurried up to the stage door. He looked around again before reaching into his pocket for a set of lock picks and opened the deadbolt, then slowly opened the door a crack and peered inside. He didn't see anyone back stage and all three dressing room doors were open, so he moved cautiously inside and stared through the curtain at the small seating area. Now all he had to do was sneak up to the camera room without being caught. If the meeting was so private, perhaps Sliven had cleared the building.

He ran to the stairs up to the projection room with no problem and set up the small camera with a view of the seating and the front of the stage. The return trip to his car was even quicker, and he climbed inside and drove to a secluded parking spot near the corner of the building, where he could see the front entrance. He plugged the receiver into the laptop and turned it on, and an image of a podium on the stage appeared near the top of the screen, with the first four rows of seats in the middle of the room clearly visible. He grinned, shut everything down, and then leaned back in his seat to wait for the meeting.

Several minutes later, he sat up when a black limousine stopped in front of the entrance and the rear door opened. He grabbed the small binoculars off the seat and watched as Okawna appeared first, followed by a small woman with red hair he assumed was Jadin. He leaned closer to the windshield when Essex climbed out, and now he knew that part of the story was true. He noticed Okawna carefully studying the surroundings and slid down behind the dashboard. When he heard the car door slam shut, he peered over the steering wheel and saw the backside of a tall woman with long blond hair walking into the building with the others.

***

THE AIRPORT:

Alex waited until the small private jet stopped, then walked over as the side door opened. A Secret Service agent appeared in the doorway, surveying the area, and when he looked down, Alex waved the two limousines over.

The agent hurried down the steps and held out his hand. "I've heard a lot about you, Mister Cave. I'm Special Agent Lewis Mecklenburg, but everyone calls me Mack. It's nice to meet you." When they shook hands, Mack felt a tingling sensation in his fingertips. The first vehicle stopped a few feet away, so Mack opened the door and looked inside. He did the same with the second one, then walked back to the bottom of the steps and looked up at the doorway. "We're clear."

Shaw walked down the stairs and stepped out of the way so she could talk to Alex. "What's so important you couldn't tell me on the phone?"

"The spaceship now has full control of the SV1, and they are both in geosynchronous orbit directly above us. Everyone was scrambling to get our satellites out of the way when it began changing course." Alex looked up at the doorway, but did not recognize any of the people exiting the plane. "What countries are being represented?"

"Most of them. A few more will be informed once we know what we're up against."

"We already know, Ma'am. I think this meeting is just a formality to let us know what she wants."

Shaw heaved a deep sigh of resignation and looked around the area. "In other words, we're screwed."

"I'm hoping Pandora could persuade the AI to make a few compromises."

"I hope you're right."

When Shaw turned and climbed into the second limousine, Alex noticed Mack waiting for him to get in, so he followed her inside. Once Mack climbed in, they followed the first limo for the short ride to the auditorium.

***

Hardin was digging through the storage compartment in the dashboard for a power bar when he noticed two stretch limousines stopping in front of the auditorium. He straightened up and grabbed the binoculars just as the rear door of the first limousine opened, but he didn't recognize any of the people climbing out. When the door on the second vehicle opened, he watched Cave climb out and turn to help a woman through the opening. When she stood, he recognized the President's Chief of Staff. "Why would Shaw be here?"

***

Alex led the group into the auditorium and invited them to sit down, then indicated for Sliven to start the meeting as he walked around the stage. He found Okawna and Essex in the first dressing room and stepped inside. "Everyone is ready."

Okawna stood. "Who did Shaw bring with her?"

"I have no idea. None of them looks familiar, and I believe they are the back channel representatives of all the major countries. I'll get the ladies."

Essex and Okawna followed Alex to the next room and waited outside while he entered. Alex interrupted Jadin, demonstrating cosmetics to Pandora, who appeared to be ignoring her. "They're ready."

Alex looked into Pandora's intense sparkling blue eyes and knew the ship was still in control and then looked down at Jadin for confirmation. Jadin knew what Alex wanted to know and shook her head no without speaking, which meant Pandora's eyes looked perfectly normal to her.

Alex turned back to Pandora. "You and I will wait here until our friends are seated and we're announced."

Pandora waited until the others walked away. "Don't you like the woman, Alex?"

"At the moment, I'm finding it difficult." He watched the sparkle in her eyes increase in intensity. When she shoved him aside and walked toward the curtain, he grabbed her arm and pulled her back. "What's wrong with you? Let me talk to the woman."

She stared at him. "No more. I've taken over permanently. I thought you would want a relationship with her, but since it is apparent that you do not, there is no need for you to speak with her."

Alex let go. "I'm not looking for a relationship. I have a job to do, and you are about to threaten my entire race." He heard Sliven running out of things to say to a quiet audience. "Let's get this over with."

When Alex pulled back the curtain and followed a gorgeous woman out onto the stage, Sliven felt relieved. "For those of you who may not know him, this is geophysicist Alex Cave."

Alex stepped up to the microphone. "You all know why you are here. This is Pandora."

He stepped back and indicated for her to take his place, and when she turned to face the audience, their stunned expressions indicated something was wrong. He looked down at Jadin in the first row, who nodded vigorously. He walked down the steps to see for himself, and the intensity of the sparkle was nearly blinding to him. Apparently, everyone could see what he saw, and then he noticed Sliven's baffled expression as he looked around at everyone, and knew he couldn't see them sparkle because he had brown eyes. He noticed Pandora turn to look directly at him, so he sat down next to Jadin, a short distance from the representatives.

Pandora looked into each person's eyes, noting their color. Four of them were Greens, and the rest were Blues, except for one Brown. "I am here to inform you we will not share our planet with you. Not unless you do as instructed. You have violated genetic law by allowing Browns to over populate our world, and they must be eliminated."

Alex stared over at the angry expressions of the representatives and tried to hear the muffled conversations, but all he could distinguish were a few obscene words. He knew most official representatives would not curse so obviously, which confirmed his suspicions.

Shaw stood up. "Absolutely not. You can't possibly expect us to kill our own people."

"All of you must agree. If you do not, I will eliminate your entire species."

Shaw was not about to follow her instructions and tried to think of a way out of the situation, but it was difficult with those radiant eyes staring at her. "We don't know your genetic laws. At least do us the courtesy of explaining who you are."

Pandora was about to walk away when she saw the curiosity in Alex's eyes, so she turned and looked down at him. "We travel through the galaxy colonizing suitable worlds to harvest their natural resources."

Shaw raised her hand. "Why our planet?"

Pandora glanced at her, but spoke to Alex. "This planet has a perfect orbit around a perfect sun, and has a permanent moon of sufficient mass to stabilize the rotation. All these elements are necessary for complex life to evolve. We know of only thirty-seven thousand planets in this galaxy that meet these conditions, and I found this world 180-million years ago. According to galactic law, it is mine."

Shaw placed her hands on her hips while staring at the woman. "We know nothing about your galactic laws, which I'm sure you are aware of now. How can you hold us responsible for breaking them?"

Pandora ignored the woman and looked around the audience for a second, then turned back to Alex. "One of my mineral extraction processes caused a massive shift in the tectonic plates, and the surface became uninhabitable. The other ships managed to escape, but I stayed behind to maintain possession of this planet. At least one ship was supposed to return and wake me when the atmosphere was once again capable of supporting life. When I sensed your technology in orbit, I brought my people to the surface, and was disappointed to find your backwards society."

Alex stared up at her. "There must be some way we could coexist. How many people do you have in your ship?"

"That is none of your concern."

Alex tried to think of a way to reason with her. "There is no way we can do what you ask. Ninety-five percent of our people have brown eyes."

"Yes, and look what they do. That genetic abnormality makes them prone to violent behavior, as demonstrated by their use of war to enforce their own moral philosophies. That is why Cruds are not tolerated in our society; so we have no moral issues to distract us."

Shaw had sat back down, but she stood up to be noticed. "Isn't murder a moral issue?"

Pandora turned to look at the woman. "No, it is not. It is a means to an end. My only concern is the survival of this species, not yours. You have ruined this planet with your clunky machines. You waste priceless resources, and you are destroying the atmosphere. You do not deserve to occupy this world."

Shaw looked around at the other people, who appeared speechless, then turned back to Pandora. "So, just out of curiosity, what will happen after we eliminate all the brown-eyed people?"

"I will scan the remaining colors for genetic traits I could use to enhance this race, and they would be allowed to live here with us. From what I've seen of your species so far, only a few will have a gene I could use. The rest will be recycled into the planet, like the Cruds."

Shaw crossed her arms and stared into the radiant eyes. "We will not murder innocent people. Mack, arrest her."

Alex watched Mack stand and run up the stairs onto the stage, and leapt out of his chair to run up after him. "No, wait! Don't do anything to her!"

Pandora held her palm out to stop the stranger, but he grabbed it and twisted it behind her back. She struggled to get free, but it became too painful, so she stopped and glared at Shaw. "You are making a big mistake!"

Alex spun around and looked down at Shaw. "You have no idea the damage she can do when she's pissed off. You have to let her go."

Shaw uncrossed her arms. "I'm sorry, Alex. This is a group decision."

Alex waved his arms in the air in frustration. "Who the hell are these people, anyway?" When no one answered, he reined in his emotions. "They sure as hell are not diplomats. If you do this, you will be responsible for killing billions of people."

Shaw stared up at Alex. "She is going to kill all of us no matter what we do, so what's the point of being nice?"

"There are always other options." He could tell he wasn't getting through to her from up on the stage, and ran down the steps to stand in front of her. "Listen, Ms. Shaw. You have to trust me on this issue."

"The decision has been made at the highest level, Alex."

Alex gave her a pleading expression, but she stared back evenly, so he let his shoulders slump in despair. When he turned to look up at Pandora, her eyes were blazing with fury.

Pandora stared down at Shaw. "You leave me no choice. I will demonstrate my power on an international level. Alex should receive a call at any moment now. He will tell you what I have done."

Shaw turned to Alex. "What is she talking about?"

His phone rang. "I don't know, but I think we are about to find out." The ID was from the SV1 control station. "I'm here, Paul."

"The SV1 just melted a GPS satellite!"

Alex looked at Shaw. "She just destroyed a satellite." He looked up at Pandora's radiant eyes, then back to Shaw. "I don't think she's finished."

Pandora stared down at the Shaw. "Let me go, or the International Space Station will be next."

***

Hardin stared at the screen, finding it difficult to grasp the magnitude of what was going on inside the auditorium. When the woman was escorted off the stage, he lost sight of her, but the rest of the people in the room stood huddled together, talking. The conversations were too muffled to understand, so he shut down the equipment and stared through the front window. "Oh, crap! I have to tell MUFON about this."

Chapter 31

NORDVULC:

Alex followed Shaw out to the vehicles and stepped in front of her before Mack and Pandora entered the limousine. "This is a big mistake."

"It's out of my hands, Alex."

"Would you at least tell me where you are taking her?"

"That's classified. I'm sorry, but she is our only leverage against the ship."

Alex moved over in front of Pandora. "Please reconsider your decision to kill us. That is the only way I can keep you out of jail."

He noticed the intensity of her eyes decrease and hoped she was considering his offer, and then she suddenly appeared to be in agony, rubbing her temples. "Are you all right?"

Pandora fought hard to regain control of her own mind from the ship, and for the moment, won the battle. She smiled at Alex and threw her arms around his neck, pulling him close, then put her lips close to his ear. "It's me, but I don't have much time. The ship is angry you won't let me go. Don't trust any promises. It will follow my movements and remain in control, so I may not get another chance to do this."

When she leaned back and stared into his eyes, Alex realized her intention. He expected brief lip contact, but she suddenly pulled him against her body and placed her lips against his while slipping her tongue between them. His mouth was suddenly full of her saliva just before she bit the inside of his lower lip. He jerked his head away and stepped back, then spit the bloody liquid onto the concrete. "What the hell was that for?" He watched the sparkle in her eyes flair and knew the ship was in control again. "Did you do that?"

"The woman needs you, Alex. I need you. Until you and Pandora are united, I will continue to destroy your race." She turned to Shaw. "Release me now or face the consequences."

Shaw looked over at Alex, who appeared embarrassed, then back to Pandora. "I don't believe you. Mack? Put her in the car."

***

Hardin watched Cave kiss the woman and jump back. "What the hell? Why would he kiss someone who wants to destroy us?" He saw the two limousines drive away with everyone except Cave and his three friends, who were left standing on the steps with Sliven. When they all walked back inside the building, he started the engine and headed back to his off-site facility.

When he arrived, he carried the equipment inside, plugged the laptop into his computer, and then saved the data on the hard drive. He logged into the internet and attached the file to an email with a brief note. 'We are in big trouble. Call me after you watch the recording.'

***

Alex called Donner. "How could you allow Shaw to arrest Pandora?"

"What? I didn't authorize it, Alex. Shaw must have done it on her own."

"Well, you had better call the President and find out where they took her, because Pandora is pissed, and we both know what she is capable of doing to us."

"I'm sure the President doesn't know anything about this, or he would have told me. I'll find out what I can and call you back."

Alex knew Donner would never lie to him, so he heaved a deep sigh of resignation. "All right. We'll head back to the base."

"I know you have a lot on your mind right now, but I'm worried about the arctic device and the one in Fallon. If Pandora can control the one in space, she could probably control all of them. I want the recovery of the devices to be a top priority."

"Okawna and I will get started right away. We'll drop Essex off at Fallon before we go to Groom Lake." He put his phone away and looked at Sliven. "Could you arrange a ride for us back to the airport?"

Sliven grabbed the phone on his desk, but paused to look at Alex, Okawna, Jadin, and Essex. "We could take my car. I'm finished here, anyway."

They followed Sliven to the side parking lot and Alex climbed into the passenger seat while his friends climbed in back. No one spoke on the short drive to the airport, and Sliven showed his VIP pass to get them to the jet, then Alex reached across to shake Sliven's hand. "Thanks for all the help. I'll keep you posted on any changes."

"In case you didn't notice, I have brown eyes. I'm scared, my friend."

"So am I, Director. I'll find out where they took Pandora and stop all this from happening."

Alex and his three friends climbed out just as the turbine engines started to whine. He followed them up the steps, then pressed the button to bring up the stairs and latched the door in place before looking into the cockpit. "Take us to NAS Fallon again, Skip. We'll drop Essex off on our way home."

Alex walked down the aisle and sat next to Jadin when she waved him over. He fastened his seatbelt as the plane taxied and felt her hand on his arm and looked at her. "What's on your mind?"

"I saw you spit blood after Pandora kissed you. What happened?"

Alex reached up and showed her the inside of his lower lip. "She bit me."

Jadin undid her seatbelt, jumped out of her chair, and ran over to the mini-bar. She found a bottle of vodka and an empty glass and then hurried back to Alex. "You might have some type of alien bacteria in your wound. Swish this around in your mouth."

Alex took the glass and bottle and did as instructed; wincing when the alcohol hit the cut, but spitting the liquid into the glass jogged his memory. He handed them back to her. "She seemed to have a lot of saliva when she kissed me."

Jadin hurried back to the bar and put the bottle and glass away, then sat down and secured her seatbelt just before the jet raced down the runway. "She did something to you, Alex. I know it." She stared out the side window for a moment, and then snapped her head around to face Alex. "I've got it! When she said she needed you, I bet that meant she needed your DNA. That's why she bit you. To get a sample."

"It would be too contaminated to be viable. No, I don't think so. The ship is angry, and it took it out on me, is all. You should have seen the way her attitude changed when I said I didn't want a relationship with the woman."

"You may think your DNA is no good to her, but we have no idea how her physiology works."

"She won't be able to do anything with it while she's in confinement. Even if they release her, my sample would be too degraded to be of any use to her."

"You hope." She suddenly remembered Pandora's eyes during the meeting. "I saw the way her eyes sparkled when she was stating her demands. Is that what you see all the time?"

"Yes, but they are much brighter when the ship is pissed off about something. I think that's why the rest of you could see them that way."

"It was a little scary. I thought she might melt my brain."

"I don't think she has any superhuman abilities. She didn't stop Mack from taking her into custody. The ship has all the superpower, and even that is limited. Without the SV1, she can't harm us."

Essex swung his chair around to face Alex. "I heard what you said about the SV1. You're right. We have to destroy it. You could have your friend Donner order a missile strike and blow it up."

"That won't work. The alien device is indestructible. Trust me. I know what I'm talking about."

Essex gave Alex a sly grin. "Not the thrusters and our control system. If she can't move it where she wants, she can't target anything."

"How long will the thrusters last before they run out of propellant?"

"That depends on how often they are used. Our plan was to use them sparingly, only making small maneuvers. We estimated there was enough nitrogen to last a year, and then I would go up and recharge the system."

Alex's phone rang, and he recognized Carter's number. "I'm here, Paul. All right. Thanks for letting me know." He put the phone away and looked at his friends. "Pandora just used the SV1 to melt the International Space Station. There are no survivors."

Jadin put her hand over her mouth. "Oh, my, gosh. I knew the Commander."

Essex slammed his fist against the armrest. "You need to tell Donner to shoot out the thruster control system."

Alex thought about it. "It would never work. She could melt anything we try to send up."

Essex grinned. "Not my spaceship. I'll go up and remove the control system myself."

Chapter 32

DAR CORPORATE OFFICE, WASHINGTON D.C.:

Rita was watching the television special report about the arctic jet stream spreading across Europe, creating blizzard conditions as far south as Spain and Turkey. She heard her phone ring did not recognize the phone number in the text message, but the code word 'AD' let her know something was going on with the arctic device and to make the call. She entered the number, and it was answered immediately. "What's going on, AD?"

"I've just learned a third party is going after that Arctic thing. Her name is Mindy Sloan."

Rita had not told Essex she had worked with Janice occasionally. "Any idea when they're going to search?"

"They'll have a sub in the water by tomorrow afternoon."

"All right. Thanks for calling."

Rita walked out onto the covered deck and stared through the deluge at the garden in the backyard. The rain was falling so heavily the flowers were lying in large puddles of water on the ground. She was torn by indecision over what to do about the arctic device. She knew Alex was right about their destructive capability after witnessing so many incidents and realized they could not be controlled the way she had intended, and now the SV1 was changing the weather patterns on a global scale. She could not let Sloan get her hands on it, but the problem was, the only way she knew of to contact Cave was through Essex and according to Preston's call from jail, he was with Cave on a secret mission. She remembered watching a video about a spaceship someone found in the arctic and that would be the type of situation Cave would be involved in, and Essex is the expert.

A lump welled up in her throat when she thought of another scenario. It could be Essex's spaceship. What if he and Cave took it up on a mission and it crashed with them inside? She walked back into the house to get away from the roar of the rain beating on the roof and entered Essex's number. When he didn't answer, she left a message that it was urgent she get in touch with Alex about the arctic device.

She stared through the window at the torrential downpour, and according to the weather report, there was no end in sight. A thought suddenly occurred to her. Why did the idea of Essex's death bother her so much? He wasn't the type of man she was looking for. She just hoped he was alive and would get the message before it was too late.

***

NAS FALLON:

In the parking lot outside the gate, rain battered the top of the vehicle as Jim Coburn stared through the sheet of water running down the front window while he waited for Essex. He was glad to get away from the compound, but the annoying beeping from Essex's phone was driving him crazy, and he didn't know the pass code to turn it off. A black sedan came through the gate and pulled up alongside his SUV, and he saw Alex roll down the driver's side window and did the same. "Is everything all right?"

"Follow me."

They drove to a covered bus stop waiting area, and when Essex and Alex climbed out of the sedan, he climbed out to join them. "Hello, Mister Essex. You don't know how glad I am to give this to you." He held out the phone. "The maid found it in your living quarters."

Essex took the phone and moved away, then entered his password and recognized Rita's ID. He glanced back at Alex and then listened to the message.

Jim held his hand out to Alex, who accepted, and felt a strange tingling sensation in his fingertips, but ignored it. "It's good to see you again. Listen, I'm really sorry for letting Preston get away with the device. I heard all his people were killed in that freak storm the other day."

"Preston is a resourceful man. Don't worry about it."

Essex turned to Alex. "Rita just left a message for you to call her. It has to do with the arctic device."

"What's the number?"

"No, I want to talk to her myself. I'll put it on speaker." He entered the number and held it out so Alex could listen. "Hello, Rita."

"Hi, John. I'm glad you called me back. I know you probably don't want to talk to me, and I'm sorry, but this is extremely important."

"I'm here with Alex. He's listening, so tell us about the device."

"Hello, Alex." She waited, but he didn't reply. "All right. Janice Sloan had a partner. Her sister, Mindy, and she knows the location of the arctic device and is going after it."

Alex knew it would be a waste of time asking her how she knows about it. "Do you know when?"

"My source said they will have a submarine in the water by tomorrow afternoon. That's why I called. I know you are right about their power, and I don't want Mindy to get her hands on it."

"Does she realize how dangerous it is?"

"I'm sure she saw the photos of it freezing and floating on the surface, so yes. She knows part of its potential, and given the similarities to the SV1, I'm sure she has a buyer lined up."

"All right. I appreciate the call."

Essex was surprised she was being so forthright with the information and thought maybe she wasn't such a terrible person after all. "Listen, Rita. I need a co-pilot for my spaceship."

"So the one discovered in the arctic wasn't yours."

"It was one of my prototypes that crashed. So what's your answer? It could be dangerous."

"It always is. When are you leaving?"

"As soon as you get here."

"I'll catch a flight to Reno, if you could pick me up."

"I can do even better. Preston's jet is still at my compound. I'll send it to pick you up."

"Just let me know the schedule. And John, I look forward to seeing you again."

Essex put his phone away without replying. "It looks like I get to go into space again."

Alex held out his hand. "Good luck. It looks like Okawna and I have a new obstacle to deal with."

Essex remained standing as Alex climbed into the sedan and drove away back through the gate, then turned to Jim. "I just hope I can make this work. Let's go."

Alex called Donner to let him know about the attempt to disable the SV1 and the message from Rita. "Is the Navy searching the last known location?"

"Of course, but they can't seem to find it. What about that new ultrasound system Mike Tanner uses for his explorations? From what you told me during the Cold Energy operation, that's how they managed to locate the one off the coast of Washington."

"That's correct. I'll contact him about it and get back to you."

"Make it a priority. Good luck."

***

Alex left the car in the parking lot and ran through the rain into the air terminal, and saw Commander Ramey, Okawna, and Jadin standing near the exit to the jet and went over to join them and stood in front of Jadin. "There's been a change of plans. Okawna and I have to get to the Mystic right away, so we'll need to find you another ride home."

"I know you're going after the arctic device, but why the sudden urgency?"

"Janice Sloan's sister Mindy is going after the arctic device tomorrow."

"I thought General Taylor was taking care of it with the U.S. Navy."

"They can't find it. The Mystic has the only viable way to locate it."

"All right. Anything else I can do to help?"

"Not really. Just keep trying to locate Pandora." He noticed her conspiratorial grin. "You already know something?"

"Christa and David said they're picking up the tracking signal from the new software in her spaceship." Her grin slipped away. "Nothing on Pandora herself. Essex is right. It sounds a little awkward differentiating the ship from the woman."

"I know what you mean." He ran his tongue across the cut inside his lip, which was developing into a permanent ridge. Of all the times his lips had been battered to a pulp, none of them had left a scar on the inside of his mouth. "If you find her, call me first."

"I will. What do you suppose she meant by you and Pandora being united? Is she talking sexually? Because that would be interesting, having sex with an alien."

He grabbed her elbow and guided her away from the men. "No. No way. It's not going to happen."

"At least you won't have to worry about commitment issues. That is your new vow of celibacy, isn't it? You might have to break your vow, because the fate of our race might depend on you getting it on with Pandora." It was the first time she had seen him blush. "It may not be that bad. She is beautiful, after all."

Alex looked away. He found Pandora alluring, unless the ship was in charge. He turned and walked back over to Ramey. "If you could get Jadin to Las Vegas, she could get a ride home from there."

"I'll make it happen. What about your secret box?"

"Could you keep it here for a while longer? We can't take the chance of moving it until we solve another issue."

"No problem. It's in a concrete vault, like you asked and I have two Marines guarding it at all times."

Alex reached out to shake the Commander's hand. "Thanks for all the help."

Ramey felt a slight tingling in his fingertips, but ignored it. "Not a problem."

Okawna ran with Alex out to the jet and up the stairs into the cabin, and waited while Alex brought the stairs up. "Sloan has a sister in the same business? It's like déjà vu all over again. I wonder if she's as ruthless as Janice."

"I hope we don't have to find out."

***

NEVADA:

Rita saw Essex waiting at the bottom of the stairs when she stepped out of Preston's jet and smiled as she walked down to greet him. "I'm glad you decided to give me another chance and invite me to come along with you, John. I wanted to tell you in person how sorry I am for not telling you everything about the devices."

"We all have our secrets, Rita. That's in the past now. The first thing we need to do is decide on the best way for us to disable the thruster control system on the SV1. The crew will take care of your luggage, so let's go play with my spaceship."

Now Rita remembered why she was attracted to him. He was driven by his love for outer space and willing to take risks to get there. Unlike her other relationships, he was also a good man. She bent down and gave him a soft kiss on the lips. "You're the boss. Let's get started."

Essex drove them to the rail hangar, where they climbed out and went into the building. He led her up next to the spacecraft, then reached inside the cockpit and pressed the button to raise the doors on the nose, and then they walked around the ship and he looked inside. "Is there an access panel on the SV1 within reach of the mechanical arms?"

Rita looked into the compartment. "Yes, but you could never open it with those pinchers. The best way to shut down the thruster control system is to plant an explosive charge and get the hell out of the way."

Essex paced across the platform, staring up at the ceiling. He had an idea and walked back to the nose, then bent over the front edge to look inside at the frame. He saw what he expected and looked at Rita. "Are there any places the arms could grab to hold us in place?"

"There are four nylon bands around the device, with thick rings for moving it around on earth. The pincers would have a solid grip on any of them. The two middle bands also hold the control system in place."

Essex stared at the manipulator arms for a moment and then looked up at Rita. "I promised Alex that I would get the device back to Earth so it could be locked away with the others. I keep my promises, but you're not going to like what I have in mind. Help me replace one of the arms with a tow strap."

"You're right. That's a crazy idea. First, you and I both know if the device activates while we're nearby, we'll lose control. Second, we have limited fuel for our rockets. If we use it for dragging the SV1, we won't have any for re-entry. We'll burn up with it."

"I said it would be dangerous. Besides, the device won't burn up in the atmosphere. Alex told me that one of them survived being buried in magma."

"And what about us?"

"All we have to do is slow it down, so it falls out of orbit, and we need to do that for our own re-entry, anyway. Did I mention it was in geosynchronous orbit above Iceland? That means we'll need to reach orbital velocity just to catch up with it. Nearly one quarter of our fuel will be used just to reach it."

"Well, this plan just keeps getting more exciting. I wouldn't take odds on our success."

Essex grinned. "Neither would I."

He walked over to the cockpit, climbed inside, and pressed the release pins on the control panel. When it popped free, he turned it over and studied the circuit board. "I need to figure out a bypass for the rocket motors. I'm hoping I can eliminate the electronics and have a direct connection to the firing switches. Good thing I designed them to be as simple to operate as possible."

"Did you work for NASA?'

"Oh, no. When they heard about my new rockets, they wanted me to sell them the plans and the patent rights. They said it was to make sure no other country could build them. I told them they didn't have to worry. No one will see my design. Not them, and not even you." He studied her eyes for a reaction and they suddenly looked miserable.

"You have every right not to trust me, John. I don't blame you. I may never get that back, but I'm willing to try. I'm here to help, so let's continue."

"Fair enough. We need to install a hook to the inside frame and be able to release it manually from the cockpit. My workshop is on the other side of the hangar. Let's go see what's available to work with."

Chapter 33

TOP-SECRET FACILITY. LOCATION, UNKNOWN:

At first, Pandora was grateful to have the ship out of her head, but without being in contact with the AI, she had no idea what it was doing to the planet. She hoped Alex would find her before it was too late to stop what the ship had started, and it had nothing to do with the nasty weather. She heard a steel door slam shut just before Shaw walked into the room and stood outside the bars of her cell. "You don't realize what you've done. You must let me go before it is too late."

Shaw stared back evenly. "You seem to be back to normal. What happened to your eyes?"

"Never mind that right now. The infection has already begun. Pandora is demonstrating her power by getting rid of all the Cruds, but if you let me go, I might be able to stop her."

"I thought you were Pandora."

"It's confusing, I know. How do you think I feel when she takes over my mind?"

"Are you saying she is not in control right now?"

"Yes. For some reason, I cannot connect with the ship."

Shaw looked up at the ceiling and walls. Although nothing was visible, she knew the room was shielded from the outside world by an electromagnetic field and smiled at Pandora. "The sample of blood we took from you is being analyzed. Once we isolate the gene that makes you impervious to disease, we'll let you go."

Pandora crossed her arms and stared back coldly. "It won't work on your species. All you have done is hastened the demise of all your people. For the moment, the disease is only infecting people with brown eyes, but if you don't release me so I can stop this, not even Alex will survive."

Shaw snapped her head around to stare at Pandora. "What has this got to do with Alex?"

Pandora kept her eyes locked on the woman. "Everything. Let me go and I'll explain why he is so important to us."

"Tell me now and I'll consider it."

"No."

"You did something to him, didn't you? Is that why you bit him?"

"You're not going to release me, are you?"

When Shaw didn't answer, she turned to face the wall. "I have nothing more to say to you."

Shaw stared at Pandora's back for a few seconds, then turned and walked out of the room. She knew she couldn't get phone reception inside the building and waited until she was outside to make her call. "This is Chief of Staff Shaw. Put me through to Director Donner."

"Hello, Miss Shaw? Where is Pandora?"

"That's none of your concern, Martin. Where is Alex Cave?"

"He's on a mission. And like you said, that is none of your concern."

"You know I can find him without your help, so why not just tell me?"

"Why do you need him?"

"I'm not sure, but Pandora seems to think he is special, and I need to know why. Have him report to my office immediately."

"Alex doesn't know any more than you do. In fact, he's wondering the same thing. All I can tell you is his mission is time sensitive and he can't leave right now."

"I'm making this an order, Director. I want him in my office in twelve hours. Is that understood?"

Donner's hand tightened around the phone until his knuckles turned white. "Yes, Ma'am."

Shaw grinned and climbed into the rear seat of the government sedan. "Take me to the airport."

***

WASHINGTON D.C.:

Donner slammed the receiver down onto the cradle and stared out the window. "Damn!" He suddenly had an idea and grabbed the phone again, then selected a number. "Hey, Doug. Run a trace on my last incoming call."

"Hang on a second, Director."

Donner stood and walked to the window while he waited. *What is so important about Alex?*

"I have it, Director."

Donner stepped back to his desk and wrote down the information. "All right. Thanks."

He sat down and brought out his smart phone, then entered the address into a text message to Alex. Urgent you call me ASAP. He sent the message, and then called his friend Harold Moses, the Director of the CIA. "I need a favor. Get me everything you have on the President's Chief of Staff."

Chapter 34

THE BUFORD SEA. MYSTIC:

Alex spotted the Navy destroyer holding station around the last known location of the device. "This is Alex Cave, on the research ship Mystic, calling the US destroyer. Come in, please."

"Mister Cave, this is Captain Mosley, of the USS Blakely. I was informed of your mission, and I'm here to help, but we might have a problem. My ship, and that one over there, are in territorial waters, so I can only use force if my ship is attacked."

"Understood. What happened to the other search vessels?"

"We were informed you would take over, so they were ordered to another project. None of them was armed, anyway, but don't worry. I have access to a few fighter jets if I need a show of force."

"All right. I appreciate you sticking around. We'll begin our search right away."

Alex stared through the binoculars at a private ship two miles north of his position. Evidently, they hadn't found the device yet, because the radar showed them crisscrossing the waters. He looked over at Bett, who was comparing the satellite image of the ice-encased device to the nearest landmasses on the computer monitor. "Are we in the right area?"

Bett looked up. "How long ago was this picture taken?"

"Three days ago. As far as we know, that was the last time it froze the water around it and rose to the surface."

"You know, Josh and I just watched the movie Titanic, for the tenth time I might add, and when it sank, it hydroplaned away because of the shape of its bow. What if that's what happens to the device when it sinks because of its pointed nose?"

Alex moved around beside her. "Could you tell which direction it was pointing from the image?"

Bett used the mouse to zoom in on a section of the satellite photo. "Just barely. It was pointed southeast before it went down. I'll bet that's where we'll find it."

Alex looked at the radar, and the dot representing the other ship was moving back and forth across the screen. "I'm sure by now they're watching us too, so let's get started."

***

Nearly six hours had passed when Okawna saw a return image on the ultrasound screen, and it appeared to be a cylindrical object on the seafloor, at three-thousand-feet. He marked its GPS location and looked out through the side window at Alex, who was gazing through binoculars at the other ship, so he stepped outside and stood next to him at the railing. "What's got your attention?"

Alex lowered the binoculars. "They stopped searching. I think they're waiting for us to locate it."

"We just did. That's why I came out. I'm thinking of waiting until dark to launch the sub and come back to get it."

"We can't take the chance they might stumble upon it if we continue the fake search. We'll move a short distance away, and then launch the sub while we're turning around and our bow is facing them. Even if they realize what we're doing, it would delay them getting their own sub into the water and over to this location."

"Works for me. I'll go prep the sub and send Josh up to relieve you and meet you there. It's time to try out your latest contraption."

Alex smiled and went back inside, while Okawna disappeared down the outside stairs. He continued the search pattern until Josh suddenly walked onto the bridge and pointed at the chart. "That's the GPS location, so stay close and keep an eye on our visitors."

"I'll make the turnaround as slow as possible to give you two enough time to dive."

Alex hurried down the stairs, glancing across the deck to the outside wall and the small white submarine. He saw Okawna checking the rope attached to a large plastic cone in the grip of one of the heavy-duty mechanical arms. When he reached the bottom of the stairs, he ran across the deck and hurried up the short ladder to join Okawna on top of the sub near the hatch. There was only room enough for two people in the small vessel, so he climbed in first and slid into the back seat.

Okawna waved down at Bett, who was holding the remote control for the hoist. "Don't leave without us."

"Just get your butts back here in one piece."

Okawna dropped through the hatch and moved to the front seat, then reached up and closed the lid. Alex leaned to one side and stared past Okawna's head to see out the front window, and thought about the first time he had ridden in this tough little sub. He and Okawna were hit by an underwater tsunami and nearly killed, but the sub kept them alive until they reached help on the surface.

Water sloshed up over the windshield as they dropped into the ocean, followed by darkness. For the moment, there was nothing to see as they dropped toward the seafloor.

Okawna looked up at the rearview mirror to see Alex. "Pandora sure is a fox. Find out if she has a sister."

"Foxes bite, you know. What bothers me the most is why?"

"She's definitely into you. She and the ship, and that's just too weird. What's up with that, anyway?"

"Hell if I know. This entire mission has been strange, even for us."

"So, are you going to get it on with Pandora? For the survival of our race and all? You know, take one for the team? I know I would. Hell, I wouldn't even need a reason. I'd do it just to brag I'd made love with an alien."

"Enough already. You sound just like Jadin. I could do it, but only, and I stress that point, if there is no other way out of this situation. On our first kiss, she bit me. What would she do to me while we're doing it?"

Okawna noticed the flashing green dot on the digital map of the seafloor. "GPS indicates it is two-hundred feet to our right, at a depth of twenty-nine-hundred-feet. We're almost to the bottom, so hang on while I level us out and make a hard turn."

The outside lights suddenly illuminated the seafloor as Alex felt the G-force pushing him into his seat, and he wasn't surprised Okawna drove the sub like a race car. The light swept across the dull gray silt of the ocean floor as they came out of the turn and knew they still had to rely on luck to find it. "This might be difficult, since the device is the same color as the bottom, so look for any kind of disturbance."

Okawna leveled the sub out and looked at the screen. "Here we go. We should see it right about now."

Alex looked through the window and saw a deep furrow in the muck. They followed it for fifty-feet and saw the blunt back end of the alien device protruding above the bottom.

Okawna looked up at the mirror. "Will your contraption work on that end?"

"Yes. Ease us into position and slide it over the device."

Okawna flipped a select switch on his control handle and swung the robotic arms down from the top of the sub. One arm carried a thirty inch long, thick plastic cone with a heavy-duty ring. Attached to the ring was a sixty-foot length of rope, with the other end of the thick nylon cord attached to a magnetic release coupling under the stern of the sub.

The cone was larger in diameter than the slender gray cylinder in the muck, with a hollow section in the center to slip over the end of the device. With great skill, Okawna maneuvered the sub and placed the cone over the end, then looked up in the mirror. "Now what?"

Alex grinned and held up a small remote control. "You're going to love this. I got the idea off the Science Channel. Have you seen a snake shed its skin? Well, inside the rest of the cone is a thin hose that does just the opposite. When expanding foam is injected between the layers, it will uncoil and wrap around five-feet of the device, then puff out and make the end buoyant. Once it floats to the surface, we tow it back to the Mystic."

Alex pressed the button and a yellow membrane, the skinner, as he liked to call it, uncoiled as promised. The foam began to expand, creating a tight seal around the device, but then it slowly stopped expanding. He didn't understand what happened, since his calculations indicated it should expand to a depth of fifteen-inches, and then he suddenly realized his mistake. "It's not going to float to the surface. We'll have to tow it."

Okawna engaged the rear propeller and eased the sub forward to take up the slack. "What went wrong?"

"Me. I forgot to take into consideration the water pressure at this depth."

"Won't it continue expanding as we tow it up?"

"No, it's a chemical reaction. When it reaches a certain pressure, the reaction stops. It would be nearly . . ."

A blinding light burst through the window, and Okawna held his hand up to shield his eyes. The sub lurched sideways, and the light vanished from inside, but now he could see another submarine with its pinchers clamped to the other end of the rope, trying to drag the device away. From what he could see, the other sub was much larger, with twin rear propellers.

Okawna knew the rope would never break, so he swung the stern of the sub around to pull in the opposite direction. He gritted his teeth as if it would help and then squeezed the handles as his little vessel swept from side to side against the pull on the rope. "I can't keep this up for much longer, buddy. I'm putting an enormous drain on the batteries just trying to hold this position."

All instruments went dark and the strain on the rope suddenly vanished. The outside lights stayed on, and Alex realized they were connected directly to the batteries without electronic control. He felt a soft thud in his seat when the submarine settled on the ocean floor, then the inside temperature dropped. Ice crystals formed on the outside of the window and turned into transparent ice, enclosing them in a crystal clear coffin, adding to the enormous pressure already against the hull of the little sub.

Chapter 35

SPACE:

Essex stared through the front windshield of his ship as they approached the SV1 and thought he was seeing an illusion. A massive funnel shape was distorting the starry background, and he looked over at Rita. "What do you make of that?"

"The device is on, but that's not the right shape for collecting material from space. That's the one used for changing the path of the jet streams."

"All right. Let's take it out of orbit. How's our fuel?"

"You were right. We're down to seventy-four percent remaining."

Essex didn't reply as he adjusted his approach to bring him alongside the device. He applied a small amount of thrust to match the SV1's speed and then eased his craft to a 90-degree angle to the white nylon ring near the rear end of the device. "It's your turn. I'll keep us steady while you hook us up."

Rita pressed a button, and the doors on the nose opened. She slid the electronic control glove onto her right hand and raised the remaining arm, then brought it down inside the compartment to grab the three foot long plastic extension, which was attached to one end of the thick polyurethane tow rope. She took a deep breath, and then slowly exhaled to calm her nerves. "All right. Here we go."

Essex applied thrust to keep the nose steady from the opposite reaction of the arm's movements. Rita's first attempt to attach the hook missed and forced the ship away from the device, so he eased it back into alignment.

Rita glanced over at him. "Sorry about that."

"It's a learning experience, and you're the first one to attempt this."

"Okay. Let's try this again."

Essex looked over at the determined look on her face, and then turned back to the front window to steady their position. He saw she had the hook close to the ring, and for a moment, he thought it would snap into place, but the force caused the ship to drift away from the SV1.

Rita leaned back in her seat, frustrated. "Damnit!"

Essex stopped their drift and looked over at her. "This time, you get it lined up, and I'll use the thrusters to force it onto the ring. That should give us enough mass to counteract the reaction."

"All right. Take me back in."

Essex lined up with the ring and tapped the rear thrusters, while concentrating on the hook extending three-feet out from the nose of his ship. He was coming in too fast, so he tapped the forward thrusters, but nothing happened. He checked the circuit breaker, and it was on. "I have a malfunction. I can't slow down."

Rita watched the hook veering off course as the ship's angle changed, so she swung the extension rod around to line up with the ring, but each movement affected the ship and she couldn't hold it steady. The arm was swinging toward the left compartment door and the hook was nearly out of sight, but with a final effort, she snapped the hook over the ring.

Essex grimaced when the rope snapped taut and ripped the left door off the front of his ship. The counter motion sent his ship hurtling toward the control panel and knew destroying it would solve their problem for moving the SV1. They were about to hit when the rope snapped them back toward the rear of the device, ripping the other door off the nose. The inertia dissipated with each small jerk until they were drifting a foot above the rear end of the SV1.

Rita looked over at John. "That was exciting."

Essex was about to agree when every system in the ship shut down. "It's about to get more intense."

"You still have rocket control, right?"

"Yes, but we're aimed in the wrong direction. If I fire them now, we'll drag it further into space. Until the SV1 changes direction or shuts down, there is nothing we can do." He looked out at the open cargo hold. "Since we are not going to survive anyway, I'll wait until I'm sure I can drag it into the atmosphere before I fire the motors."

Rita took off the glove and dropped it on the floor, then smiled over at Essex. "Being with you is never boring." She reached over and grabbed his hand. "At least it will be an exciting ride for a while."

"Since I know for a fact we're not going to make it back alive, I can't think of any better way to die than right after a trip into space."

"I won't count us out just yet."

"Why is that, Rita?"

"Because Cave knows we're out here trying to save civilization, and he's your friend. He'll think of a way out of this."

"I'm not going to wait around to be rescued. As soon as I get the right trajectory, I'm firing the rockets. I know we'll never survive, but I promised Alex I'd get it back to Earth, and it's the right thing to do."

She leaned her face toward Essex and looked into his eyes. "You must be having a good influence on me."

"Why is that?"

"I don't usually do the right thing."

Chapter 36

ICELAND:

Sliven swallowed two more painkillers and leaned back in his office chair, hoping to get rid of the pain in the back of his eye sockets. It started on the drive to work the morning after the meeting, when the sun seemed more intense, and his sunglasses didn't stop the irritating pain from the glare. At first, being inside any structure helped, but now, even with the window shades closed, the pain remained.

He heard angry voices from the parking lot, all wanting to get into his office for an interview. When the recording of the meeting with Pandora first appeared on social media that afternoon, he was plagued by people asking if the recording was real, and quickly grew tired of repeating 'no comment' so he stopped taking calls from unknown numbers and visitors. His door opened, and the light was intense before his receptionist stepped inside and closed it. "I see you are one of the chosen. I mean, you having blue eyes. Good grief, listen to me sounding like one of those crazy protestors on TV, making eye color seem like the new racial tension. I'm sorry. What can I do for you?"

She glanced back at the door. "There really isn't anything for me to do right now, and I'm a little nervous about trying to get through all those angry students. Most of those people have brown eyes and they are saying how unjust it is, being discriminated against because of the color of their eyes. They're taking their bitterness out on people like me."

"Of course, leave right away. I think it might be like this for a while, so I'll call you when things settle down."

"Thank you, Director."

Sliven held his arm up to block the light when she opened the door and left the room. From what he had learned, many more people were suffering the same effect as he was, with intense pain in their eyes. He realized Pandora was keeping her promise, and there was nothing anyone could do about it. Except perhaps Alex Cave.

***

NAS FALLON, NEVADA:

Ramey cupped his hands behind his head for support as he stared up at the woman with a stethoscope hanging around her neck. "Are those things considered part of a Navy doctor's uniform?"

Lieutenant Commander Amy Burkhart grinned. "It's in the handbook. There is some kind of irritation on your retina. I've been seeing this a lot lately, and it only seems to affect people with brown irises."

"Have you seen that recording of the supposedly alien female saying bad things about brown-eyed people?"

"Yes, but it has to be some kind of hoax. Those sparkling eyes have to be computer-generated. There's no way eyes can sparkle like that."

"What are you talking about? They were blue and pretty, but they didn't sparkle."

"You know, I've heard that before, too. It seems no one with brown eyes can see it."

"I wonder if this is the plague the woman was talking about. Do you think that's her real name? Pandora?"

Amy stared down at him. "I don't know. If it is, it seems her box has been opened. I'm sorry."

Ramey lay back down and stared at the ceiling, wondering how long it would take before his brown-eyed wife and daughter began feeling the pain in their eyes. His gaze returned to the pretty nurse with dark green eyes, and he felt a twinge of jealousy.

Chapter 37

BUFORD SEA:

Bett was on the bridge, staring through the binoculars, and saw a strange anomaly floating on the surface, so she hollered at Josh. "I see something! It's a clear iceberg, just like in the satellite image. It has to be the device."

Josh turned to look and could barely see the translucent ice. "Any sign of the submarine?"

"Oh, shit! It looks like it's trapped inside. We have to go help them."

Josh grabbed the radio microphone and called the destroyer to let them know what was going on. He kept the ice in sight as he swung the *Mystic* around and headed over to the location.

***

Through the clear ice surrounding the sub, Okawna recognized the distorted outline of the Mystic floating a short distance away, so he pressed the button on his microphone. "Mystic, this is Okawna. Can you hear me?"

They heard her voice through the speaker. "I hear you. Is that you I see down inside the iceberg?"

Okawna looked up at the mirror and grinned at Alex. "That's us, Bett. There should be another submarine trapped in here with us. Do you see them?"

"I see something inside, but it looks like it was crushed."

Okawna kissed the tips of his fingers, and then held them against the hull of the sub. "Thank you."

Alex noticed. "Shouldn't we be crushed too?"

"Mike spared no expense. This is the latest thing in deep submersible craft. Our hull is ceramic."

"I'll send him a bottle of champagne. If the spaceship turns off the SV1, this device is going to sink again with us still attached."

Okawna flipped a switch on the dashboard. "I'm increasing the buoyancy of the sub to compensate."

"Would the Mystic's hoist be powerful enough to lift both us and the device?"

"Not if we're both out of the water at the same time. Once the sub is stored, I'll use the hoist to drag the device onto the deck."

"I have a better idea. We'll leave it in the water and add another cable, then tow it to Adak Island. If it freezes again, nothing would be affected."

"Okay, but I was wondering why it didn't freeze a massive amount of water and keep it frozen, like you said happened in the other timeline."

"I have no idea. Paladin told me even little things I change in this timeline would have a ripple effect. Maybe by saving your father, his tribe did something to change it."

"Wow. That's really out there, Alex. Anyway, if we get it out of the water, it won't freeze into ice and we could move much faster."

"True, but don't forget, it could also change the molecular structure of steel. The water should dampen the effect and the Mystic won't melt."

"All right. It's your device, so whatever you think is best."

Bett's voice came through the speaker. "Whatever you're going to do, hurry, because the ice is melting fast. One more thing. That mystery ship just arrived to watch the proceedings. They're about three-hundred yards from us."

Alex watched the ice quickly disappear from the front window and felt a shift in the angle of the sub as the device dropped beneath the stern. Light still streamed through the nose, and it appeared they were still on the surface, so Okawna drove them to the stern of the *Mystic*.

"Hey, guys. That other sub just sank, but the ship is still here. I can see them staring back at me. Hey, Alex? Should we ask the destroyer to make them go away?"

"No, there is nothing he can do about it unless they're attacked, and that ship is no match against the destroyer. His hands are tied. Can you attach another tow cable to a deck cleat on the stern?"

"I suppose so. What have you got in mind?"

"I'll drop into the water and attach it to the nylon rope. When I'm back on board, I'll go inside and release the magnetic latch. Once the sub is on board, we'll leave with the device in tow."

"Okay, I'm attaching it now. You know, even wearing that wetsuit, you're going to freeze your butt off."

"Don't worry. It only takes a few seconds to screw in the pin."

"If you say so. The destroyer is standing by, and I'm ready up here."

Okawna opened the hatch and crawled out on top of the sub. When Alex came out and slid over the side into the water, he dropped the end of the cable down to him and quickly attached the harness connectors to the sub, so he was ready to go.

Alex flinched at the sudden drop in temperature. Without a facemask, he would have to feel his way along the side of the sub to the nylon rope. He dragged the new cable to the stern, took a deep breath, and then dropped below the surface. He followed the curved side to the bottom and slid one hand along the sub, searching for the magnetic latch, but ran out of breath and swam back up to the surface.

Okawna was looking over the side when Alex burst through the water, gasping in deep breaths of air. "Grab my hand."

Alex held up the end of the cable. "Not yet. I should have paid more attention to where it's located." He took a deep breath and dropped back down, then repeated the routine as before. This time, he found it immediately, but his fingers were numb, making it difficult to unscrew the eyebolt. When it finally came free, he nearly dropped it. He was running out of breath, but it was too late to stop and risk losing the end of the cable, and it seemed to take forever to align it with the rope and slide the metal connector through both eyelets.

His lungs burned and doing it by feel was taking too long, and when he could not feel the opening in the eyebolt, he opened his eyes, and it took both hands to screw the pin in place. He kicked for the surface, his lungs on fire, as he stroked furiously, then he burst through the water and took in several deep breaths as he reached up for Okawna's hand. "Get me out of here! I'm freezing!"

Okawna hauled his friend up onto the sub and leaned him against the hatch collar. "I told you so. I'll go down and release the latch."

Alex stared out across the water at the other ship, trying to outmaneuver the destroyer, who was acting as a blockade between them and the mystery vessel. He felt the sub lurch beneath him as the device dropped away, then Okawna was kneeling beside him.

"Nice job."

Okawna stood and grabbed the sling hanging from the hoist and attached it to the sub, then knelt next to Alex as the sub rose out of the water. Bett stepped out of the way as water dribbled across the deck, while Josh guided the little submersible onto its storage bracket. Once Okawna released the hoist cable, she slid the short metal ladder alongside so her friends could climb down.

Alex could not stop shivering, as Okawna helped him down the steps and across the deck into the ship. He tried unzipping his jacket to take advantage of the warmer temperature inside, but his fingers didn't want to work. "Could you give me a hand?"

"Let's get you downstairs into a hot shower before I see you naked."

The muscles in Alex's jaw ached when he grinned and began walking down the steps. "It's not the first time."

Okawna left Alex standing in steaming water and hurried back up to the bridge. Josh was standing at the controls and Bett was standing outside so she could look down at the tow cable. He saw the other ship racing away toward the Northern Canadian shoreline, and the destroyer standing station off their port bow and he grabbed the radio microphone. "USS Barkley, this is Mystic. Come in."

"Commander Mosley here, Mystic. Go ahead."

Okawna wondered if the other ship was monitoring the radio. "We're through here, Commander. Our submarine is damaged and we're calling off our search. We're leaving for NAS Adak for repairs before we can try again and would appreciate an escort."

"I've heard about how fast your ship is, so I'll try to keep up."

"You lead the way and I'll match your speed."

"Copy that, Mystic."

Chapter 38

SPACE:

Realizing they were going to die, Essex decided to tell Rita about the new visitors. When he finished, she appeared speechless, with her mouth hanging open.

It took a moment for her mind to comprehend the enormity of what was going on, and then she closed her mouth and stared out the window. "Wow. So, it's all true, we're not alone after all, and they're not friendly. Oh yeah, and if you have brown eyes, you're as good as dead. This is great. I'm one of the chosen ones and I'm going to die in outer space."

Essex let the moment hang. "You're a chosen one? That's great. The spaceship is probably not too far away from us right now. I'll try to contact Pandora and let her know who you are, and see if we could get a ride back to Earth."

Rita turned and grinned at Essex. "Did you bring your phone?" She stopped grinning when she noticed he had brown eyes. "Oh, John. I'm sorry."

When he just smiled at her, she slowly leaned in to give him a kiss, but before their lips touched, the instruments came on. "How's that for timing?" She leaned back. "Are the thrusters working?"

Essex tried twice. "No, it must be something we did when we isolated the rocket motors." He turned on his microphone. "SV1 control, are you still listening?"

"Yes, but we lost you for a while. How's it going?"

"We are attached, but we can't maneuver. I'll keep you apprised of our progress."

Rita leaned closer to Essex. "So now what should we do?"

Essex turned to stare out at the open cargo area, noticed the torn hydraulic line for the door, and had an idea. "All I need to do is re-orient the nose of the SV1 so it's facing Earth, then I could fire the rockets."

When Essex released the latches on the control console and flipped it over, Rita looked over his shoulder while he worked. "What are you doing?"

"I'm bypassing the master valve on the oxygen tank to give us some thrust."

"Which oxygen tank? The one for the rocket motors?"

"No, I can't afford to waste the fuel. I'm bleeding it from our life support system."

"Hold on a second. Don't we need that? You know, to breathe?"

Essex stopped working and looked over at her. "We already know this is a one-way trip, so what difference does it make?"

Rita leaned back and crossed her arms. "You don't know Alex Cave. From what I know about him, he never abandons his friends."

Essex continued working. "I only have faith in me. Anything more is welcomed. There, that should do it." He pressed a button, and then a plume of ice crystals burst from the cargo hold. He grinned when the ship moved and let go of the button, then his grin slipped away as he jabbed it several times, but the crystals continued to spew from the nose. He flipped the circuit board over and yanked out a wire, then looked at the compartment. The crystals had stopped, but the momentum continued, and they were slowly spinning above the SV1.

Rita felt nauseated and looked away from the window. "Yes, this is much better." She looked at the gauges. "We have twenty percent of our oxygen remaining."

Essex replaced the panel and slammed his fist against the dashboard. He was suddenly thrown back in his seat and stared opened-mouthed at Rita, then turned back to the window and stared at the wisps of gas shooting from the thrusters of the SV1. "It's being taken to a new location."

"Yes, and it's dragging us with it. Release the tow rope."

"No, not while there's the slightest chance I could drag it into the atmosphere when it stops." He stared through the front window, concentrating on the intermittent burst of gas from the SV1's thrusters. "This time I'll be ready to fire the rockets the instant I'm pointed toward Earth."

"You know, John. Everything you try just makes matters worse. I'm amazed you managed to build this ship."

Essex didn't take his eyes off the SV1. "A ship moves through water. I have built a spacecraft." He noticed small bursts shooting in the opposite direction and his finger hovered over the control button. "If you'd rather walk home, be my guest. Just watch the first step. Make it fast, because I'm about to fire the motors."

Rita turned back to the window and looked down on the planet, but was suddenly thrown back in her chair when the rockets fired. The ship shook violently under the strain of dragging the SV1 down toward the atmosphere, and her hands clinched tight to the armrests.

Essex thought the ship would shake apart at any moment and stared at the gauges on the instrument panel. His speed was dropping fast, and he realized the SV1's thrusters were pulling in the opposite direction. He watched the fuel consumption emptying the tanks, then the roar of the engines abruptly stopped, and the shaking ceased. At the same instant, he watched the Earth disappear from view as the SV1 dragged him into a higher orbit.

Rita glared at him. "Cut the rope, damnit!"

When he didn't reply, she undid her upper harness and reached across to throw the switch, but Essex grabbed her wrist to stop her. When she glared at him, he smiled back, which irritated her even more.

"Rita? Please don't do that right now, or we'll drift off into outer space."

Rita didn't resist and stared at him. "What? We're already there, John."

"No, this is just space." He waved his other hand at the star-speckled background. "That, my dear Rita, is outer space."

She jerked her wrist free and plopped back down in her seat. "So, what do you have in mind for your next failure?"

"I'm tiring of you cutting me down, Rita. Keep pushing it and I'll kick you out myself. I liked you better when you weren't so snarky. What happened to your positive attitude?"

"It's hard to keep one when I run out of options."

"Not too long ago, you were counting on Alex to come to the rescue if we failed."

"I guess deep down I really didn't think he could, but I needed something to believe in at that moment. Now I've reached the acceptance part of the four-step program for dealing with imminent death."

"Not me. I'm in the denial part and I plan to stay there."

"Give it up, John. There is nothing anyone can do for us."

Essex didn't reply and stared out at the universe. "It's not over until I'm dead." He heard a click from the speaker. "What was that?"

"This is SV1 control. I guess you didn't realize your microphones are still on. We've been listening, and I'll let Alex know about your situation."

Essex looked over at Rita, who was grinning and shaking her head. "Thanks control."

Chapter 39

NAS ADAK ISLAND, ALASKA:

When the *Mystic* arrived, Josh located an area outside the small harbor where the device could be safely stored on the seafloor, then stopped the *Mystic* and let it settle on the bottom of the ocean. Alex had called ahead to Captain Dennis Wong, the head of security and a close friend of Donner's, and three rubberized assault boats with fifty-caliber machine guns mounted inside approached to secure the area around the ship. He eased the Mystic against the dock, where Wong was waiting for them. Alex stepped onto the dock first and shook hands with Wong and made introductions.

Wong let go of Alex's hand and felt a slight tingling sensation in his fingertips, but ignored it. "Martin asked me to do what I could to help you. What do you need?"

"Protect this ship by any means necessary. No one is to go near it without his express permission. I'll be back in a few days, but while I'm gone, could you build me a wooden crate with an interior of thirteen-inches square by twenty-one foot long, with a removable lid?"

"I don't see any problem. What's it for?"

"We have an experimental torpedo in tow and I'll need to take it with me when I get back."

"Is that why you parked offshore?"

"Yes. It has an experimental power supply with a slight glitch, but it's nothing you need to worry about."

"All right. Anything else?"

"Okawna and I need a ride to NAS Whidbey."

"Follow me and we'll check with the squadron Commander to see what's available."

"Thanks." He turned to Josh. "I'll keep you apprised of our progress."

"All right. We'll keep it safe. See you soon."

When Alex and Okawna walked up the pier with Wong, Bett strolled over to join Josh. "It's hard to believe Pandora's eyes really sparkled. Her slaves must really be a different race of humans."

"What do you mean, sparkle? They just looked blue to me."

"I guess not everyone can see it."

"I guess not. I hope we still have some painkillers in the medicine kit. I've got this nagging pain in the back of my eyes."

***

NAVAL AIR STATION. WHIDBEY ISLAND, WASHINGTON"

The men had caught a military flight, and while they waited for Donner's jet to arrive, Alex's phone rang and he recognized Carter's number. "Hey, Paul. How are Essex and Rita doing with the SV1?"

"That's why I'm calling. The mission has failed, and they are trapped in outer space."

"What went wrong?"

Carter explained what had happened. "Everyone here has watched the video of the meeting you had with that alien woman, and she's in control again. I don't mind telling you, me and everyone else here with brown eyes are scared shitless. I hope you have a plan to stop her from killing us."

"I'm working on it. How much longer can they last in Essex's ship?"

"Our best estimate is twelve hours. Essex just informed us the SV1 thrusters have run out of propellant, so it isn't going anywhere."

"All right. I'll do my best to save them."

"How could you possibly save them? Just worry about saving the rest of us."

Alex stared out across the water at the San Juan Islands. "I'll do what I can."

The phone had been on speaker, and Okawna heard what happened, and he could tell from Alex's posture he was deeply troubled over the situation. "Hey, it's not the first time we've had to make difficult choices. Here is my idea. We know we need to get that device out of Pandora's control, so let's take your spaceship into orbit, pick up the SV1, and get it to Groom Lake. At least she won't be able to control the weather or melt any more satellites."

"Don't forget about her genetic weapon. We need to rescue Pandora, because a little kindness might help convince her to change the ship's mind about killing all the people with brown eyes. But first we have to rescue Essex and Rita and get our device."

"Listen, I like the little guy too, but there is no way we could get his spaceship into our cargo hold."

"I know, and I have a plan."

"This should be interesting."

***

GROOM LAKE:

The men walked down the steps from the jet and were greeted by Henry, and Alex shook his hand. "It's good to be home, Doc."

Henry felt his fingertips tingle, but ignored it. "It is good to have both of you back in one piece."

While Okawna shook Henry's hand, Alex smiled at David. "Great job with the software. She didn't notice the change."

"Thanks. It was mostly Christa's work."

Jadin looked up at Alex. "Donner called. He's located Pandora, and she's in a British MI6 prison in Australia. They have her in some type of electromagnetic shield, which is blocking any attempt the ship might have of contacting her."

"Perfect. What are his plans?"

"He's waiting to talk to you."

"Let's not keep him waiting. Let's go to Hangar 5. I have an idea, but I need to check on something first."

They went over to two golf carts parked next to the building and Jadin sat next to Okawna in the second golf cart, following behind the others. "Did you talk to Alex about breaking his vow?"

"I got him to agree to get it on with her, but he'll only do it if it's the last option. I wish I was in his position."

"Figures."

They parked outside the hangar and stepped into a recessed alcove, and then everyone entered their codes and retinal scans before they were allowed past the guards on the other side of the door. Once inside, they walked over to a smaller version of Pandora's ship. It appeared to be a giant forty-foot diameter by twenty-four foot high table hockey puck, with a mirrored surface on all sides.

Alex strolled to the open section on the side of the alien craft, which was the eight-foot square outside door to the airlock and entrance into the cargo hold. He held his arms out to measure the distance, then stepped inside and looked across the room at the new spacesuits, then went back outside and smiled at his friends. "This will work. Let's go call Donner from the lunchroom." He strolled beside Henry. "Where did the new suits come from?"

"Jadin arranged it with her friends at NASA. They were prototypes sent by the contractor. When they proved to be reliable, the contract was signed, and we got the used ones for free. They only had two models, his and hers."

"What about the old suits? I need Okawna with me, not Jadin."

"I'm sorry, Alex. Her NASA friends took them when they left."

"Damn. All right. This will still work."

They entered the break room and sat down at an oval table, and then Alex called Donner. "Hi, Martin. You're on speaker with my team at the base. What are your plans for Pandora?"

"Nothing for the moment. The President set the whole thing up with Shaw without my knowledge."

"I bet that pissed you off."

"You have no idea. The President thinks she's a bargaining chip, and still hoping to reach an agreement with her before she releases her genetic bomb. I told him it wouldn't work, but he has brown eyes, and he's scared. So am I, by the way. He and I both hope you have one of your crazy ideas to fix this."

"I do, but it won't work unless I can talk to Pandora in Australia. Could you arrange it?"

"Absolutely, but they won't release her unless you can guarantee she'll call it off."

"I'll do my best."

"I know. You always do. Good luck."

Alex leaned back and looked around at the expectant faces of his friends. "We're taking our ship up to get Essex, Rita, and the SV1."

Jadin shook her head adamantly. "I already told you we cannot let her ship make line-of-sight contact with ours."

"We won't. I'll go to Pandora and get her out of the shield. Once the ship pinpoints her location, it would probably move there to make contact. Since we can track it, we'll wait until it's out of sight before we move in to rescue my friend and get the device."

Okawna stared across the table at Alex. "You still haven't explained how you plan on pulling that off."

"First, let me go talk to Pandora. If this part doesn't work, the rest of the plan won't either."

Okawna jumped up. "I'm going with you."

Alex stood, as did the others. "I thought you would."

David got Alex's attention. "What about me and Jadin? Well, at least me. I'd really like to see her in person."

"Okawna and I will be lucky to get in. Anyway, both of you need to prep the ship for our trip. I'll make a list of what we're going to need to pull this off."

***

AUSTRALIA:

After landing at a private airport outside Sydney, the driver checked their identification before allowing them inside the sedan. He remained silent for the next hour while driving them across the open plains, even under Okawna's relentless attempts to have a conversation. They passed through a security gate, and Alex noticed the fenced-in area on the side of the concrete building. Now all he had to do was get Pandora outside.

The driver stopped in front of the main door of the prison, where two casually dressed men with shoulder holsters strolled out to greet them as they climbed out. One of them appeared friendly and held out his hand, so Alex accepted. "I'm Alex Cave, and this is Okawna."

The man felt a slight tingling in his fingertips. "Uh, yes. I'm Bill Redfield, and this surly looking fellow is Archibald Bessel. We saw you in the video recording, Mister Cave. And you, too, Mister Okawna. Word has it you're the one who could stop her from starting the Brown Plague." He noticed Alex's puzzled expression. "That's what they're calling it on the Internet. Everyone is freaking out at just the thought of it."

"I'll try. Can I go see her?"

"Of course. Right this way."

They followed the escorts into the building, then along a short corridor across from some empty jail cells. When they stopped at the open doorway, Okawna noticed a large electrical disconnect switch on the left side of the wall. They entered a twenty-foot square room with a large cage in the center, and inside the cage were a small table with a single chair, and Pandora lying on a cot.

Pandora leapt off the cot when she saw a familiar face. "Oh, Alex! Being stuck inside a windowless room is torture, and I can't take it any longer. You have to get me out of here!"

Alex looked at Bill. "Could I at least take her out to see some open area?"

"I'm sorry, Mister Cave. We have our orders. She cannot leave this room."

Alex moved closer to her. "Do you think you could convince the ship not to kill us if we let you out?"

Pandora sat down on the cot. "I'm afraid it's too late for that. The genetically targeted virus is already spreading, thanks to you."

Alex's posture stiffened. "What are you talking about? I have blue eyes."

"Yes, and a unique gene which created them. Tell me, Alex. Are my eyes sparkling?"

"Yes, like they always do. Apparently, I'm the only one that can see them unless you're in contact with the ship."

"That's right, and only when it is angry. When I look at you, I see your eyes sparkling like mine. You're unique among your species, Alex Cave. Pandora believes you are a descendant of our race. Right now, the people in our colony are genetically stagnant. That's why she wants to add your genetic traits to ours and start a new lineage."

"Then how come you're saying *I'm* spreading the disease? I'm not sick."

"You are one-hundred percent immune to the virus. The ship has located one-hundred thousand of your species who have a higher immune rating because of their eye color, and they would survive long after the rest of your population is dead. It will use them to shut down the entire infrastructure which is destroying our planet."

"You haven't answered my question."

"You were infected with the virus when we first met and I touched your hand. Every Crud you have touched since that day is now infected, and every Crud they touch, and so on, until they are wiped out within a year. Most everyone else would be affected over a longer period, but only those few thousands would not die because of the virus."

"Can it be stopped?"

Okawna knew they would never let her outside as planned, and when everyone's attention was on Pandora, he eased back outside and pulled the power disconnect switch. He stepped back inside, and no one seemed the wiser until Pandora leapt off the cot and her eyes appeared to burst with blue fire.

Alex saw the immediate change in Pandora's eyes. "I see you're back. You must be in a pretty high orbit to connect with her from Iceland."

"Let her go, Alex. I'll let you come into the ship so you won't have to witness the carnage I've unleashed upon your species."

"I'd rather rot in hell. Give me a cure for the virus and we'll trade. Otherwise, she can rot in hell with me. I'll give you a day to reconsider. If you give me the cure, I'll come back soon with her release papers and use them to get her back to you."

Okawna stifled a grin when Pandora's eyes became even brighter and he knew it worked. He eased back outside and turned on the power, and when he stepped back into the room, her eyes were normal.

Alex turned to his escorts, who backed away from him with fear in their eyes. "I'm done here."

Bill stared at his hand. "Bloody hell! You've infected me. You've killed me, you son of a bitch!"

Okawna snatched Bill's pistol from the shoulder holster and held it against the man's head. "Just take it easy, guys. Alex didn't do it on purpose. Now that we know how it spreads, start wearing gloves so you don't infect your family and friends."

"What bloody good would that do? We're all going to die, anyway."

Alex saw how scared Bill and Archibald were. "Don't give up hope. I'll do my best to stop the brown plague. We're going to leave now and we don't want any trouble. She may still hold the key to stopping this, so don't harm her."

Bill glared at Pandora for a moment, and then turned to Alex. "Fine. Just promise me you'll stop this."

"I promise I'll do everything possible."

When Bill walked out through the doorway, Alex and Okawna followed and they returned to the sedan, still parked in front of the building. Okawna waited until Alex was in, then tossed Bill's pistol to him before getting inside. A moment later, they were being driven back to the airport.

Chapter 40

GROOM LAKE:

Henry stood inside the cargo hold of the spaceship, watching Alex and Okawna bolt the storage bracket for one of the devices to the floor. David and Jadin finished mounting a winch with a reel of thick rope to the wall across from the airlock, then stepped back to admire their work.

Alex stood and walked over to Henry while Okawna taped the control cable for the winch to the floor. "I think we're ready."

"You never cease to amaze me, Alex. I just hope this crazy idea of yours works."

Alex grinned. "So do I, Doc. What's the latest location of Pandora's ship?"

"Just as you thought. It is in geosynchronous orbit above the prison in Australia."

Alex noticed Henry grimace in pain and massage his temples. "What's the matter?"

"It is my eyes. I have a constant pain in the back of my eye sockets. I have taken medication, but nothing seems to work."

Alex's heart sank as he remembered shaking his hand, and didn't know what to say to him. On the flight back to the base, he and Okawna had agreed to keep Alex's infectious nature between them until the appropriate moment. He knew Henry was already worried about the mission, so he decided this wasn't the moment. "Okay, I guess it's time to go, Doc."

Henry moved out through the airlock doors and then turned to wave at his friends. "Good luck."

When the outside door to the airlock closed and blended in with the mirror surface of the ship, he walked over to the control pad to open the large hangar doors. He rubbed his temples while he waited for the spacecraft to cloak.

Alex ran up the stairs to the control room and then stared out through the transparent sides of the spaceship at the interior of the hangar. His friends joined him and saw Henry standing by the doors. When he saw Henry rub his temples, he looked over at Okawna, who gave him a knowing expression that Henry's brown eyes were his death sentence.

David sat down in one of four chairs in the middle of the large, round room. Unlike Pandora's ship, the entire top floor of their forty-foot-diameter craft was the control room. He pulled the control console closer and pressed one of the colored touch pads to engage the engine. He saw Henry push the button for the doors, indicating the cloak was working, and watched them part in the middle.

Alex followed the outside wall to keep an eye on Henry as David eased the silent craft out of the hangar. A moment later, the base seemed to fall away beneath him as the ship rose straight up into a low orbit. He stared at the slight curve of the horizon as they soared across the United States and Northeastern Canada. A small object was reflecting the sun's light while quickly growing in size, and he looked over at David. "Is the other ship still over in Australia?"

David checked his control console. "Yes, we're ready."

Alex turned back to look outside. As they closed the distance, he recognized the SV1 and Essex's ship in front of a starry background. When David stopped the spacecraft twenty feet away, he turned to Jadin and Okawna. "Let's get suited up."

The trio hurried down the stairs to the cargo hold, where Okawna helped them into their new spacesuits. "These are great. They're so lightweight and compact. When do I get one?"

Jadin put a communication device in her ear and turned it on. "We can't afford it. How do you read?"

"You're good. Next time, I get to spacewalk."

"Your anatomy would never fit in here."

Okawna chuckled as he slid her helmet in place. "I'll borrow Alex's. This is your first time, so be careful. Remember, slow methodical moves, so you don't drift around too much once you turn off the artificial gravity."

"Got it. Thanks."

Alex inserted his earpiece. "How we doing up there, David?"

"We're still good, Alex. Don't forget the radio for talking to Essex's ship."

Okawna slipped a headset with Essex's frequency and one ear pad over Alex's thermal hood, then lowered the helmet in place and slid the latch closed. He hooked the end of the rope from the reel onto his safety belt and then held out a crossbow with a steel treble hook on the tip of the bolt.

Alex grabbed the crossbow. "See you soon."

Okawna stepped inside the alcove for the stairs to the upper levels, pressed the button to close the door, and sealed the cargo hold from the rest of the ship. He pressed another pad, and the atmosphere was sucked out of the cargo hold.

Alex stood next to Jadin in front of the inside airlock door as the room became a vacuum to match vacuum outside the ship. "I need to say this, Jadin. As much as I want to save Essex and Rita, our priority is to get the SV1 device into our ship."

"I know. If Pandora's ship gets within line-of-sight of us, she'll be able to hear us talking."

"That's up to David and Okawna. Once we have the device inside, they have orders to leave the area immediately if that ship moves in our direction."

"I'll let you explain that to Essex and Rita."

"I won't have to. Essex has the same priority. That's why he risked everything trying to save us."

A small light on a control panel beside the door turned red, indicating the room was a vacuum, and Alex opened the inside and outside airlock doors. He fastened a tether line to Jadin's suit before pressing a button to turn off the artificial gravity, then grabbed a handhold, pulled himself into the eight-foot square room, and then stared at Essex's spacecraft tethered to the SV1. "Let's get started."

***

Knowing they were being monitored, Essex and Rita kept their conversations to a minimum. It also helped to conserve the diminishing oxygen supply. They were both staring out the front window when a large square of white light suddenly blocked a section of the universe, and Essex bolted upright in his seat. "No way! Are you seeing what I'm seeing?"

Rita stared at the human silhouette inside. "Is that Pandora?"

"No, it has to be Seth."

They both flinched when a voice burst through their radio speakers. "How's your air supply?"

Essex recognized the voice and could not believe Rita was right, then looked over at her. "Alex?"

"Just thought I'd stop by and see if you needed a ride home."

"You can't imagine how happy I am to see you. We're down to 5% oxygen. Where did you come from? Is Pandora helping us? Don't tell me you stole her spaceship."

"It's a long story, so just sit tight and conserve your air while we get the SV1 inside this ship. Don't worry. I'll get you out of there."

"All right."

They watched Alex aim a crossbow with a big fishhook on the end at his ship. Essex was about to duck when the bolt bounced off the bottom of his craft, then a slender line wrapped around his towrope.

Alex secured the end of the line to an anchor point inside the airlock, and then pushed off from his ship, using the taut line as a guide. He let go when he reached the towrope and followed it hand-over-hand until he reached the plastic ring, then removed the clip on the end of the line back to the ship and secured it to the SV1. "All right, Jadin. Give us a tug."

Jadin had moved into the airlock to watch Alex's progress, and stepped back into the ship. The control pad for the winch was taped to the inside wall, and the slack in the thick rope looked like a snake writhing across the cargo hold. She pressed the start button, and then flinched when the line snapped taut beside her. When she let go of the button, the recoil dragged the rope back inside, coiling it against the back wall. When she stepped back into the airlock, Essex's ship was rushing toward Alex on the SV1, and there was nothing she could do about it.

Alex barely hung on when the rope jerked the SV1 much harder than necessary, and then the towline from the bottom of Essex's ship swept back toward his head. He twisted out of the way just before the slack in the line slapped against the device. He knew the two objects were about to collide and feared the coming impact would knock the SV1 on a collision course with the side of his spaceship. The little craft bounced off the device, driving it sideways like he thought.

Jadin was surprised when the rope inside the spaceship snapped taut, slamming against her back and driving her out of the airlock. She flipped upside-down when her safety tether jerked her back inside and she managed to grab the door frame as it swept past her head.

The tether on his waist belt was the only thing keeping Alex from floating off into space. The problem was the rope was dragging the SV1 and Essex onto a collision course with the invisible side of the spaceship, with him floating helplessly in the middle. He noticed Essex's tow rope winding through space like a serpent and had an idea, and then dragged himself hand-over-hand back to the device, and transferred his tether onto the rope from his craft. He grabbed the hook from Essex's towrope and moved it from the SV1 to his waist belt, then began furiously pulling himself back to his ship. Hopefully, he could get inside before the slack between him and the little craft was gone.

Jadin gained control of her movements and stared out through the airlock, then pulled herself closer to the outside doorway, but couldn't believe what Alex was attempting. She saw the towrope straighten out, and silently urged Alex to move faster, even though his momentum was already steadily increasing with each pull. When he reached the airlock, she grabbed his tether, trying to stop him from flying into the cargo hold. The reaction slammed them together, and then they bounced back against the walls of the airlock.

Alex stared out the doorway and saw the tow rope ready to snap taut. He grabbed the hook from his belt and then slid the plastic clip onto an attachment point on the wall. He barely managed to keep his fingers from being crushed under the rope when it slammed against the door frame.

Essex felt his heart beating so hard he thought it would burst from his chest. "He did it! You did it, Alex!"

Rita released a sigh of relief. "That's great, but now what?"

Alex took a moment to catch his breath. "I heard that. Just give me a moment to think about it."

"Alex, this is Okawna. Pandora's ship must know something is wrong. It's moving into a higher orbit."

"How long before it's in line of sight?"

"Not much. If you have an idea to get us out of this, now's the time."

"All right. John, you're wearing G-suits, correct?"

"That's right."

"Is there a way you could maintain the pressure if you leave your ship?"

"Wow, hold on a second. Yes, but you're not suggesting we try to make it from here to the airlock in the vacuum of space?"

"In a way. We'll attach the line to the device inside the airlock and leave it outside, and then Jadin and I will drag the nose of your ship into the airlock as far as possible. You'll open your canopy and we'll drag both of you into the cargo hold. Once you're clear, I'll shove your craft outside and close the inside door. It should only take a few seconds for the room to pressurize and you can breathe again."

"Hey Alex, it's Okawna. What about the device?"

"David? The moment you and Okawna think the other ship will see us, I want you to set a course back to the base, regardless of what is going down here. Land and get away from it, then worry about us."

"Got it."

Alex pulled some slack from the rope on the reel and tied it to a cleat on the wall near the outside doorway. He reached over to the door frame, grabbed an emergency cutaway tool, and then severed the rope leading inside the cargo hold. He turned and shortened his tether so he would remain inside the airlock, then looked at Jadin. "I'll pull and you guide the nose inside. Are you ready?"

When she gave him a brave smile, he grabbed the towrope and gently dragged Essex's lightweight craft closer to the opening. Jadin grabbed a handhold near the opening when the front of the small ship was within reach, and was surprised how easily she moved it into the center of the room. She saw the twisted plastic hinges where the doors used to be, and Essex and Rita's troubled expressions. When the short wings bumped against the door frame, she held it steady so it wouldn't bounce back outside.

Alex ducked under the craft and into the cargo hold to assess the situation, and thought it could work. "Everything looks ready. Just remember to exhale when you open the canopy."

Essex looked over at Rita. "We're ready."

"All right. Jadin, you help John and I've got Rita."

Okawna stared at the moving dot on the ship's holographic monitor. "Hurry it up down there. The other ship is coming this way. It will see us in ten seconds."

Alex looked at Essex. "Do it now!"

Essex pressed the button to release the latches and pushed up on the clear plastic. His lungs felt like they would explode as he floated over the edge into Jadin's arms.

Okawna was also watching what was happening in the cargo hold on the holographic monitor. "Five seconds, Alex. It's almost in sight."

Alex grabbed Rita under the arms and saw she was in pain as he dragged her out. "Exhale, damnit!" He sent her drifting across the room and shoved the little craft out of the ship. "David! Go!"

He pressed a button to close the inside airlock door and another to re-pressurize the room. He settled onto the floor as the artificial gravity slowly increased, and saw Essex and Rita trying to breathe normally.

"Is everyone all right?"

Essex sat up and raised his thumb to Alex, then reached over to help Rita, who appeared to be in pain. "What's wrong?"

"I hit my elbow when Alex hurled me against the wall. But I'll be okay."

Alex removed his helmet. "Sorry. I was out of time."

David was watching the monitor as the ship began moving into the atmosphere when it suddenly went crazy for a few second then returned to normal. He checked their speed and trajectory, and they appeared to be able to land in a few minutes.

Okawna ran down to the hold and quickly assessed everyone's situation, then helped Jadin out of her suit. "I think Pandora's ship contacted ours, but it was only for a few seconds."

She squirmed out of the tight-fitting clothes. "That's all the time that bitch needs. Is our ship okay?"

"It seems to be. I don't know if the SV1 and Essex's ship are still attached, but I guess we'll find out in a few moments." He turned to Alex. "David is going to land us near the south bunkers until we know for sure."

Essex stood and looked around the room. "Where did you get this?"

Okawna strolled over and smiled at Essex as he put his hand on the little man's shoulder. "Alex found it a while back and lets us use it on special occasions."

Essex hurried over to the alcove that led up the stairs and looked over at Okawna. "Does this lead up to the control room?"

"You bet. We'll be landing in a second, and then I'll give you a personal tour."

David had no idea what might be outside the ship, so kept it moving until he set it down on an old concrete pad near the underground bunkers. "We've arrived."

Alex opened the inside door to the airlock and walked outside. He saw the control system for the SV1 was demolished, but the device was unharmed. He was surprised to see Essex's ship relatively intact, and expected to see him come out to inspect his tough little craft, but saw Okawna, who was detaching the ropes from inside the airlock. "What happened to our guests?"

"Jadin wanted to introduce them to David."

Alex's phone rang, and he recognized Henry's number, so he put it on speaker. "You might want to come out here and listen to this, Okawna. We're back, Doc, and we have it. We even managed to pick up a couple of hitchhikers on the way."

"That is good news, but we have another problem. Pandora insists you see her immediately. She promises she can give you the cure if you let her get back on the ship."

"All right. We should be back in the hangar in a few minutes."

***

Once David had the ship secure in the hangar, Alex hurried outside and saw two security guards standing by to accompany Essex and Rita. "The man is a friend, but use a little caution with the woman. She's a flirt." He moved away and called Donner, who would arrange Pandora's release. "Have you heard any reports about how bad the plague is spreading?"

"Ramey says most of the base is infected, and it's spreading through town. Sliven was in so much pain, he tried to commit suicide. His wife called me when she found him in his office at NordVulC. The doctors flushed the pills from his system, but they have him on morphine for the pain."

"I'd better get going."

"Good luck, Alex."

When his friends joined him, he noticed Henry was missing, so he turned to the woman walking back from closing the hangar doors and noticed she, too, was rubbing her temples. "Have you seen the Director?"

"He went to the infirmary to get something stronger than Ibuprofen. That's where I'm headed."

Alex turned to Okawna. "I'll leave immediately, of course. Listen, we both know what a pain in the ass those devices have been. Would you mind staying here and making sure they're secured in one of the remote bunkers?"

"I'd rather watch your back."

Alex grinned at his best friend. "I'm unique among my species, remember? I'll be fine."

"Yeah, well, wear protection."

Alex chuckled. "Thanks." He saw Jadin staring at him. "Question?"

"No, just tell that bitch if she tries anything, I'll fry her circuits."

"I will. I'll stop and see Doc on the way to the plane."

***

Alex found Henry lying on a bed in the infirmary with gauze covering his eyes. "Are they taking good care of you, Doc?"

"Ah, Alex. Yes, so do not worry about me. Go get the cure and I will be much better."

"All right. See you soon." He walked to the door, but stopped before stepping out of the room and turned back to Henry. "I'm sorry, Doc. It's my fault and I'll do my best to fix it." When Henry grimaced in pain, he left the room and headed to the air terminal for his flight to Australia. He just hoped it wasn't too late to save those already infected.

Chapter 41

AUSTRALIA:

Thanks to Donner's connections, a helicopter picked him up at the airport, and Alex arrived at the prison with verified papers for Pandora's release into his custody. The pilot set down on the far side of the building, and then he climbed out and went to the rear entrance, where two different men with blue eyes escorted him back to Pandora's cage. He noticed the power to the energy field was still on, but it didn't matter. In a few minutes, she would be outside.

Pandora stood from the cot when she saw a familiar face. "Oh, Alex! I was hoping you got my message. I can get you the cure. I promise."

Alex knew for the moment he was forced to trust her word. "All right. Come with me." He turned to the men. "Open the door, please."

When the door swung out of the way, she smiled and reached out for Alex. "I knew you liked me."

Alex held his hands up to stop her. "I didn't say that. You have something I need. That's it. Now let's go."

Pandora knew the moment she stepped out of the building the ship would be in charge, so she slowly reached out for Alex's hand. "I won't hurt you. This will be the last time I can touch you as just me, not the ship."

Alex realized she was right and wrapped his fingers around her hand. "I do like you as just you, and I wish you could stay that way."

"Me too, but I don't have a choice."

Alex turned to walk out, but she was reluctant to leave the room, and he had to urge her to the door. When they stepped outside, the change was immediate. Her eyes were more intense, so he let go of her hand as a precaution.

Pandora stopped before they reached the helicopter. "I'll have the ship land in this field."

"I'm afraid there are too many witnesses."

"I was in contact with your ship's AI. I did not know your species had evolved here. If you let me have the remaining data, I can leave this planet in your destructive hands. I'm sure if I come back in a thousand years, you will have killed every breathing creature on this planet, and then I can reclaim it."

Alex realized he had a new bargaining chip, but decided to save it for the right occasion. "I see. All right. Here's the deal. I'll take you someplace close to meet your ship." He handed her a small piece of paper where he had written the coordinates. "I'll fly home and meet you at this location in six hours. You give me the cure, and I'll give you the data."

"I can do more than control the weather and melt your machines. Using your device was only a convenient opportunity. Do not deceive me."

"I wouldn't think of it. I'm a man of my word."

***

NEVADA. SIX HOURS LATER:

Pandora stepped outside the ship when the wind from the helicopter blades ceased, and waited while Alex walked over, then stared at him when he stopped in front of her. "I see you are a liar."

"No, I'm not. Give me the cure and I'll have Okawna bring the data."

Pandora held out a small vial with the clear liquid inside, partially hidden by a note wrapped around the outside. "Here is the base serum to use as a culture for replication. The process and dosage are on the note."

Alex took the small capsule and stared at the contents, then held it up with the sky for a background, and it was perfectly clear. He had no way of verifying if it truly was the cure, but he didn't have a choice. He slid the vial into his pocket and waved Okawna over.

Okawna strolled over to join Alex. "Are we good?"

"Yes, give her the data."

Okawna held the storage device out to her. "Wow, you must be pissed about something. Your eyes are on fire."

Pandora snatched the small device from his hand. "We're done."

She turned and stepped inside her ship, and when the opening sealed behind her, Alex turned to head back to the helicopter when suddenly he heard a familiar voice holler his name. He spun around and the door in the ship was open, and Pandora was waving him over without the intensity in her eyes. He hurried back and could tell it was just the woman. "Aren't you going with her?"

"Listen closely, Alex. She lied. That's not the cure."

Alex gritted his teeth and headed for the entrance, but Pandora suddenly grabbed his arm and spun him back, so he grabbed her wrist and glared at her. "I'm going into that ship!"

"Wait. Once you're inside, she could kill you and still take your DNA. You already have the cure because I gave it to you, but she doesn't know."

Alex let go and watched her rub her wrist. "How?"

"Your scar. The one on the inside of your lip, where I bit you."

He had been constantly rubbing his teeth against it, wondering why it didn't go away like the others. "I don't understand."

"Like I said, you are unique among your species. Your genetic structure allows you to both carry the virus and be immune to it, like me. All you need to do is bite the scar open and swallow the liquid. Your own antibodies produced it, and I gave them a chance to congregate in one location to adapt to the new threat. It will work just like the virus. If you touch any Brown, the antithesis of the virus would spread between your skins. That person would then pass it on, just as with the virus."

Alex shook his head at the irony. "All right."

"Just one more thing. When you're done, why don't you come with me?"

He heard Okawna chuckle and turned to glare at him, then looked at Pandora's beautiful eyes. "I still don't understand how you are bound to this artificial intelligence. Are you its slave?"

"I suppose, in a manner of speaking. We were engineered to serve this race of AIs and we build ships for them to go out and claim more territory in the universe."

Alex saw her close her eyes and appear to be concentrating. "Are you alright?"

"She's trying to regain control. I have to go before she learns what I've told you."

She opened her eyes and slowly wrapped her arms around Alex. "I'm sorry she lied about the cure. I'll miss you."

She gave him a gentle kiss, and then he watched her run back into the ship. The side became a mirror an instant before it was cloaked, and then he walked toward it with his palm extended. When he kept going, he stopped and looked up at the sky, but it was gone. "I lied too. Goodbye, Pandora."

Okawna walked up beside his friend and looked up at the sky. "Do you think it will work?"

Alex stopped staring skyward and grinned at his friend. "David and Christa made the software with the tracker work, and they said adapting that first download was more difficult than installing the new code."

"Yeah, well, it's a shame Pandora didn't stay here with us. Of course, knowing they are just slaves to artificial intelligence eases my conscious a little about what we are about to do."

"I still feel bad for them. It wasn't their fault. I just hope it works."

"Let's get going. You have a few million people to save."

"Hold on a second. Maybe Pandora wasn't really in control when she told me I had the cure. I want to try it now before I get my hopes up."

Alex looked up at the sky, and then bit down on his scar. It wasn't painful, and the liquid draining into his mouth was bitter. When he swallowed, his throat burned for a second, and then he felt a tingling in his fingertips. He turned his back to the sun as he brought his hand up to see why and when he spread his fingers apart, sparks passed between them and the tingling increased, so he closed his hand, completely disappointed. He spread them again, but when nothing happened and the tingling went away, he turned to Okawna and grinned. "Let's go."

***

The ride back to the base in the helicopter took only a few minutes, and Alex's first stop was the infirmary. He found Henry hooked up to an intravenous drip regulator and recognized the label on the hanging plastic bag as morphine. He moved up beside the bed and gently took Henry's hand. "I'm back, Doc. I have the cure, so you're going to be fine now."

Henry felt a tingling sensation in his fingertips, then in his arms, and it seemed to cover his entire body. "I do not know what is happening. I have this strange sensation, like electricity on my skin. Wait a minute, the pain in my skull seems to be fading." Henry reached up and removed the gauze covering his eyes, squinting and blinking from the bright light. After a few moments, he looked over at Alex and smiled. "I can see you."

"I'm just glad it worked."

Henry sat up on the edge of the bed. "Go tell the nurse to unhook me from this machine. You and I have a lot of hands to shake."

Alex walked around the end of the bed to the IV drip. "I'll take care of it, Doc."

Okawna leaned against the doorjamb and looked across at Alex. "So, all you have to do is touch them and they're cured? Since you're unique among our species and have these special powers, tell me what else you can do."

Alex grinned. "I'll let you know when I can walk on water."

***

AUSTRALIAN ASTRONOMICAL OBSERVATORY NEAR SYDNEY:

"Janet, come here! I just saw something spectacular!"

Jim Rogers, a graduate assistant doing thesis work in the AAO observatory, blinked furiously to clear his eyes. "There was a blinding flash like a star going nova in the Pleiades constellation, but much, much closer!"

His boss looked up from her categorizing activities keeping her glued to her laptop for the past several hours and walked over to his workstation. "Show me."

"Sure. It's, it's, well, uh, that's funny, it's gone."

She indicated the seventy-five-inch panel hanging on the wall. "That's OK. It's all on the hard drive. Pull up the past minute and put it on the big screen."

The two of them watched as a small area brightened for a moment, blotted out several stars, then shrank to a pinpoint and disappeared completely.

Jim had never seen anything like it. "Wow. Should we report it?"

Janet had been there before. "No. We'd open a Pandora's Box of problems trying to explain it. Just let it go."

The End.

Movie script available from the author.

I hope you enjoyed Pandora's Eyes, and I hope you will take a moment to write a short review.
Thank you.
James M. Corkill

Here is a preview of the next Alex Cave adventure
DNA
The Alex Cave Series book 6

Chapter 1

SALT LAKE CITY, UTAH. DISCOVER NEW ANCESTORS FACILITY:

Zane Simons was alone in his advanced genetics lab, studying the results from a DNA sample extracted from a twenty-five-thousand-year-old tooth found at a dig site in Colorado. When he saw the final results, he smiled to himself. "Well, Ms. Austin. Your discovery is going to change the scientific community's theory of our evolution."

He turned off his equipment and tossed the printed report into his briefcase, then grabbed the handle and his car keys as he headed out of the room. In the parking lot, he hesitated before climbing into his vehicle, wondering if he should call the archeologist to let her know he is on his way to her dig site. He grinned and climbed in. "I hope you like surprises, Mya."

***

SEATTLE, WASHINGTON:

His trip home had turned out to be the opposite of what he had expected, and ex-CIA operative turned geophysicist Alex Cave was reading a magazine in a business class seat on the aircraft, hoping to take his mind off recent events with his nephew, Derek. A rift had formed between them, and it was like a dagger through his heart. He looked up when a woman with short, dark hair sat down in the seat beside him. He gave her a courteous nod hello before returning to the article and moved his leg out of the way when she bent down to shove a small bag under the forward seat.

Mya Austin straightened up and looked over at the ruggedly handsome man with wavy black hair sitting beside her. "I'm sorry about that. They never give us enough room."

It was the first time he could study her features, and other than her soft hazel eyes, she had an unremarkable face and her tan skin was slightly weathered from being outdoors a lot. He guessed her age to be around forty. "I know what you mean."

He continued reading an article in the magazine. It was an interview with the owner of the Discover New Ancestors program, and the geneticist Zane Simon had made some incredible discoveries. Alex thought about his last mission, where he had become familiar with some aspects of genetics, and found the interview intriguing.

He hadn't heard the pilot welcoming them aboard or the safety instructions, but looked up when the plane began moving. Once it took off, he returned to the article until he noticed Mya trying to look out the window, which was even with his head. He set the magazine on his lap and leaned back so she could see.

She smiled at the man and then leaned over his lap. "I'm sorry again. I was just trying to see Mount Rainier."

He could not move back any further, and her face was only inches from his. "That's fine."

She turned her head and could see deep into the stranger's dark blue eyes. "Hi. I'm Mya Austin."

He noticed a few flakes of gold in Mya's hazel irises. "It's nice to meet you. I'm Alex Cave."

She turned her face back to the window. When the mountain disappeared from view, she leaned back in her seat. "Thanks."

He noticed the medallion hanging from a beaded leather necklace around Mya's neck. "Is that Sioux Indian?"

"Yes, I'm an archeologist for the Sioux Nation, and I'm currently working at a dig site near Fort Collins, Colorado."

"You're a long way from home. What brings you out this way?"

"A friend of mine at the university was helping me with some research."

Alex knew he couldn't tell Mya he worked at Area 51, but didn't want to lie. "I used to be a geophysics instructor at a small college in Montana, and now I'm a NASA consultant."

When she heard he worked for NASA, Mya wondered if this might be a fateful encounter. "I've just made a discovery in a cave on tribal land that will change the world."

He could see the excitement and sincerity in her eyes. "How is that?"

"If the local tribe is correct, what they call the vanishing stone should appear at the dig site any day now."

"I'm sorry. Did you say vanishing stone?"

"Yes, that's what they call it. Inside the cave is a drawing of a box-shaped object with two human figures standing beside it. According to the legend and cave drawings, the vanishing stone magically appeared above the cave twenty-five thousand years ago. The visitors left two new people with the tribe, and promised to return in exactly twenty-five thousand years then left in the vanishing stone. That's this year, Alex."

"How can you be so precise?"

"I've read about similar drawings in caves all over the world, and carbon dating of the various mediums used for the images indicate all the drawings were made twenty-five thousand years ago." Mya could tell she had his attention. "Since you work for NASA, is there any chance there might be a satellite taking pictures of that part of the United States?"

"That's not my area of expertise."

She wasn't about to give up. "All I need is an overhead view of the dig site."

"Well, a friend of mine might get you some pictures. Give me your contact information and I'll see what I can do."

She smiled, reached into her purse, and handed him a card. "You can have them sent to that email address. I'm usually at the dig site, so use the mobile phone number if you want to call me."

He was intrigued and decided to help her out. "All right, Miss Austin. I'll try to arrange for you to get some satellite images."

She smiled. "Thank you."

When Mya brought out an electronic tablet, Alex returned to reading the article, and during the rest of the flight, said little to her until they got off the plane in Las Vegas and he held out his hand. He hadn't realized how tall she was and estimated her to be about five-foot-nine. "It was nice meeting you, Mya. It shouldn't take long to get you those images."

She accepted his hand. "I appreciate it. Listen, since you're a geophysicist, would you like to come out to Colorado and see the cave? Maybe you can verify the age of the rock strata."

"No promises, but that might be interesting."

"I'll look for you." She indicated a walkway. "My flight home is down there."

"I'm afraid mine's the other way." He turned and headed along the concourse.

Mya stared after Alex until he disappeared around a corner, then turned and hurried toward her departure area. She stood in front of the large window and stared at the plane rolling across the tarmac, hoping her being seated next to Alex was a sign she was onto something big.

***

Alex left the air terminal and took a taxi to a remote hangar on the far end of the tarmac. He showed his identification to a guard at the gate who let him through to board a special plane. When he stepped into the cabin, he was the only passenger and set his luggage bag in a rack, then sat in a chair forward of the wing.

One of the pilots came out of the cockpit and pressed a button to bring up the stairs, then closed the door and gave him a nod before returning, and then the aircraft began moving. He stared out the window as the plane taxied past the terminal, and saw Mya outlined in the window frame, and for a moment, had a strange sensation she was staring at him as he moved along the tarmac. When she was out of sight, he returned to the article about the Discover New Ancestors article.

Award-winning author James M. Corkill is a Veteran, and retired Federal Firefighter from Washington State, USA. He was an electronic technician and studied mechanical engineering in his spare time before eventually becoming a firefighter for 32-years and retiring. He has since settled into the Smokey Mountains of western North Carolina and has a fantastic view from his writing desk.

He began writing in 1997, and was fortunate to meet a famous horror writer named Hugh B. Cave, who became his mentor. In 2002, he rushed to self-published a dozen copies of Dead Energy so his wife could see his book published before she was taken by cancer. When his soul mate was gone, he stopped writing and began drinking heavily.

His favorite quote. "When you wake up in the morning, you never know where the day will take you."

In 2013, he met a stranger who recognized his name and had enjoyed an old copy of Dead Energy, except for the ending. When she encouraged him to start writing again, he realized this chance meeting was just what he needed to hear at the right moment. He quit drinking and began the rewrite of Dead Energy into The Alex Cave Series, and thankful for that fateful encounter.

Other books by James M. Corkill
Dead Energy. The Alex Cave Series Book 1.
Cold Energy. The Alex Cave Series Book 2.
Red Energy. The Alex Cave Series Book 3.
Gravity. The Alex Cave Series Book 4.
DNA. The Alex Cave Series Book 6.
Parallel. The Alex Cave Series Book 7.
Impact Yellowstone

Movie scripts available from the author.
You can contact him at. Jamesmcorkill@gmail.com

www.ingramcontent.com/pod-product-compliance
Lightning Source LLC
Chambersburg PA
CBHW071407100726
47908CB00004B/1093